Ring of Terror

RING OF TERROR

Michael Gilbert

Carroll & Graf Publishers, Inc.
New York

Copyright © 1995 by Michael Gilbert

Originally published by Hodder & Stoughton, London

First Carroll & Graf edition 1995

Carroll & Graf Publishers, Inc.
260 Fifth Avenue
New York, NY 10001

Library of Congress Cataloging-in-Publication Data is available.

ISBN 0-7867-0193-5

Manufactured in the United States of America

10   9   8   7   6   5   4   3   2   1

To Donald Rumbelow,
the only man I know who
talks and writes sense about
the Siege of Sidney Street.

1

Luke Pagan was standing in the shadow of a lime tree on the border of Sir George Spencer-Wells' coverts. In this year, which was the sixth in the reign of His Majesty, King Edward VII, Luke was fifteen years and four months old. It was late November and the tree was nearly leafless, but even when the full moon slid out from behind the clouds the boy was not easy to spot. It was partly the place he had chosen to stand in; but, even more, the fact that he was as motionless as the tree itself.

His father, Hezekiah Pagan, who was Sir George's head keeper, had taught him that standing still depended on control. Control of breathing and control of thinking. Think hard and you would have less cause to fidget. It occurred to him that this was one of the few pieces of instruction that his father had given him. For the rest, in his efforts at self-improvement, he had had to rely on hints picked up from newspapers and magazines.

In the *Daily Mirror* he had found an account of the exercises of Eugene Sandow, the physical culture expert. Also an advertisement for Vitaloids ('Are you weak and nervous? Try one box. Your strength will be increased and your whole system braced and invigorated'). Unfortunately neither the exercises, which were time consuming, nor the tonic, which was expensive, had seemed noticeably to increase his muscular power. He had then decided that agility might be more important than brute force. This idea came from an article in the *Strand* which described the feats of Harry Houdini, his almost miraculous escapes from bonds and chains, and exposed some of the secrets of the master of escapology. He had also picked up, from one of his father's friends who came from Cumbria, some of the tricks and devices of North

Country wrestling. To practise these he had provoked fights with boys larger than himself and had won most of them. This did not make him popular: in the schoolboy code it was creditable to knock an opponent down; to trip him up was foreign and despicable.

'Don't you worry,' his father had said. 'Put'm on's back. How you got'm there don't signify.'

Supplementing these efforts at physical improvement he was being coached by the vicar, the Reverend Millbanke, in English, Latin, Greek and theology. This was paid for by Sir George with the object of fitting Luke for a career in the Church. Both men regarded him as a promising candidate.

'*Mens sana in corpore sano*,' said Sir George quoting almost the only Latin he knew.

'Indeed,' said the vicar, 'the Church militant will acquire a champion armed at every point.'

Luke had been standing there for nearly two hours when someone passed within a few yards of him, evidently unaware of his presence. The young stranger was carrying a type of snare of which his father particularly disapproved.

It was a noose of steel wire anchored at the far end to the ground. When he had finished arranging the snare across the rabbits' runway the intruder moved off up the path. As he went Luke moved behind him, a shadow among shadows.

Four times more a snare was set. Four times more, as the intruder moved away, Luke pulled the snare up, until he was carrying five of them dangling from his left hand.

The sixth halt was in front of an open-fronted shed built of logs and planks, which Hezekiah had put up and which he used as a store and a shelter. If caught out in one of the sudden storms that blew in from the North Sea across the Suffolk flats he would sit in it smoking his pipe until the weather improved.

The intruder, having set his last snare, had wandered into the shed to examine the old coats and other oddments that hung on the walls. Finding nothing of interest he turned and came out. Luke was standing with the six snares in his hand.

The intruder looked, first at the boy and then at what he was carrying. Then he said, in a voice that proclaimed his status, 'What the hell are you doing with my traps?'

'Picking them up,' said Luke. His own voice was unexpectedly cultivated. A fact that seemed to surprise and annoy the other boy.

'Then you can bloody well go back and set them again. And see that you do it carefully.'

'They're not traps,' said Luke. 'They're snares. Cruel and illegal snares. We'll have none such in this wood.'

'And who the flaming hell gave you any right to say what I could do and what I couldn't?'

'My father told me about these snares. He told me to remove any I saw and to arrest anyone I found setting them.'

'And are you proposing to arrest me?'

'It depends on you. Give me your name and address and some evidence of your identity and I'll be happy to leave the rest to the police.'

'Sure you can have my name. And my address. I'm Oliver Spencer-Wells. I live at the Court and my father owns these woods.'

Luke could see now that it was a boy of about his own age and of much the same height, but more heavily built. He said, 'All right. I know you.'

'I'm glad about that.'

'You can go. You'll get a summons in due course.'

'For trespassing in my father's wood?'

'For setting illegal snares.'

'That's easily remedied. Because right now *you're* going to reset them for me. When I've taught you a lesson.' He threw himself at Luke, his fists whirling.

Luke met the attack in the way he had been taught. Dropping the traps he stretched both his arms out, rigidly, in front of him, fingers extended. As his opponent tried to close with him Luke's arms went underneath his and he ducked his head to avoid the flailing fists. So, for a moment, the two boys stood locked, body to body. Then Luke slipped a foot under one of his opponent's heels, lifting him and twisting him as he did so. The next moment he had him pinned down and was kneeling on his arms with one hand on his throat. Their faces were so close together that when Oliver spat at him the muck landed fairly on Luke's face.

Using his free hand Luke pulled a handkerchief out of his pocket and wiped his face. Then he said, 'If that's all you've got to say, suppose you get up and go home.'

He shifted his weight off Oliver's arms and got to his feet. Oliver lay for a moment, as though debating whether to move or not. Then he got up. His face was scarlet and his mouth was ugly.

He said, the words coming out in vicious spurts, 'I know you. You're Hezekiah's cub.'

'Correct.'

'And you're my father's sucking clergyman. The one he's paying for to get into the Church. The rector's been teaching you to talk like a gentleman. Even if he can't teach you to behave like one.'

'He's been teaching me more than that. Latin and Greek. We're just starting on Hebrew.'

'You can stop all that. As from now, you'll get no more help from him or us.'

'Isn't that for your father to say?'

'I can tell you what he'll say. He'll say that he was dragging you up, by your collar, from the ditch. Now he'll let go of you, so you can sink back into the mud where you belong. Latin and Greek! What you need to be taught isn't Latin and Greek. It's respect for your betters.'

When Luke said nothing some of Oliver's anger seemed to drain out of him. He said, 'Look here, you reset those traps and we'll forget all about it. Right?'

'Like I told you. They're not traps. They're instruments of torture.'

'Then you set the comfort of six rabbits above your career?'

'Put like that, it sounds silly. But yes, I suppose I do.' He picked up the traps. 'Have to take these with me. Be needed as evidence.' He swung round on his heel and left Oliver staring after him.

When Luke got home it was after midnight, but his father was waiting up for him. He said, 'I caught a boy who was setting snares and I pulled them up. Here they are.'

'And you got his name?'

'Yes, I got his name.'

'Good. We'll tell constable in the morning and he'll have him up in front of Bench.'

'Who do you think will be sitting on the Bench?'

'Sir George, like as not. And what are you grinning about?'

Luke explained what he was grinning about. His father, trying to keep the shock out of his voice, said, 'You're a bloody fool. You won't find it no joke, that I can tell you for sure. Sir George ain't the man to take a slap in the face and say thank you for it.'

'Maybe his son won't tell him. I had to put him on his back. He'll not be proud about that.'

'He'll surely tell him,' said his father. He sat for a time in silence while the clock on the shelf above the fire ticked away the minutes. For the first time that night, as he saw the distress on his father's face, Luke was sorry for what he had done. Finally his father said, 'I'll have a word with Reverend Millbanke. Leah can drop a note at the Rectory on her way to school. Sir George thinks a lot of Rector. Maybe he'll be able to work something out for us.'

The Reverend Francis Millbanke arrived after breakfast. He had a mop of grey hair and the pinkness and smoothness of his face belied his sixty years. A scholar of Sidney Sussex College, he had been offered preferment more than once, but had refused it on the grounds that since he was perfectly happy at Bellingham any change could only be for the worse. His popularity was great. It did not stem from his sermons, which were way above the heads of his congregation, but from his desire and ability to get on with everyone from the highest to the lowest.

He said, 'All I could gather from your note, Hezekiah, was that you were worried. Sherlock Holmes would have had no trouble in deducing that from your writing, which was more nearly illegible than usual.'

Hezekiah grinned. He said, 'Certainly I was kerflummoxed and I expect it showed. Any event, I'm no great hand at writing.'

'Tell me about it.'

'You'd better have it from the boy.'

Reverend Millbanke's face grew steadily more serious as the recital continued. Finally he said, 'There's only one thing for it. You'll have to go along and apologise to Sir George. He's really quite a reasonable man.'

'That's not what his people tell me,' said Luke. 'Mrs Parham says there are days when he does nothing but grunt and growl and no one can get any sense out of him at all.'

'That's when the demon gout has got him by the big toe. It would make Saint Peter and Saint Paul bad tempered. Incidentally –' a faraway look came into the Rector's eyes – 'have you ever thought that the real reason his disciples were so ready to follow our Lord and rough it with Him was that they were young men? If they'd been twenty years older they'd have thought twice about it and stayed with their lobster pots.'

Luke said, 'I always thought that the reason they followed our Lord was because He was such a remarkable teacher.'

The Rector came out of his abstraction. 'Don't change the subject, boy. This is an emergency and must be treated as such. I'm sure you realise that if Sir George indicates that he doesn't wish me to continue as your tutor I should be obliged to fall in with his wishes.'

'Of course.'

'And even if you were to continue educating yourself – I could probably let you have the necessary books – when it came to the point and you succeeded in passing the entrance exam at theological college you could hardly expect your father to find the fees.'

Hezekiah shook his head sadly.

'And even supposing you managed to scramble your way through college without Sir George's help, what would be your chance of going any further? Sir George is patron of a number of livings and it had been his intention to nominate you to one of them. You could hardly expect him to do that now. And if he raised his voice against you, no one would have you.'

Luke said, 'When Oliver was thinking what he could say in order to hurt and insult me, he called me his father's sucking clergyman. I'm not sure that he wasn't right. Considered as a clergyman I am, in every sense, his creature.'

'Then you'll see him?'

'I'll have a word with Mrs Parham first. If she says he isn't in one of his bad moods, I'll have a try at apologising.'

'Yes, certainly talk to Mrs Parham first. She knows Sir George as well as anyone. And she wouldn't have put up with him for thirty years if he was the sort of ogre he's made out to be.'

'There's just one thing that puzzles me. The faults were all on the other side. So what am I going to apologise for?'

The Rector thought for nearly a full minute before he spoke. Then he said, 'I'll tell you what you're apologising for. When you thought you were dealing with a poacher, what you did was right. When you found it was Sir George's son, it was wrong.' He raised a hand to prevent Luke from interrupting him. 'If you're going to be a clergyman – a parish priest – one of the things you'll have to remember is to keep a sense of proportion. Not to try weighing up absolutes of right and wrong. In this case you were putting three years' work at risk for three minutes of ill-judged self-justification. You may not know this, but Sir George and I looked on you as a boy of exceptional promise. I can remember being impressed – oh, many years ago – when you were at the village school and I came to teach you all Divinity. A sad waste of time for the most part. But your comments and your questions were far above anything your fellows could produce. That was when our plans for you were made. They must not be thrown away for a single night's misunderstanding.'

One part of Luke's mind was ready to accept what the Rector said. Another part was in revolt against it. He said, 'I understand that some men are placed above others and the ones below must respect the ones above. But that doesn't seem to me to be what Christianity teaches us. Christ was quite prepared to challenge the classes above him. I mean, all the scribes and the pharisees and that lot. He was always ready to argue with them. He even took a whip to them when he cleared the Temple.'

'That may have been all right in those days,' said the Rector sadly. 'But not today. Not in England. The classes are set and fixed. You can't argue them away. Remember what the hymn says, "God made them high and lowly and ordered their estate".'

Hezekiah brought them down to earth.

'You realise, boy,' he said, 'that if Sir George takes against us, I could lose my job. *And* we could be turned out of house. It belongs to him, not me.'

This hit Luke between the eyes. He was almost too upset to speak. He said, 'You don't think – could he really – ?'

'I don't say he would. I only say he could.'

'Then of course I'll apologise. I'll go right round today.' In spite of his consternation he managed to grin. He said, 'I shall have to think out pretty carefully how I'm going to say it. After all, it was Oliver who was breaking the law. And he attacked me. Not me him.'

'Watch your grammar,' said the Rector. 'The subject of the verb "to attack" should be the nominative pronoun. You should have said, "Not I."'

This made them all laugh, which was, no doubt, the Rector's intention.

The heavy, nail-studded door at the back of Bellingham Court opened on to a flight of steps which led down to a passage flanked by doors on each side, a subterranean area of cold stores, wine cellars and game larders. In his childhood Luke had feared it. He had thought of it as a cemetery.

This was partly the fault of his grandfather. The old man had been versed in the mythology of death. In his own childhood he could remember how heavy stones were laid on newly dug graves to prevent their occupants emerging and he had entertained the little boy – sometimes frightened, but resolute not to show it – with stories of vampires and ghosts and of men who turned into wolves as the light began to fade. So it was that when Luke had to carry messages to Mrs Parham he had hurried down that particular passage, fearing to hear the pheasants and partridges coming back to life and fluttering their wings to escape from the hooks on which they hung.

Now, he was too old for such fancies, but none the less he wasted no time in making for the far end of the passage and climbing the steps which led up to the kitchen quarters, a more temperate zone. Here lived and worked the platoon of maids who served the house, under the joint generalship of Parkes the butler and Mrs Parham the housekeeper.

Luke had once calculated that if you added the outside staff, the gardeners and grooms and stable boys, you could easily reach a total of thirty people. It seemed a great number to be looking after Sir George, who was a widower, and his two sons; but when he had mentioned this to his father, Hezekiah had not been impressed. 'It might seem strange to you,' he had said, 'but think of it this way. Sir George is giving employment, from his own pocket, mark you, to thirty men and women. It stands to his credit, not to his discredit.'

In truth, it was a style of living that was already becoming uncommon. In Sir George's case, the money needed to keep it up did not come from the farms on the estate. As Sir George pointed out to his cronies, the miserable rents which the farms paid scarcely met the repairs which, as landlord, he was bound to carry out.

The real money came from Sir George's share in the silk- and cotton-spinning industry brought over by Huguenot refugees from France two centuries before. One of Sir George's ancestors, when leasing them the site near Lavenham for the factories they wanted to build, had stipulated that, instead of a rent, they should allow him a share of the profits. This had proved to be a very lucrative investment.

Mrs Parham welcomed Luke warmly and he rewarded her with a smile which, had he known it, was already beginning to flutter the hearts of the local girls.

She said, 'What good wind blows you here? Don't tell me you've come to see an old woman, because I shan't believe you.'

'Then you'd be wrong, Mrs P,' said Luke. 'Because I did come to see you. Though it's true I had a second reason.'

'I knew it. Something you want out of me. In the old days it would have been my home-made fudge. But I guess you're too old for sweets now.'

'Never too old for your home-bake. But the thing I really wanted was a piece of information.'

'Indeed. About what, might I ask?'

'About Sir George. I need to know how his gout is.'

'At the moment, thank the Lord, it isn't troubling him.'

'And he's at home?'

'When I saw him about half an hour ago he was in his study, writing letters.'

'Then I'd better go straight up.'

'Before his gout comes back, is that it?'

Luke knew that she was longing to be told what it was all about; and although in the past he had confided many of his secrets to her as a surrogate mother, his own being dead, he felt that in this case he had to keep his counsel.

He departed, up a second flight of steps, emerging through a baize-lined door into the front hall of the house. Here he paused to collect himself.

He had crossed Sir George's path many times, at shoots and on other outdoor occasions and had observed him in church, trying not to go to sleep as the Rector plunged more and more deeply into Hebrew history and philosophy, but he had never contemplated a face-to-face encounter. How was he going to manage it? Should he stump in, say, 'I'm sorry for what happened yesterday,' and stump out again?

By now the simplest words seemed to be sticking in his throat and his hands were clammy. It was determination which took him along the passage and pride which knocked at the study door.

Sir George looked up from his writing and said, 'Come in, boy. Shut the door. What can I do for you?'

'There's something I wanted to say, sir.'

'Wouldn't it be easier if you sat down?'

'No, sir. I'd rather stand. The fact is – well, my father and Reverend Millbanke both thought I should come along and apologise –'

'I'm not interested in what other people thought. What I'd like to know is what *you* thought.'

'I thought the same. It was silly of me. I should have realised that Oliver – that your son – would have told you what he meant to do and got your permission.'

'My son told me nothing. He knew he could go anywhere he liked on my property and he only told me this morning about his rabbiting. He should not have used illegal snares, but that was for me to tell him, not you.'

'No, sir. I realise that now.' Luke drew a deep breath. 'If it would make up for it, I'd be glad to set some of our dead-fall traps where he set his. And I'd let him have any rabbits they caught.'

'Handsome,' said Sir George. 'But not necessary.'

Gaining confidence from the comparative friendliness with which this was said, Luke added, 'I was fearing you might be planning to visit my sins on Father.'

'Meaning?'

'Meaning that you might dismiss him.'

'You can put that idea right out of your head. What? Get rid of the best head keeper I've ever had and at the beginning of the

11

shooting season? That would, indeed, be cutting off my nose to spite my face.'

Sir George paused for a moment, then added, 'In fact you may well be wondering why I should be bothering my head about a boys' quarrel. But there's more behind it than you think.' He got up and walked across to the window. 'There's a dangerous spirit abroad in the land. An evil spirit. It comes creeping up like one of our fen fogs. One moment the sky's clear. The next you can hardly see your nose on your own face.'

As he spoke he was looking out across the expanse of lawn to the line of wind-stripped beech trees which guarded the far end. Luke realised that he was really talking to himself.

'God alone knows what propagates this evil, or why people encourage it. Radical politicians, do you think, trying to make a name for themselves in the House? Agitators stirring up trouble, so that they might find pickings in the chaos they create? You can see the symptoms of it everywhere. Workers starting to combine against their employers. Tenants against their landlords. Everyone who fancies that he has too little of this world's goods trying to snatch something from those who have more than he has. And one sign of it is very clear. The growing and open disrespect of the lower classes for the class above them. Every time an example of it occurs, whether in big things or in small things, the upper class *must* stamp on it. If they fail to do so, they are acting as traitors to their caste.' Sir George swung back on Luke. 'So now you know why I was upset.' He gave a short grunting laugh. 'Really, you're apologising to the wrong person. It's Oliver you should be addressing yourself to. I don't mean for stopping him from using illegal snares. Maybe you were within your rights there, though it might have been done more respectfully. What was unfair was taking him unawares when he wasn't expecting it and tripping him up.'

Luke said, 'If that's what he told you, he was lying.'

There was a long silence. The boy would have given anything he possessed to take the words back. If he had been only a few years older he would have realised that up to that point he was winning. He had only to keep his mouth shut to consolidate his gains. Now he had thrown everything into the discard.

He waited for the storm to break, but there was no storm.

What happened was almost worse. Addressing him coldly and impersonally, as though he was delivering a judgement from the Bench, Sir George said, 'One thing is clear to me. You are totally unfitted to be a clergyman of the established Church, in any shape or form or any place. Should you try to pursue your intention of so doing I should regard it as my duty to use all means in my power to prevent you from getting further.'

Having said this he sat down to continue with his writing and Luke went out of the room, closing the door quietly. He was leaving behind him something that had been part of his life for the last three years.

As he shut the study door, the door next to it opened and a young man came out. Luke knew him by sight, though he had rarely met him. It was Sir George's elder son, Julian. Unlike Oliver he did not accompany his father on his sporting forays and never seemed to put in an appearance at church. Also he was much away from home. Until recently at Eton and now at Cambridge.

When the village discussed him they called him either 'odd' or 'modern'. The terms, which were not really intended as insults, were almost synonymous and arose partly from Julian's appearance, but more from his occasional visits to the village pub. Here it was his custom to order drinks all round and having thus ensured himself a captive audience, to lecture it on current political topics.

He now grabbed Luke by the arm and said, 'Come inside. I want to talk to you,' and dragged him into his room.

Luke offered no resistance. He was not frightened of Julian, assessing him as a less formidable opponent than his younger brother.

Also the room, which he had never been in before, was

intriguing. The pictures on the wall would have supported the village verdict, being daubs of colour, apparently applied at random to the canvas. One of them Luke saw was entitled *Womanhood Observed*, but turned out, disappointingly, to be a composition of blue and crimson triangles and circles.

And there were books: shelves full of them, piles on the window ledge and a heap of what was evidently Julian's current reading on the table by the small sofa. Luke was more interested in books than in pictures. A careful course of English literature, as prescribed by the Rector, had recently embraced both poetry and philosophy. As he was being hustled past the pile on the table he had only time to look at the top one. He recognised the name of the author, Bernard Shaw, whom he knew to be an exciting and much criticised playwright, though this one could hardly be a dramatic work, being entitled *The Common Sense of Municipal Trading*.

'We can't talk standing up,' said Julian. 'Come and sit down over here.'

He dragged him to an armchair and sat down beside him. The chair was a large one, but not really broad enough to accommodate two people and Luke found himself pressed against Julian who increased his discomfort by putting one arm round his shoulders.

'I thought I must tell you this. There's not much goes on in Dad's study that can't be heard in here. So I got the full force of his standard lecture on the *trahison des clercs*. Not that I needed to listen too hard. I knew it by heart.'

'What did you call it?'

'*Trahison des clercs*. That's a French expression. There's no exact equivalent for it in English. It means that if you belong to a certain class you should stand up for it and defend it if it's attacked.'

'That seems sensible.'

'It's all right if you don't imagine, as Dad seems to do, that it applies only to *your* class. Perhaps I shouldn't talk about my father like this, but you're a sensible kid, I know.' He gave Luke's shoulders a squeeze. 'He's really just a silly old buffer. As old fashioned as the Tower of London and as difficult to shift. What he refuses to accept is that the lower classes have every right to their own sort of solidarity. The right to combine for war against their superiors. Why shouldn't a group of tenant farmers gang up to force their landlords to lower the exorbitant rents he's charging? Why shouldn't workmen combine to secure a rise in their wages and strike if they don't get it?'

'Reasonable,' said Luke. Julian's body was pressed so tightly against his that he could feel the warmth of it coming through.

'But he's quite right when he says that it's not only the big things. Little things matter, too. Like workmen not remembering to call the boss "sir" and tenants failing to take off their caps when the landlord passes them. And you not knuckling under when you realised that it was Oliver – I offer no excuse for his conduct – who was setting illegal snares. You can realise now why he was forced to tell lies about Oliver being treacherously attacked by you. What he couldn't get away from was the fact that Oliver finished up on the ground. You *must* have cheated to put him there. Otherwise you were a better man than he was, which was unthinkable.'

'You may be right,' said Luke. 'All the same, I shouldn't have said what I did. Your father's gone out of his way to help me in the past. I should have thought about that and held my tongue.'

'I disagree. Most emphatically I disagree. It's always right for the under-class to speak out against the over-class. I'm only sorry that in this particular case it worked so much to your detriment. You're such a nice kid. Everyone in the place likes you. I know that. If only there was something I could do to help. Anything at all.'

Julian had shifted his position slightly and his face was very close to Luke, who could see the sweat starting up on his forehead and a tiny dribble at the corner of his mouth.

He wants to kiss me, thought Luke. Am I going to let him? To stop him, I should have to hit him. And if I hurt him, that will make more trouble.

The problem was solved for him by Sir George, who chose that moment to give tongue from the next room.

'I don't know who you're talking to,' he bellowed, 'but just stop gossiping and come here. I've something I want to tell you.'

The alacrity with which Julian responded rather contradicted the disparaging way in which he had been talking about his father. He jumped up and trotted to the door. Luke extracted himself from the sofa and followed him. When they were out in the passage he muttered a quick, 'Goodbye. I'll be thinking about what you said,' and was through the green baize door before Julian had got into his father's room.

He realised that what he needed most was time. Time by himself; time to think things out before he talked to his father and the Rector, both of whom would probably be waiting for him at home. Above all, time to plan. In spite of his haste to get clear he realised that it would be a mistake to slide out without saying goodbye to Mrs Parham, though he was sorely puzzled about what he could say to her. Another problem, in a day of problems. When he got there, the housekeeper's room was empty.

He caught sight of one of the maids coming out of the kitchen and said, 'I'm sorry, I don't know your name.'

'I'm Debbie.'

'Well, Debbie, would you be kind enough to give Mrs Parham a message from me. Tell her I looked in, but her room was empty. I'll try to see her later.'

'Do anything for you,' said the girl, with a slanting look out of her dark eyes. 'And pleased to do it, I'm sure.'

Luke looked after her as she scuttled back into the kitchen. Evidently she liked him. Fine. He liked people to like him. Just so long – he grinned as he thought of Julian, squeezing down beside him on the sofa – just so long as they didn't start liking him too much.

He found his father and the Rector waiting for him and gave them as truthful a report as he could manage.

'Until that moment,' he said, 'everything seemed to be going pretty well. He'd no hard feelings against you, Dad. In fact, he described you as the best head keeper he'd ever had.'

'I can see from your face,' said the Rector, 'that that's where things went wrong. What happened?'

'What happened was I lost my head. He accused me of cheating, of catching his son unawares and tripping him up. Heavens above! If he could have seen it. Oliver announced that he was going to teach me a lesson and came rushing at me, his arms going like a windmill. I did what I'd been taught, stretched my arms straight out so that he couldn't reach me and when we clinched, rolled him over.'

'Good,' said his father, the light of old battles in his eyes. 'Good.'

'Good that you defended yourself,' said the Rector. 'Bad that you accused Sir George of lying. For all you knew he was only repeating what Oliver had told him.'

'That's just it. I didn't accuse *him* of lying. What I said was, if that's what Oliver told him, *he* was lying.'

'Just as bad,' said the Rector. 'It was the honour of the family that you were attacking.'

'I can see that now,' said Luke. He had no wish to pursue the matter. It was sterile. What was done was done. It was the future that mattered. It was clear that his father thought so, too.

'You'll not enter the Church,' he said. 'That road's barred. So what are you going to do?'

'I've got an idea about that. I haven't had time to think it through. But one thing seems clear. I didn't ought to throw away—'

'Ought not.'

'Sorry, Rector. I ought not to throw away all that you've been teaching me for the past three years. There must surely be some way of using it.'

The Rector said, 'My mind's been moving in the same direction. You've learned the fundamentals of mathematics and though your English grammar is still sometimes faulty, no doubt it'll improve. And you've a good grasp of the Classics. There are schools that would welcome you as an usher.'

'Not Eton or Harrow?'

'Not Eton or Harrow,' agreed the Rector with a smile. 'Nor even my own old school at Winchester. But I'm told that there are board schools and village schools looking for teachers. In three years' time you'd walk into a job. Meanwhile you'd be living at home, helping your father and I could lend you books so that you could carry on with what I've tried to teach you.'

Luke said, 'What I'd really like to do is master a modern language.' Sensing the Rector's disapproval, he added hastily, 'I don't mean dropping the Latin and Greek, sir. Just to have something to go alongside them.'

'Good,' said his father. 'That's good. Two strings to your bow.'

The Rector said, 'Yes, a good idea. But what languages had you in mind? And how are you going to do it? I'm afraid I shouldn't be much use to you as a modern language teacher, even if Sir George allowed me to do it.'

'I thought I might start with French. Some of your parishioners – ones who work in the spinning mills at Lavenham – they came from France, didn't they?'

'Originally, yes. Huguenots who came over to avoid the repression and massacres in France. But since their families have now been here for two centuries or more, I imagine they will have forgotten all the French they ever knew.'

'But there must surely be younger ones. People who have come over recently and only just begun to speak English. If you could find one of those, I could teach him English while he was teaching me French.'

The Rector thought about this. Then he said, 'Even better if we could find some sort of job in the mills. It'd be unskilled work, but it would bring you in a few shillings. Enough to pay for your food and lodging with one of the families.' Seeing the look on Hezekiah's face he added quickly, 'Of course, you'd come home every weekend.'

'Aye, I'd be glad of that. The boy's a great help to me.'

'If we pick the right family, one with young folk in it, newly come from France, it should work very well.' The Rector's eyes kindled with enthusiasm. 'You were quick to pick up dead languages. You'll pick up a living one fast enough. I warrant that in a year or two you'd be bilingual. Then we could add another language. German, perhaps, or Italian. Why, by the time you were eighteen, you could set your sights as high as you liked.'

But not on one of the great public schools, thought Luke.

Recently the Rector had introduced him to the works of Charles Dickens and he was now halfway through *David Copperfield*. He remembered how Mr Mells had been despised by the boys at Mr Creakle's academy and how he had finally lost his job when it was revealed, by the despicable Steerforth, that Mr Mells' parents were living in an alms house. Small doubt that this would have been the reaction of public schoolboys like Oliver – there was a lot of Steerforth in Oliver, he thought – when it was leaked to them, as it surely would be, that his father was a gamekeeper.

The thought did not worry him.

He had no intention of becoming a school master.

2

Luke was squatting in a doorway in a narrow, unlighted and stinking alley in the east end of Whitechapel, watching a house which belonged to a widow called Triboff.

To arrive at that spot he had followed a young Russian, whom he had observed hanging round a coffee stall. His name was Tomacoff and he was known to be a messenger for members of the *émigré* ring. The fact that he was dawdling over his second cup of coffee, with occasional glances at his watch, suggested the possibility that the recipient of his message was not expected to be at home until a late hour. When he had delivered his message he might be entrusted with a reply. If he could then be followed, he might lead to where another member of the ring was holed up.

Near midnight, with the streets silent and empty, it would not be easy to follow undetected, but it was worth trying. There was a light showing showing in an upstairs window. From time to time the shadows of two men moved across it. All he had to do was to wait and make no movement that could be detected from the window.

To help you keep still, had his father not said many years ago, control your thoughts as well as your body. The events of the six years since he had been forced to abandon the road to the Church had certainly given him plenty to think about.

In many ways, the first year had been the hardest.

He had put in a full day at the spinning mills of the brothers Laurent, fetching and carrying for everybody and paid less than anyone. The weekday evenings had been spent in the house of Antoine de Maître-Huquet, a distant relative of the Laurents newly arrived from France. Here he had consumed his first real meal of the day and for an hour or more than two young men had talked to each other, first in English, then in French, correcting each other's grammar as they went. After which he had bicycled the six miles back to Bellingham. It was often after midnight before he reached his bed.

So for five days in the week. At the weekends his father had expected him to help with the manifold jobs around Sir George's preserves and coverts. Whilst so engaged he had contrived to avoid meeting Sir George, or his sons. He was helped by the fact that Oliver was away for much of the time, either at school or, later, at Cambridge, while Julian was rarely at home, pursuing a course of political self-education in Germany and Spain.

After a year Antoine had decided that there was not much more he could teach Luke who was, by that time, a competent French conversationalist, with little grammar but an expanding vocabulary. So ended Act One. Act Two had been different and in some ways easier.

A Russian tutor had been located. This time it was not to be informal conversation, but steady professional coaching, which would have to be paid for. Luke had saved a certain amount from his Lavenham pay and his father had insisted, despite his protests, on supplying the deficiency out of his own pocket. Knowing what he did about his father's finances it had sometimes occurred to him to wonder where the money was coming from.

Living at home, with two or three hours of solid coaching every afternoon, he had made rapid progress. Commenting on this, his tutor had repeated what the Rector had observed, that his pupil seemed to have a natural aptitude for tuning in to the rhythm of a new language, something akin to an inborn talent for music. So rapid had been his progress that he was soon able to read and enjoy the books that he was given for homework. Sergei Aksakov's *Chronicles of a Russian Family* and *The Childhood of Bagrov the Grandson*, plain fare, but nourishing; then to more exciting stuff. Ivan Goncharov's *The Precipice* and Nikolay

Gogol's *Taras Bulba* with its account of the doings of the Zaporozhian Cossacks.

In the course of this study and particularly in Goncharov's novel, which deals with the traumatic introduction of a nihilist into a conventional family of Russian gentry, he had found that he was imbibing something quite apart from the story. It was a matter of feeling.

From the French books, most of them nineteenth-century reminiscences of life in Paris, he had concluded that, in spite of their revolution, the French had, quickly and thankfully, reverted to a caste system. It was encapsulated, for his tutor Antoine, in the possession of the precious 'de'. 'You will perceive,' he had said, 'that although we have no aristocrats in France we still value the concept of aristocracy.' The Russians, on the other hand, did still have their Tzar, with his satellite court, supported by a land-owning over-class. But, underneath it, he could feel the passions stirring; passions that had burst out, even as he was reading, in flame and blood on the decks of the battleship *Potemkin* and down the Odessa Steps. Flames ruthlessly extinguished, but burning all the hotter for being confined underground.

On one occasion towards the end of the second year, his father had brought back from shooting Dr Ramsden, the head of Lavenham Grammar School, a prestigious grant-aided establishment. Luke remembered him coming into the cottage, looking round cautiously as though suspecting owls in the rafters or rats under the floorboards. He had refused a chair, maybe fearing that if he sat down he would be committing himself too far and had listened, standing in front of the fire, to Hezekiah's enthusiastic account of his son's progress. After which he had offered them his advice.

Luke, he considered, ought to start at the foot of the ladder, seeking a post in some small church school. He should be able to secure such a position without great difficulty, particularly if backed by a recommendation from the vicar. What use fluent Russian would be to village children was not immediately apparent, but Luke, who was growing older and wiser, had confined himself to agreeing with every word that Dr Ramsden had uttered.

This was easy, since, as has been noted, he had no intention of becoming a school master.

His secret ambition had been planted, years earlier, by a bundle of dog-eared copies of the *Strand* magazine. Here he had stumbled into the colourful, the ensnaring world of Sherlock Holmes; of Baker Street, Dr Watson, hansom cabs and pea-soup fogs. His only objection to them was that the official police force seemed to be unduly depreciated. Inspector Hopkins was sometimes approved of. Lestrade, on the other hand, seemed to grab the wrong end of the stick with masterly regularity. It was all very well for Sherlock Holmes. The author dealt him all the cards. Luke thought that in a number of the cases he could have done as well as Holmes himself.

Was that someone looking out of the window? Surely the curtain had shifted. Or were his eyes beginning to play tricks? As the moments went by and a further quarter struck from a nearby clock he relaxed and resumed his thinking.

It was on his eighteenth birthday that he had finally revealed to his father what his plans were. His father had accepted this change of direction with unexpected composure. It was almost as though the thought of his son as a humble usher had ceased to appeal to him, too. A few mornings later he had driven Luke in the trap to Ipswich and, after making sure that he had enough money for his immediate needs, had said goodbye to him, swung the trap round and clattered off without looking back.

Arrived in London, Luke had presented himself at the recruiting office of the Metropolitan Police. This had turned out to be a cold and dusty room in the corner of Scotland Place. Most of the other recruits seemed to be ex-soldiers, with the army polish still on them.

The intelligence test, so-called, had been a farce. The physical examination which followed had proved an ordeal. The recollection of being forced to strip naked and to submit to a police surgeon pawing his body, still had the power to upset him. The other recruits had taken it in their stride; no doubt their army experience had hardened them to indignities.

That same afternoon he had been sworn in as a constable and posted to 'L' Division, where he was billeted in a station house and shared a room with three other recruits. He was allocated a sergeant for the first few weeks as guide, philosopher and friend.

Sergeant Hamble had completed over forty years of service and could offer him little in the way of up-to-date advice. He despised the modern police helmet and spoke warmly of the top hat he had worn as a recruit. 'Lined with best quality steel,' he said. 'You could sit on it if you were tired and stand on it if you wanted to look over some wall or fence. Couldn't do that with the modern helmet, now, could you?' He also considered that the rattle was better than the whistle that had replaced it.

In his dreams Luke sometimes saw the sergeant, his top hat at a rakish angle, advancing down the street whirring his rattle like a demented football fan. But such gleams of humour were few and far between in an existence that seemed to be uniformly and unendingly grey.

That he was lonely was natural. He was exchanging a place where he had known and been known by everyone for a place where no one knew him or cared anything about him. This might have been anticipated and in his heart of hearts he suspected that it was good for him. He had to learn to stand on his own feet. What had really upset him was the lack of action and movement.

Of all the divisions in London, 'L' had seemed the least exciting. It was neither one thing nor the other. Not a countrified division, like 'P' or 'R' which ran south into the fields and woods of Kent; nor a central division like 'M' which lay immediately to the north of them with one end just across the river from Westminster ('the Government is vitally concerned by this development, Mr Holmes. Any help you can give will be much appreciated'), the other end embracing the garish riverside of Rotherhithe and Jamaica Road, the land of W. W. Jacobs.

And what had 'L' got to offer, for God's sake?

Clapham, Brixton, Camberwell, Peckham. Places as dull as their names; places full of dull people, the cycle of whose lives seemed to be Saturday night drunkenness and Sunday morning repentance.

Nor had the situation been improved by the character and disposition of his superior officers. The division had been headed by Superintendent Garforth, the plain-clothes men were under Divisional Detective Inspector Cridland. The two men loathed each other. What time they could spare from inter-departmental fighting was spent in keeping the lower ranks in their place.

When Garforth learned that Luke was competent in French and fluent in Russian his first reaction was to distrust him. The next was to make use of him in the most tedious manner possible. There were court documents that needed translation and for the whole of one week he had been loaned to a neighbouring division to take down everything that was said at an Anglo-French trade conference, translating into English any comments made. His thirty-two-page report went into Garforth's desk and, Luke was certain, never saw the light of day again.

It was at the end of that particular week, at the darkest hour of his depression, that the clouds lifted. Joe Narrabone arrived. And better still, he and Joe had managed to get a room to themselves. Joe had been at the village school with Luke. He had been no sort of scholar, regarding the study of books as a waste of precious time. He had a genius for getting into trouble and wriggling out of it. He had been unquestionably, and with no near rival, the bad boy of the village.

Standing behind the form mistress, who was covering his exercise book with corrections, he had spent his time attaching the end of her skirt to the chair she was sitting on; so firmly that, the other boys being too weak with laughter to help her, the poor lady had been forced to hobble into the next-door classroom, dragging the chair with her, to report the outrage to the headmaster. This had earned Joe a record flogging, which he had repaid by climbing into the headmaster's bedroom carrying a sack with a dead dog in it. As he explained to Luke with a gap-toothed grin, he had arranged the dog in the bed, with its head tastefully exposed on the pillow.

He was suspected of this outrage, but nothing could be proved.

His elders and betters had prophesied fates for Joe ranging from transportation to the gallows, but he had been unimpressed. Luke, being his total opposite in character, had naturally become his closest friend, a friendship which had produced one practical advantage. Joe had poached, consistently and successfully, in all coverts except those belonging to Sir George.

After leaving school Joe had continued his career of rowdy misconduct and petty crime; until, as he explained to Luke, he got reformed.

'T'wasn't religion nor nothing like that,' he explained. 'Fact is, I got cotched selling pheasants I'd picked up. Told the beak I'd found them in the road, but somehow he diddun believe me. Result was, I got a proper whipping. Oh boy, don't you ever try it. At school all they did was tickle you. This hurt. I diddun want no more of it. So I made up my mind. You know what they say – if you can't beat 'em, join 'em. And here I am.' He had added, sitting on the bed drumming his boots on the floor, 'At school you was always held up to me as a good example. A sort of saint, with one of those custard pie things round your head.'

At this point Luke had thrown a pillow at him and they had rolled on to the floor, trying to hold each other down. The noise had brought in Sergeant Hamble who had separated them and lectured them on the virtue of co-operation.

'I don't know what you boys was quarrelling about, but whatever it was, you must make it up and try to be friends.' They had promised to try and when the sergeant had departed had lain on their beds almost ill with suppressed laughter.

From that point life had started again.

They had managed to get posted to the same patrol and had quartered the streets of Clapham, Brixton, Camberwell and Peckham looking for some excitement in those depressingly unexciting parts of London.

It had arrived unexpectedly.

One morning the sergeant who was briefing them had told them to keep a particular eye on a meeting at the Brixton Town Hall. 'It's them wimmin,' he said, speaking the bi-syllable as though it was synonymous with 'vermin'. 'I expect you've read about 'em in the papers. Suffrajetters they call themselves.'

Recently Luke had picked up a paper which had intrigued him by its slashing cover picture. This showed a young lady equipped with a sword called 'Equity' and a shield labelled 'Purity'. She had need of both of them, since she was being pounced on by a dragon with scaly wings and long claws identified as 'The Press'. He noted that it was the official organ of the Woman's Social and Political Union, which had achieved notoriety as the militant branch of a more decorous body, the National Suffrage Union. It was the WSPU, it seemed, who were organising this particular meeting. The brainchild of the Pankhurst family from Manchester, their battlecry proclaimed their aims: 'Women, speak out. No pulling of punches. Fight. Suffer if you must, but never, never keep quiet.'

'I dunno what they call themselves now,' said the sergeant. 'They keep changing their names. But I can tell you what *I* call 'em. I call 'em trouble. This meeting's to raise money. What for? Why, so's they can make more trouble. Watch 'em close. If you see a breach of the peace, you know what to do.' What exactly this was he had left unexplained.

Luke and Joe had rearranged their beats so that they met behind the Town Hall, a gaunt yellow building overlooking the railway on one side and a canal on the other. The noise inside the building reminded Luke of a hive of bees getting ready to swarm. As he was thinking this, the noise increased, in tempo and in pitch. Not bees. Hornets.

'Something's happening round the side,' said Joe. They doubled back the way they had come. As they turned the corner a door burst open and a man staggered out. His shirt was torn open at the neck and his face was running with blood. As he hesitated, undecided which way to turn, the furies on his heels caught him.

The young lady who was leading the pack dived for his ankles like an expert Rugby footballer. The two who were following her piled on top of him, clawing and scratching.

Breach of the peace, thought Luke. What do we do now? The idea of attacking a well-dressed and clearly upper-class young woman was unappealing. By the time he reached the point of action half a dozen more had come out and formed a circle round the trio on the ground. Some were shouting, others were offering advice. They were divided between a suggestion that the man be thrown on to the railway line or, alternatively, into the canal.

'Must stop this,' said Luke. He caught hold of one of the women in a half-hearted way, and tried to pull her off her prey. She was unexpectedly strong. While she was resisting, two of her friends had grabbed him, one by the collar, the other by the hair. He felt that in a short time he would be on the ground himself.

The situation was saved by Joe. He was a great deal less inhibited than Luke. He hit one of the women who was attacking him with an upper-cut which felled her, and he dealt with the two on top of the man by banging their heads together hard. Then he advanced on the crowd of supporters, kicking them on the shins and stamping on their feet. This was more effective than punching.

Luke, meanwhile, had helped the victim to his feet. Reinforcements were pouring out of the door. A tactical withdrawal was indicated.

He and Joe each grabbed one of the man's arms and they ran for it – down the side alley, through an open gate and along the canal bank. Joe paused once, to knock the closest of their pursuers into the canal, a move which conferred a double benefit on them, since the rest of the pack halted to rescue their friend and the pursuit slackened.

They crossed the canal via a bridge, dived down an alley and emerged into a side road.

'Pub here,' said Joe.

He thundered on the door, which opened after a clanking of bolts and was shut and bolted behind them. It was a middle-aged lady who had let them in. Luke supposed that Joe knew her, since when he put one arm round her waist and kissed her, she offered no objection to this treatment, but clucked with concern when she saw the state of the victim's face and bustled off for hot water and sponges. By the time she got back he seemed to be better.

'I'll have that jacket,' the lady said. 'Sooner we get the blood off it the better. And put some of this on them scratches.' It was a bottle of yellow stuff labelled 'Poison'. When Luke looked at it doubtfully she said, 'I keep it in the bar to use on my customers. Not killed one of them yet.'

She made off with the jacket and the man submitted to having his face dabbed.

'If it stings,' said Luke, who had been brought up on this well-known medical theory, 'it's a sign that it's doing you good.'

'Looks like a Red Indian, dunnee,' said Joe critically. 'A new sort. A Yellow Indian. He could do with a bit more on the chin.'

By the time they had finished painting, the landlady was back with the coat, which she had roughly sponged and pressed, a bottle of brandy and four glasses.

The man said, 'It wasn't only the scratches.' He felt the back of his head. 'I got quite a bump there when I went down.'

'If you were concussed,' said Luke, 'I don't think you ought to drink alcohol.'

'That's a fallacy,' said Joe. 'I've been concussed more times than you've had hot dinners and brandy's the only thing that done it any good.'

While the man was sipping his brandy cautiously, with pauses to make sure that it wasn't doing him any harm, Luke said, 'We ought to introduce ourselves. We're the latest thing in recruits. I'm Probationary Constable Pagan and this is Probationary

Constable Narrabone. Both of "L" Division. We haven't been here long enough to know everyone by sight. You'd be in the Detective Branch, of course.'

'The aristocrats,' said Joe, 'compared with us poor foot sloggers, that is.'

'Actually,' said the man, 'I'm not in "L" Division.' He paused for a moment as though deliberating whether to go on, then he added, 'As a matter of fact, I'm not a policeman. I'm working at the Home Office. I was sent to report on this meeting. I thought I was safely tucked away in a dark corner of the gallery, but those women must have spotted me.'

'Eyes like cats',' agreed Joe.

'I'm everlastingly grateful to you for what you did,' said the man. He had hoisted himself to his feet and found that he was tolerably steady on his legs. 'I've got to get back as quickly as I can. Could I ask you a favour? When you make your report, could you leave me out of it as much as possible? Describe me as an innocent member of the public, set on for no reason by those women. Something like that.'

'Do what we can,' said Luke.

'And I'm sure that this lady—'

'I'm not one to blab,' said the landlady. 'And if you must go, though I think you'd be wiser to sit still for a bit, I'll show you a back way out, in case those creatures are still prowling round.'

While she was gone the two probationary constables sat warming their feet at the fire, sipping their brandy and wondering how long they could make this useful diversion last.

'One thing I did think a bit odd –' said Joe.

Hold it. Two men at the window now. Two shadows quite clear on the curtain. They seemed to be looking out. And were they signalling to someone? And if so, who to? Luke felt a trickle of apprehension at the thought. The alley-way was a dead end running up to the railway. No one had gone past him since he arrived, so whoever it was, was either up on the railway or, more probably and more disturbingly, had got there before him and had been standing as still as he had been.

It was some minutes before he could detach his thoughts from this unpleasant possibility and bring them back to the story that he was telling himself. It was worth the effort, because he remembered that Joe had said something important.

'One thing I do think a bit odd,' he had said. 'We told him our names, didn't we? OK. So why didn't he tell us his?'

'Perhaps he's in the Secret Service.'

'He wouldn't be in no service at all if we hadn't been there to lend him a hand.'

The landlady, who was back by now, having seen her guest safely away through the cellar-flap, said, 'Did I understand that you was wanting to know something about him? Well, I can tell you this much. His name's Hubert Daines and he lives at 173B Cromwell Road.'

'How on earth—?'

'Couldn't resist taking a peep in his jacket pocket. Found two or three letters addressed to him.'

Luke made a careful note of both the name and the address. In view of what they had promised, they could not use them when they made their report, but he had a feeling that they might come in handy sooner or later.

The landlady waved aside Luke's offer to pay for the drinks. 'He paid for them,' she said. 'Paid up handsome.' They finished their own drinks quickly. Although they had an excellent excuse for having left their beats they felt they might have stretched it a bit far.

'Have to talk fast,' said Joe, 'to talk ourselves out of this.'

He was right.

They had missed two points and were reported, reluctantly, by Sergeant Hamble. Their account of an unnamed bystander whom they had rescued from the hands of the suffragettes, had been received with cynicism. It appeared that, after the ejection of the spy, the meeting had closed with a number of resolutions advocating varying degrees of violence and had then dispersed peace-fully. The organisers denied all knowledge of intrusion by a spy.

Luke and Joe were warned that they would face a disciplinary board, at Area level, which, since they were still only probation-ers, might mean dismissal from the Force.

At this point, when things looked black for the two young con-stables, a letter had arrived. Addressed to Superintendent Garforth, it was typed on a double sheet of handsomely embossed Home Office notepaper and signed by no less a person than an Under-secretary of State. It congratulated the Superintendent on the measures he had taken to keep a poten-tially dangerous meeting under observation and control. It applauded the vigorous steps taken by his officers in protecting a member of the Home Office staff from assault and damage and said that the whole episode reflected great credit on Garforth and on the organisation at his division. The Under-secretary would be sending a copy of his letter to the Home Secretary.

Luke and Joe were now wheeled up for a second helping. The letter was read out to them and they were told that, in all the cir-cumstances, their offence of missing two consecutive points could be overlooked – provided that it did not occur again.

Luke had derived two impressions from all this: that Hubert Daines must have an unexpected pull with the senior ranks in the Home Office; and that he was a very shrewd man.

A second episode was imprinted on Luke's memory, as much for the uneasiness which it had caused him at the time as for its unexpected outcome. It had occurred eighteen months after his and Joe's brush with the suffragettes.

Their probationary period was long past and they were by then established members of the rank and file of 'L' Division. Luke, in spite of a tendency to use words of more than two syllables and to read works of literature in preference to the penny press, was toler-ated by his fellow constables on account of his unfailing good nature and generosity. Joe was popular. His skill in evading the consequences of his more outrageous manoeuvres commanded respect among his friends and suspicion among his superiors.

Both of them had acquired a number of commendations and the tiny pecuniary awards which occasionally went with them – money which disappeared immediately in a round of celebratory drinks.

Superintendent Garforth's view of them was ambivalent. Both were unquestionably good at their jobs and would come up, in due course, for promotion to sergeant. This was a step which neither of them would have viewed with unmixed pleasure. They knew that the real way up was through the ranks of the CID.

Transfer from the uniformed to the plain-clothes branch did not normally occur until after three or four years of service, but in exceptional cases it could be expedited and take place after one complete year. DDI Cridland had early spotted their CID potential and shortly after the conclusion of their first year's service had approached Superintendent Garforth with the prospect of their transfer. Garforth had immediately, and inevitably, opposed any such move.

It was at this juncture, that the second episode occurred, which Luke remembered, not only for its unpleasant beginning, but for the important results which finally stemmed from it.

One of the local attractions was a courtyard at the bottom of Brixton Hill. It had been taken over by a group of enterprising businessmen who had set up stalls selling all manner of portable property, from costume jewellery and watches to fruit and vegetables. It was usually crowded. The arrangement of 'Shoppers' Paradise', as they had named it, was that you selected your purchases and carried them over to a cashier's desk in a central booth. The openness of the transaction would have made shoplifting difficult, but the police had been instructed to keep an eye on it.

One morning Luke, who was on duty, observed a young man who seemed to be behaving oddly. He would push through the crowd towards the cashier's desk, pause there for a moment then, seeming to change his mind, make his way back towards the entrance. He showed no interest in the goods displayed in the stalls and Luke began to wonder what he was up to. The next time he moved into the crowd he followed him cautiously, keeping a few yards from him and a screen of shoppers between them.

Suddenly, and it happened so quickly that he could hardly believe his eyes, he saw the young man's hand slip into the shopping bag of a lady in front of him and extract her purse. He was about to drop it into his own pocket when Luke, lunging forward, caught hold of his wrist and took the purse from him.

The young man did not resist him, but bellowed out, 'Take your hands off me, you crazy bluebottle.'

'That's right,' said a bystander, 'you leave him alone. And what are you doing with that purse, eh?'

At this the young lady swung round and said, 'That's my purse. Let me have it back at once.'

'Excuse me, madam,' said Luke. 'It was this young man who stole your purse. I saw him do it.'

'A pack of lies,' said the helpful bystander.

'And I'm charging him with it. I'll require you and him to come with me to the station.'

'Don't go,' said the helpful bystander. 'Are we going to let ourselves be trampled on by a Jack-in-office what's been caught stealing money and is trying to put it on to an innocent man?'

The crowd seemed to be with him and was turning ugly when a second constable appeared. This was PC Farmer, a large and formidable person, and when Luke had rapidly explained the situation to him he said, 'Right. You come along with us. You and the lady. And that witness. Where is he?'

But the witness had disappeared.

Back at the Station Sergeant Hamble listened, first to Luke and then to the young man, who repeated his story and added that if the police persisted in such a ridiculous charge, he had a number of highly respectable friends who would vouch for him. The sergeant said that if he would give them his own name and address and details of his friends, he would be allowed to depart, being remanded to appear in due course and answer the charge.

The young man thought about this and said, 'You shall have my name, which is George Taylor. But not my address or the details of my friends. When this insulting charge has been dismissed, as it will be, you will release me and apologise. And I trust,' he added, eyeing Luke malevolently, 'that steps will then be taken against the actual thief.'

The sergeant said that if he persisted in refusing his address he would have to be held, in custody, to appear before the magistrate.

This took place on the following morning. The magistrate, Mr Horace Lamb, was shrewd but fair. It was one man's word against another. The woman was neutral. She had no idea who had taken her purse. The helpful bystander had disappeared and no other witnesses had come forward. As the matter stood it seemed to turn on the character of the accused. If he had indeed led a blameless life, never straying from the straight and narrow path, it seemed incredible that he should have chosen such a public occasion to depart from it. On the other hand it was equally unlikely that a young policeman should have embarked on a career of crime in such a place and in such a manner. In the end, the magistrate decided to adjourn the hearing for seven days.

'This will give you time,' he said to Mr Taylor, 'to think again about your refusal to identify your family and the friends who will speak for you. You realise, I hope, that their evidence may be decisive.' Mr Taylor said that his friends would have to be consulted, but he was sure they would speak for him. The magistrate said, 'Very well,' and looked at Luke, who had nothing to say.

He was certain that the self-styled George Taylor was a professional thief and that the helpful bystander had been an accomplice. He had a week to prove it. For God's sake, how did he set about it? Joe said he would ask around and see what he could ferret out. Sergeant Hamble recommended prayer. Luke went up to Scotland Yard and began a desperate search through the photographs in the Rogues' Gallery.

There were hundreds of photographs. Thousands. Front view, side view, even back view. After a bit they seemed to merge together. They became a composite picture of criminality which haunted him in his sleep. When, on the third day, suddenly and without the least doubt, he found Mr Taylor, he was so relieved that he laughed aloud.

A man who was also studying the photographs turned round and Luke recognised him. It was Detective Inspector Wensley, the DDI of 'H' Division. Known throughout the force as Fred and by the criminal population of East London as Vensel or the Weasel, he looked as unlike a senior policeman as it was possible for a man to look. He had a long, white, sad face which sloped down from his forehead to a prominent jaw. His upper lip was adorned by a splendid moustache which made him look more like a walrus than a weasel.

Plucking up courage as he noted the twinkle in Wensley's deep-set eyes, Luke had poured out the whole story.

'Good,' said Wensley. 'I had a very similar experience myself during my early days in Whitechapel. It's a common ploy among the light-fingered gentry. If I might suggest it, your next step should be to examine the man's record. If he's a professional criminal there will certainly be previous convictions.'

Luke said he had thought of this, but would the rules allow him to bring them to the magistrate's attention?

'There's an answer to that,' Wensley said. 'Not, perhaps, strictly legal, but very effective. I take it you will be conducting your own defence? Good. You'll do it much better than the sort of third-class barrister you could afford. Records of previous offences are on dark blue paper. I'll assume you find one or more of them. You hold them in your hand in such a way that the prisoner can see them and you say to him, "You are aware, I take it, that lying on oath is a crime, for which you can be severely punished. So I want to ask you one question. You have based your defence on your good character, so I'm entitled to ask you whether you have ever been convicted of a criminal offence." He'll be a very bold man if he doesn't say "yes". Then you can rub it in. How many times and what for? I'm sure I can leave it to you.'

His confidence was not misplaced. Taylor, real name Abrahams, was convicted of attempted theft and Luke received a commendation.

Wensley, who was in court when this happy conclusion was reached, had taken him aside afterwards to congratulate him. What followed seemed predestined. As soon as he discovered that Luke was a fluent Russian speaker he had applied his considerable weight to effect what Luke had been praying for, both for himself and Joe. A transfer to the Detective Branch and a transfer to 'H' Division. Superintendent Garforth had fought hard to retain Luke, but his opposition had been steam-rollered. Opposition to Joe's departure had been a good deal less strenuous.

This had all happened six months ago and Luke had had time to appreciate why, in the eyes of the Force, the 'H' in 'H' Division (which embraced Stepney, Whitechapel and Poplar) stood for Horror. Notwithstanding the dangers and difficulties he had enjoyed life enormously.

Hold it. The door of the house he was watching was being opened, cautiously. Someone was going to come out. Was coming out. He craned forward, and the movement saved him. A blow, which would have fallen squarely on his head, fell instead on his left forearm. He whipped round, got his right arm round his attacker's neck and pulled him down.

Footsteps running up and a rain of blows from his new attacker. A lot of them fell on his opponent as they rolled together on the ground. Then a crack on the forehead which dazed him.

When the mist had cleared a little he levered himself up on to his knees. He could hear two sets of footsteps running away round the corner and disappearing into the distance. He was in no shape to follow. His left arm felt as though it didn't belong to him, his head was still spinning. He felt sick.

He was sick.

This restored him sufficiently for him to get to his feet and stagger towards the only destination that mattered – his bed. As he went, there were two thoughts in his mind. The first was that there was something wrong with his arm. Something very wrong. And it wasn't only his arm, now. His legs were misbehaving. As they buckled under him and he went down face first into the gutter there was another quite independent thought in his mind. There had been something odd about the second set of footsteps. Something he ought to remember.

3

For some time there had been nothing firm, nothing to cling on to. Flashes of consciousness had been followed by intervals of darkness which were too disturbed to be called sleep.

In these intervals he seemed to spend most of his time walking down the Ratcliffe Highway, a frontage of buildings with nasty, dark, dangerous little alleys between them. Every other building was a tavern. Between the taverns were shops that catered for sailors. Peering through the windows as he strolled past he could see sou'westers and pilot coats, thigh-length rubber boots, sextants and bosun's pipes, knives and daggers. Why, you could fit out a whole ship from each shop, he said. Ship, shop. Ship, shop. Clip, clop. Hansom cab coming up behind him. Dodge before it runs you down. The effort he made to escape jerked him back to consciousness.

A man with a beard, whom he had seen before, was smiling at him. He said, 'That's right. Cheated the parson this time. Lucky these youngsters have got such hard heads, isn't it, Mrs Hutchins.' There was a woman with him who reminded him of Mrs Parham. He remembered her as one of his regular visitors, who gave him hot sweet drinks which made him sick.

On one occasion, most remarkably, it had been DDI Wensley who had stared down at him, looking like a mournful seal, and said something that sounded like 'bloody young fool'. After that it was the motherly woman again. This time she had given him a cold and rather bitter drink which he had succeeded in keeping down.

Then he really had slept.

When he opened his eyes he saw Joe, perched on a chair

beside his bed, reading a magazine. All he could see of it was the picture of a girl with beautiful legs which, very reasonably, she was making no effort to keep hidden. Wanting to see more, he hoisted himself up on to his elbows

''Ullo 'ullo,' said Joe. 'The sleeping beauty has awucken. And you're not supposed to sit up.'

'Why on earth not?' said Luke, sitting up.

'Bin at death's door, haven't you?'

'Nonsense,' said Luke. 'I'm as fit as a fiddle.'

'Whole thing was a fiddle, if you ask me. Three days in the infirmary and Mother Hutchins clucking over you, like as if you was her long-lost son.'

'Have I really been here for three days?'

'Best part of. Every precaution known to science has been took.' He was examining a chart which hung at the foot of the bed. 'This one shows your temperacheer. And here's a list of ticks and crosses. Nothing to say what that is. Might be the number of times you wet your bed.'

'Don't talk nonsense,' said Luke. 'Tell me. Did old Wensley come and have a look at me? It seemed like him and I thought I heard him say "bloody young fool".'

'Taken by and large,' said Joe, 'that seems to sum up the general verdict. Letting yourself be knocked on the napper by a couple of cheap Ruskies. Mind you, I'm beginning to wonder if we was quite as smart as we thought we was, getting ourselves transferred to this division. Talk about the bloody Tower of Babel. Squareheads, Polacks, Guineas, Johnnies and hundreds of thousands of Shonks. Fourteen to a room and one bed. Either they take it in turns, or some of them sleep on the floor.'

'Uncomfortable either way,' said Luke. 'That's a lovely black eye you've got. Been fighting someone?'

'In this part of the world, life's one long fight. How'd I get this shiner? I got it yesterday. Rescuing a sailor from a fate worse'n death. From death too, like as not.'

'Tell,' said Luke, settling himself comfortably.

'Well, I was proceeding along Cable Street, getting dark, and mist coming up from the river, and I was thinking as how nice it would be if I was back home with my slippers on and a glass of something in my hand when I saw these three men coming along, arm in arm. Friendly types, was my first thought. When they got up to me, I saw the two on the outside was nasty-looking hunkies.' Joe demonstrated what he meant by frowning ferociously and sticking his jaw out. This made Luke laugh.

'Laugh away,' said Joe. 'It weren't funny. Not really. The one in the middle was a sailor – not much more'n a boy – and as anyone could see, he was drunk as parson's cat. Couldn't hardly stand up. I said, "You leave that boy alone."

'"We leave him, he falls down," said the tough character on the right. "We take him home."

'"I know just where you're taking him," I said. "Somewhere you can finish emptying his pockets. And then empty him into the river. Not tonight, though. This ain't your lucky night".'

'He didn't seem anxious to let go of the boy, which handicapped him somewhat, so I hit him.' Joe smiled at the thought. 'A four o'clock one. Right on his snozzle. He let go the boy then and come for me. So I kicks him in the goolies.'

'Wasn't that a bit rough?'

'I had to protect myself, didn't I? Then I got me old whistle out and blew it. Always creates a good effect. The other man took one look at his friend lying on the ground trying to be sick and cut off smartish down one of the side streets. The only one who didn't seem to appreciate my efforts was the boy. He said, "You've hurt my friend. Only friend I've got," and blow me down if he didn't square up and belt me in the eye. It was what you might call a parting effort, because as he did it his knees gave way and if I hadn't grabbed him he'd have finished flat on his face. I got him up over my shoulder and left the field of battle as the crowd started to gather. One of the men knew me and gave me a hand with our gallant tar and we got him into the church refuge just round the corner. When we got him there he fell flat once more and this time, just to show how comfortable he was, he started to snore. It didn't seem to worry the refugers.'

'I expect they're used to that sort of thing. What did they do with him?'

'They said they'd put him to bed. He'd be all right in the morning. I wasn't too sure about that, so I went round next morning and had a word with the boy. He was called Bill Trotter and he was off the brig *Alice*. The usual story. Came on shore with a friend from another ship. Both of them with their pay in their pockets. Friend went off with a girl, leaving young Bill on his tod. Easy meat for the squareheads. Seeing he was still a bit shaky I went back with him to his ship.'

'The *Alice* you said.'

'Right. One of the "A" line – *Alice, Annabel, Audrey* and *Amelie*. They call them brigs, but really they're brig-rigged schooners. They do most of the east coast work, up to Scotland. The "B" line – *Betsy, Belinda, Beatrice*, that lot – they're more enterprising. Sometimes compete with the "A"s, but mostly they push out across the sea, heading for Copenhagen and Gothenburg. Now –' Joe wagged a schoolmasterly finger at the invalid – 'I'm not telling you all this just to give you a lesson in geography. I had an idea when I was talking to young Trotter and his mates and sampling some of the Highland dew they'd brought back from one of their trips to Edinburgh. Lovely stuff. I'd've brought some round for you, only I remembered what you'd said about alcohol being bad for concussion.' Observing the look in Luke's eye he hurried on. 'My idea was that these boats wasn't only cargo boats. They've got accommodation – limited but comfortable was how they described it – for one or two passengers. Businessmen who like to take things easy, people like that. So what about you asking for a couple of weeks' convalescent leave and getting a bit of sea air into your lungs?'

'Attractive,' agreed Luke. 'How long should I have to be away?'

'That's what I asked Bill. The *Amelie's* due to leave for

Newcastle on Saturday. How long the trip takes depends on the weather – sometimes they have to beat about for days – and how long they're held up at the other end, that depends on the cargo. They'll be carrying cement in bags and timber. Clean stuff and easy to unload. Coming back it'll likely be iron-ore for smelting. They could be tied up at the other end for a week or more. Shouldn't be more than ten days, though. If it was going to be more'n that they'd come back empty. Can't hang around. That's losing money.'

As Joe had been speaking the idea had been growing in attraction. Fishing trips out of the Orwell or the Stour, with a night at sea and return on the morning tide, had been almost his only relaxation during the years of his Russian study and the North Sea no longer had the power to upset him. Calculating dates and times he said, 'It looks as though I'd have to put in for fifteen days. Saturday to Monday fortnight.'

'The skipper wouldn't say no to that. You're his white-headed boy. When he heard you'd been hurt, the tears were streaming down his face.'

Having nothing handy to throw at Joe, Luke said, 'Then you think he'd agree?'

'It wouldn't be his say-so. Not entirely. He'd have to fix it up with Josh.'

This reference to Superintendent Joscelyne, the head of 'H' Division, gave both of them pause. Although the Superintendent did not control the day-by day working of the plain-clothes branch, all administrative decisions stemmed from him. He was not positively unfriendly, as Garforth had been, but had maintained, so far, a massive neutrality in his dealings with those two young hopefuls, Detective Pagan and Detective Narrabone. So far as he was concerned, they were on probation.

'There's just one thing,' said Joe. 'It mightn't be a good moment to bother the skipper. He's got a lot on his plate. I've noticed, if there's any sort of nonsense anywhere and a Russian or a Yid's involved – which there usually is – then it doesn't matter which division it happens in, it's "Send for Wensley".'

'That must be good for him, career-wise. Surely he's heading for the top.'

'He may be heading for it, but it won't do him much good if he dies of overwork before he gets there. Last time I saw him he was looking like death warmed up.'

'Surely not as bad as that,' said Wensley.

He was noted for walking softly. When on the beat he was reputed to have tacked strips of bicycle tyre to the soles of his regulation boots.

Joe, unperturbed, said, 'I don't know how much of that you heard, sir. But I was proposing a sea voyage for this young tear-away's health.'

'Yes. I heard that bit. Not a bad idea. But I've had a better one. We'll sell it to the superintendent as one week's convalescence and one week's work. If you feel you're up to it.'

'I'm all right now, sir, really,' said Luke. 'Two or three days at sea and I'll be on the top line.'

Wensley examined the temperature chart, stroked his splendid moustache and said, 'All right. Here's how it goes. I've got friends in most of the east coast ports, up as far as Edinburgh. They keep an eye on arrivals, and if they think they are going to interest me, they telephone me, or drop me a line. That way I've had some very useful tip-offs. My contact in Newcastle is a man called Farnsworth. Carter Farnsworth. He's well placed, you see, because he's head of the Water Guard and combines that with being deputy head of Customs. Any suspicious characters who arrive, the docks police send them along to him. Well, about a week ago this Russian turned up on a boat from Libau, which was interesting, because anyone who wants to slip out of Russia is liable to make first for Poland, which isn't a difficult border crossing. Then they try Danzig for a ship and if they can't find one next choice is Libau or Riga. When the police wheeled him in, Farnsworth had him stripped naked and searched. A proceeding which he resented, violently. First thing they found was that he'd got two passports. One which he produced, in the name of Ivan Morrowitz. The other, tucked away in a very secret pocket, in the name of Janis Silistreau. That one had his picture on it, so it may have been his real name.'

'Do they *all* have two names?' said Luke.

'Two's a poor score. One man I've been dealing with recently used six. And none of them turned out to be his real name. Anyway, as well as a second passport, Farnsworth found a number of papers in Russian handwriting. This didn't mean a lot to him, as neither he nor anyone in his office could deal with Russian current script. He wasn't very happy about putting them in the post to me, but if you found them interesting I'm sure he'd lend them to you and you could bring them back with you for our Home Office friends to look at. Right?'

'Right,' said Luke, delighted that at last some practical use was to be made of his knowledge of Russian.

'Next point, if this Morrowitz-Silistreau character is heading for London, as I've no doubt he is, it'll be useful to know what train he's on, so that we can have him followed when he arrives. And last, and most important, don't overstay your leave. If the *Amelie* is really hung up waiting for a return cargo, you'll have to miss your return sea trip and come back by train. We're not over-staffed and things are beginning to heat up down here. Normally, I wouldn't be sorry about that, because –' Wensley's fingers opened and shut – 'when things heat up is when we get results. But just at this moment, everything's moving a bit fast, in different directions, so don't hang about too long admiring the Northumbrian scenery.'

'Or the Northumbrian lasses,' said Joe.

Luke promised to bear these instructions in mind. He, too, liked it when things started moving.

On the Friday morning Joe walked down with him to the docks. The quayside was crowded. There were three ships anchored in tandem alongside and two more in midstream awaiting attention.

Ship-building might have gone north to the Clyde and the Mersey, but ship-handling was still the prerogative of the London docks.

The *Amelie* sailed at dusk. With the wind behind them, they were soon out into the mouth of the river. Luke, on deck and inhaling the cold air in grateful gulps, felt health and strength building up fast. Which was as well, since before long the wind had swung from the south-west to the south-east and had freshened. By Sunday evening it was coming straight out of Russia and the sea had got so ugly that they pulled into the Wash and spent the night in the lee of Boston Stump. Luke began to fear that they might lie there for days, but they ventured out, on Monday morning, into a sea that was moderating as the sun rose.

'I've often noticed it,' said the skipper, an Ulsterman, who was inclined to be friendly to Luke on the grounds that a normal passenger would have been incapacitated by that time. 'The sun kills the wind.'

Good progress from there on saw them safely round South Shields Point and by four o'clock on the Tuesday they were gliding sedately up the Tyne with the tide behind them. When they reached the main disembarkation point on the famous mile-long quay, Carter Farnsworth, a short red Northumbrian, was there to meet Luke as he stepped ashore.

After a friendly greeting, coupled with enquiries about his old friend the Weasel, he led Luke into his office and got down to business.

'That's the man who calls himself Ivan Morrowitz,' he said, pushing three photographs across. 'That was the name in the passport he produced. The photograph in the passport was so messy that it was useless. So I had these new ones done. A remarkable face, don't you think?'

The forehead and eyes of an intellectual were contradicted by the mouth and jaw of a fighter. Luke looked at them for a long moment, then said, 'A thinker and a soldier. That's a dangerous combination.'

'When we searched him we found a second passport hidden on him. The name on that one was Janis Silistreau. It rang a bell and I had one of my boys look him up in the public library. He found him, too. In which section do you think?'

'Soldiers, economists, politicians?'

'None of those. He found him in the literature section, under "Poets". Originally from Simferopol', in the Crimea. Came up to Moscow and made a name for himself there. Seems he's written a lot of stuff and been published in Russia, Poland and Germany.'

'And in England?'

'Not yet. That may be coming next. He certainly speaks our language well enough. Now, about those papers.' He showed Luke a sheaf of papers which had clearly been rolled up tightly. 'Had 'em inside the leg of his trousers. We've smoothed 'em out and cleaned 'em up a bit, but I couldn't find anyone in my office to translate 'em. I could have sent 'em to the university, but that would have meant spreading things further than I wanted, just at present.'

As he was speaking Luke was slowly deciphering the first of the documents. Although written was basically the same as printed Russian, there were inevitable shortenings and elisions in the script. The document seemed to be a report, though it was not clear from whom or to whom, describing the different groups of Russians, Poles and Latvians currently to be found in London. There were one or two names and addresses which must, he thought, refer to leading characters in the groups. 'Casimir Treschau' occurred more than once.

'If all the papers are like this,' he said, 'they'll be manna in the wilderness for Wensley.'

'I thought they might be important,' said Farnsworth. 'And that's why I'm keeping them safe until you go.' As he spoke he was stowing them back in his briefcase. 'Our friend has settled in with a gang of Russian immigrants who work in the docks. Good workers, too. The locals don't like 'em much, but I prefer to have 'em together, under our eye. We could pull this man in for further questioning if you liked. Speaking their lingo, as you do, you might be able to get something out of him.'

Luke said, 'I don't think I'd get anything more than you have. What I would like to know is the moment he shows any signs of leaving here and heading south.'

'Understood. Now, what are your plans? I gather you're here part on sick leave, part on business. Having disposed of the business, let's think about the next bit. Have you any ideas?'

'First I must find a hotel for the night. Then I thought I'd start off tomorrow on a walking tour.'

'Your second idea's a good one. You'll find a lot of lovely country behind this grey old town of ours. The *Amelie* won't start loading until after the weekend and I doubt she'll start back much before the end of next week. That gives you at least eight days. In that time you could walk right along the Roman Wall from Haddon to Carlisle and back again.'

'Sounds perfect,' said Luke.

'Right. Now as to your first idea, that's ruled out. You're not staying in a hotel, you're staying with me.'

The way it was spoken, it sounded more like an order than a suggestion. Luke agreed to it gratefully.

'We'll go in my automobile,' said Farnsworth. 'I call it an automobile because to call it a motor car would insult it.' It was a splendid vehicle, powered by steam. Once heated up, it moved away from the quayside with regal deliberation and sailed off up the Scotswood Road to the Farnsworth residence, where he was welcomed by Emmeline Farnsworth, who was the same size and colour as her husband and just as friendly. Here he spent a dreamless night and started out next morning powered by a Northumbrian breakfast.

Eight days later, in the early evening, he arrived back at the house feeling as fit and as happy as he could ever remember. Much of his happiness evaporated when Mrs Farnsworth opened the door and he saw the look on her face.

'What is it?' he said. 'Has something happened?'

'Yes,' said Mrs Farnsworth flatly, 'something's happened. Go in. Carter's there. He'll tell you about it.'

Wondering what could have upset her he went through into the living-room where he found Farnsworth sitting in front of the fire smoking his pipe. He seemed to be unworried.

'You mustn't listen to my wife,' he said. 'Women take these things too seriously.'

'Women have got more sense than men,' said Mrs Farnsworth, who had followed Luke into the room. 'If I've told you once, I've told you a dozen times. You've got to clear them Russians out. Right out.'

'They're hard workers.'

'They're murderers.'

'We've got no proof of that. And now Silistreau-Morrowitz has taken himself off I'm not looking for any more trouble.'

'What happened?' said Luke.

'What happened was that I was stupid. Twice over. Those papers, you remember I said I'd keep them safe in my briefcase? Of course, I ought to have lodged them in the bank. That was my first mistake. My second was sticking to my usual routine. Every evening, around five o'clock, I'd walk down from my office to the Customs shed at the end of the quay to pick up any items they might have for me. *Every* evening.' He brought his fist down on the arm of the chair with a force that nearly cracked the wood. Luke could see that he was not quite as relaxed as he was pretending to be.

He said, 'I suppose the Russians jumped you and got your briefcase.'

'Guess again. If they'd tried anything like that, I'd have given them something to think about. No. What happened was I was passing the iron-ore loading bay. They'd been using an outsize scoop on a swivel arm. They'd swing it out over the hold of ship and could put in a couple of hundredweight or more at a time.'

'I saw them doing it,' said Luke. 'It seemed a quick and sensible way of loading the ships.'

'Very sensible.' Farnsworth gave a laugh, but there was not much humour in it. 'They'd been working at it when I went past. Now they'd knocked off for the night and normally the scoop would be swung back alongside the building. I happened to notice that, for once, they'd left it out, over the quayside. Maybe that sounded a warning. I don't know. But as I was going to step under it, I glanced up and I saw the scoop starting to open. I did the only thing possible. I jumped for it.'

'Jumped where?'

'Into the water,' said Farnsworth with a grin. 'I heard the solid thump as a hundredweight or so of ore came down on the place I'd been standing a split second before. A few lumps hit the water with me, but they didn't bother me. I was underwater and swimming hard. When I surfaced I realised I'd dropped my briefcase. Too late to do anything about that. There was a strong tide running and it must have been halfway to the North Sea. Not that I was worrying just then about the papers. I was thinking first about getting back on to dry land, which I did, via a ladder two hundred yards downstream. Next thing I was worrying about was how the thing could have been rigged. As soon as I'd changed into some dry clothes I tackled the man who was running the loading operation. He said it was two of the Russians who handled the crane. Reliable men, he said, who'd never failed to swing the scoop back alongside the building when they knocked off. Must have been intruders. Boys, perhaps, playing with the machinery. Panicked when they saw what they'd done and run off. It sounded thin to me, but difficult to prove anything.'

'You were lucky to get away with nothing worse than a ducking.'

'Agreed. Pity about the papers, though.'

Emmeline Farnsworth, who had been listening with growing impatience, said, 'The way you keep on about those papers. What do they matter? Don't you realise that but for the grace of

God, you'd have been under a heap of stones, squashed as flat as a black beetle?'

'Well, I wasn't,' said Farnsworth. He shook his head, as though clearing such ideas out of it. 'But one thing did make me think that Silistreau was behind it. My deputy, who came round that evening to find out how I was, told me that Morrowitz – as he called him – had packed up and pushed off on the train that very same afternoon. As you may imagine, I grabbed the telephone and left word for Fred Wensley. The four o'clock train stops at York for an hour and doesn't reach London till half past ten, so he'd have had time to get the arrival platform covered.'

Mrs Farnsworth, who was as little interested in trains as she was in papers, muttered something uncomplimentary about a husband who couldn't look after himself and if he didn't clear those Russians out she didn't know what would happen next.

'They'll be no trouble now the big man's gone,' said Farnsworth. 'And I've got some news for you, young Luke. The *Amelie*'s nearly finished loading and with any luck she'll be away on the evening tide tomorrow. Better get a good night's rest. Might be another rough trip.'

In fact the sea was as calm as the North Sea ever condescends to be in winter. Luke, standing by the stern rail and watching the roofs and towers of Newcastle disappearing into the evening mist, was thinking about Mrs Farnsworth's expression, 'squashed flat as a black beetle'. It was an exaggeration, of course. The contents of the skip would have knocked Farnsworth on to his face and would certainly have dazed him. Long enough for Silistreau lurking in one of the nearby entrances to dart out and pick up the briefcase, and perhaps kick Farnsworth's head in for good measure. What was really worrying him was not the damage Farnsworth had escaped by his prompt action, or the loss of the papers. It was a growing appreciation of the sort of man they were up against: a man of influence among his fellow emigrants; a man clever enough to devise and organise in the short time he had been there, such an elaborate and nearly successful ambush.

As Luke turned to go he glanced out to sea. What he saw was a cloud, so black and heavy that it looked solid. The skipper, behind him, said, 'Yon's a present from Russia.'

'Stormy weather, is it?'

'Not so much a blow as a dowsing. There's a bucket of rain in it, aye, and sleet and maybe snow. 'Twon't be much pleasure for anyone to be up here while they're hosing that little lot over us.'

Certainly, in the next few days the deck was no place for anyone not properly protected by oilskins against the wet and by thick clothing against the bitter cold. Luke spent most of the journey in the cuddy talking to members of the crew as they were allowed down, one after the other, to get some warmth into their bodies.

The skipper had to spend a lot of his time aloft and when he did come below was in no mood for talk. On one occasion, observing Luke's depression as he huddled over the stove, he said, with a grim smile, 'Cheer up, lad. Nothing lasts for ever.'

Luke said, 'I was born and brought up on the Suffolk flats and I thought the North Sea had no more surprises for me.'

''Tisn't from the sea, this little lot. It's from the land behind the sea. There's a powerful devil lives there, did you know? Slings a bucketful of hate at us from time to time. Just to let us know as he hasn't forgotten us.'

Having said which, he stumped off to get a few hours' sleep, leaving Luke alone with his thoughts.

So there was a devil in the north-east. A devil who rolled out a great black cloud to show that he was there; to show that he hated them.

The stove had burned low and he was shivering. He piled on more wood before creeping off to his own bunk. 'Nothing lasts for ever,' he said to himself and tried to get to sleep with that small grain of comfort.

It was not until the last hours of the trip that the weather relented. At four o'clock, on the evening of January 3rd, as the *Amelie* swung out of the river and edged into Shadwell Basin and the East Dock, a pale sun looked out from the clouds. Luke, who was standing on deck watching the operation of docking, raised his eyes.

To the north, less than a mile away, a thick column of smoke stood up against the evening sky.

4

The streets were oddly quiet and empty and he noticed that many of the windows were shuttered. Away to his right the smoke he had seen was billowing up. Now that it was growing dark he could see the sparks and fragments of burning wood that were whirling up in it. The silence of the street he was in magnified sounds from that direction and he could hear the noise of a considerable crowd. That was understandable, though why such a large crowd in a part of London where fires were a common occurrence? And why the shuttered windows?

No matter. He would hear all about it from Joe. He hitched his bag on to his other shoulder and made for the second-storey apartment which they shared at 15 Osborne Street.

Joe was at home and fast asleep. He moved not a muscle at the noise of Luke's entry. It looked like the sleep of exhaustion. Luke let him lie, dumped his bag and headed for Leman Street.

Here the mystery deepened. The only man in the police station was the desk sergeant, who was writing so busily that he looked up briefly, acknowledged Luke with a grunt and went on writing. Clearly he was not to be disturbed.

Retracing his steps Luke headed for the fire, which must surely be the key to the puzzle. As he turned into Sidney Street the sounds of the crowd grew louder; a babble of excitement so high pitched that it was close to frenzy. There was a solid line of uniformed police across the road. They were reinforcements, Luke noted, from 'K' Division to the east and 'J' to the north.

Half the inhabitants of Stepney seemed to be there, squashed six deep behind the police line, others leaning out of the windows or perched on top of the buildings on either side of the street. The roof of the brewery on the corner was a grandstand, fully occupied. Despite the excitement, nothing much seemed to be happening. The fire brigade were attending to what was left of the building at number 100, their efforts punctuated by the occasional crash of falling timber. He thought he saw Wensley among a bowler-hatted group on the pavement. Very odd. He controlled his curiosity and hurried back the way he had come. If he was going to get a sensible explanation of what it was all about, there was only one thing for it. He was going to have to rouse Joe.

This was easier said than done.

Knowing that food ranked high in Joe's list of life's attractions, he spread out on the table between the beds the remains of the generous supplies that the cook on the *Amelie* had seen him off with. Cold cooked sausages, two or three pies, a hunk of cheese and a bottle of beer. Then he rapped repeatedly on the table, chanting 'Arise and shine', 'Come and get it' and other suitable slogans, until Joe rolled over, opened his eyes, said, 'What the bloody hell,' and sat up.

'Brought you some food,' said Luke.

'So I see. Ugh. Mouth full of shit. All the same, if I started with the beer, I dunno, I might manage to swallow a crumb or two.'

Luke filled a tooth glass with beer and pushed it across. Joe emptied it, returned it for a second helping, swallowed most of that and then seemed strong enough to tackle one of the pies.

'Now,' said Luke, 'before you fill your mouth again, perhaps you can tell me what it's all about.'

'What it's all about is that you're a lucky bugger. A very lucky bugger.' He awarded this important announcement a full stop in the form of a further chunk of pie.

'Understood,' said Luke patiently. 'I'm a bugger and I'm lucky. No truth in the first statement. Maybe some in the second. Now, let's hear what you've all been up to.'

Joe finished his mouthful so deliberately that Luke guessed he was giving himself time to think. Then he said, 'The moment your restraining influence was removed – how long ago was it? Best part of three weeks? Seems like three months – all hell broke loose. It started with a crowd of Russians – Letts, Poles maybe; they all crawl out of the same hole as far as I'm concerned – breaking into the Harris jeweller's shop. You know, the new one in Houndsditch.'

'Houndsditch? Wouldn't that have been a matter for the City boys?'

'Too right. The front of the shop, being in Houndsditch, is indeed in the City. The rear part, known as Exchange Buildings, is in this division. So, it might have fallen out either way. As it happened the man who heard the break-in – they didn't seem to mind how much noise they made – headed for the Bishopsgate Station. Result, half a dozen of the brightest and best of our City chums surrounded Exchange Buildings and called on the people doing the housebreaking to come out and show themselves.'

Joe stopped for a long moment.

'So what happened?' said Luke impatiently. Then, seeing the look on Joe's face, repeated more gently, 'Tell me. What happened?'

'What do you bloody suppose happens when men without guns face up to a crowd of bastards who've got guns and are prepared to use 'em? Result. Three of our men were killed. Nothing clever. No marksmanship needed. Just press the gun into the man's side and pull the trigger two or three times. Bound to do some damage that way, aren't you?'

'Anyone –?' Luke hesitated to put the question.

'Anyone we know? Yes. Sergeant Tucker—'

'Daddy Tucker?'

'That's the one. And Bob Bentley.'

'Not the one whose wife—'

'Yes. His wife was pregnant. If they'd known, I suppose it would have made them even happier to think that she might have died from the shock. And the baby as well.'

It was clear that Joe, who usually took life lightly, was angry, upset and bitter.

'You said three.'

'The third I didn't know. A constable called Choate. He was the best of the lot. Got his arms round one of the bastards and wouldn't let go. As they were rolling on the floor a second man came up and emptied his gun into them. Finished Choate, but wounded the other man too. Wounded him badly. They got him away somehow. Wensley says he died two days later. Unlamented. So that was the score. One of them to three of us. That was when we really got going. Started to take Whitechapel and Stepney to pieces. Well, you know what they're like. Everyone seems to be related to someone else and as soon as you start asking questions they all clam up and if things start to look too dangerous, why, they scuttle off down one rat hole into another before you can grab hold of their slimy tails. We were at it night and day. Particularly night. Got nowhere, until a couple of days ago, two of the bastards were located.'

'In that house in Sidney Street?'

'Right. We pushed two vanloads of men into the street to block it off. After that, things seemed to get stuck. They wouldn't come out. We couldn't get in.'

'Couldn't?'

'One narrow doorway. Staircase with a turn in it. Man waiting behind the bend with a gun. Would have been an easy way to commit suicide. Not surprisingly, after what happened at that jeweller's shop, no volunteers. So they called out the Army. Scots Guards from the Tower. After that it was a game of ping-pong. Both sides shooting at each other. Two against two hundred. They kept it up for hours. And it was first blood to them. They put a bullet into Sergeant Leeson. You remember Ben? Tall fellow with a squint.'

'Yes, I remember Ben. Was he killed?'

'Next door to it. Had to be got to hospital. The trouble was he was stuck in a doorway opposite number 100. They got him out at the back, ran a ladder up and hoisted him on to the roof of one of the brewery outhouses. Our one and only Fred was helping him up and got stuck on the roof. He was lying in the gutter with the bullets parting his hair, and a rumour got into the papers that he'd had it.'

'But he hadn't?'

'The old weasel? Not him. Ripped some of the roof tiles up and dropped through the hole.'

'Good for Fred.'

'He came out of it all right. He was about the only one who did. The two Russians copped out. Shot or fried. Not sure which. All the same, not a good result for the home side. The buzz is, Josh has been sent for by the Commissioner. He's probably getting his balls chewed off right now.'

Luke said, 'Good show.' Joe returned to the pie.

Winston Churchill looked with satisfaction at the arrangement of the table: sufficiently formal to be intimidating; sufficiently informal to allow for a certain latitude in the proceedings if that seemed called for.

He was flanked, on his right, by Haldane Parker, in charge of the Home Office Aliens Department and on his left by Vernon Kell, head of the newly created Home Security Section MO5. Aligned opposite him were the heads of the uniformed and the CID sections of the two divisions concerned – Superintendent Stark and DDI Morgan of the City Police; Superintendent Joscelyne and DDI Wensley of 'H' Division.

Neither of Churchill's supporters was looking entirely comfortable. Vernon Kell was thinking that the Home Secretary looked like a plump schoolboy who finds himself, in the absence of the master, in charge of the class and is enjoying himself. Haldane Parker, a long-established senior civil servant, thought the meeting was irregular and unnecessary. It would achieve nothing that could not have been better achieved by a memorandum in quintuplicate, with one copy to the Prime Minister, as *ex officio* head of national security, and the other four copies planted where they would be best placed to needle the police.

Churchill, though exuding his normal bouncing self-confidence, was not, be the truth told, entirely comfortable either. As Home Secretary he found himself forced to apply the Aliens Act. When in Opposition he had voted against it and had, on one occasion, succeeded in talking it out.

A less confident man might have found this embarrassing. Being an experienced politician he rode over the difficulties with the ease of a practised horseman, taking the jumps as they came.

He addressed the four policemen in front of him as though they had been a hostile political audience.

'What I said at the time I saw now. Shut out the alien – if diseased – always. If immoral, as soon as you find out. If criminal, after you have convicted him. But do not shut out people merely because they are poor. And do not throw upon police and Customs House officials duties which they are unable properly to discharge.'

His audience had all read this glib stuff, which had been widely reported in the press, and they were well able to see the weakness in it. Sensing unfriendly reaction he adopted the normal tactics of a politician in a corner. He went over to the attack.

'I have studied the reports of the Houndsditch jewel robbery. I found them in some respects incomplete, but nothing can alter one astounding, inexplicable fact. A terrorist, mortally wounded, as it now appears, was supported by two other terrorists from Houndsditch to Grove Street, where he finally lay down to die. A distance, gentlemen, of more than half a mile, through the streets of London, *without a single policeman taking any notice of them.* In the light of this extraordinary episode, you will forgive me if I speak plainly. Nothing which I may have said at any other time is to be interpreted as meaning that the police can relax or rest on the somewhat tarnished laurels they may have gathered from the battle of Sidney Street. We must do better. A lot better. And the first thing is this. Any man with a record of violence in his own country must be watched and put under restraint *before* and not *after* he has used guns or explosives. Is that clear, gentlemen?'

He interpreted four sombre nods to mean agreement and added, in a more conciliatory tone of voice, 'If we work together, government and police, I am sure we can do it.'

When the meeting broke up, Vernon Kell collected the two CID men and took them to his own office. As soon as the door was shut Morgan, who had a Welsh temper, exploded. He said to Kell, 'I gather you're in Intelligence. Right? And intelligent too, no doubt. Then would you mind telling me how the bloody hell we're expected to know - by divination, I suppose – that an immigrant who turns up without papers and probably using one of several alternative names, had a record of violence in his own country? Are we supposed to find this record tattooed on his bottom?'

Wensley grunted agreement.

'All right,' said Kell. 'Don't take it out on me. You've been listening to a politician washing his own neck. They all do it. It's a form of catharsis. Now, let's consider practicalities. If we can set up some form of liaison between the Home Office and the police, we might be able to tackle the job.'

Wensley said, 'What had you in mind?'

'Just at the moment we're on reasonably good terms with the Foreign Office. A matter of personalities. They could be helpful. As you know, they have so-called military attachés – a polite name for spies – in most of the important countries, including, of course, Russia. They could alert us if any particularly notorious bad hat had slipped out of the country and was heading for England.'

Morgan said, 'I'd have thought that if he was all that notorious his own Secret Police would have stopped him.'

'Yes and no. Sometimes they might stop them. Sometimes they might even send them.'

The heads of both policemen jerked up. The idea was clearly new to them and disconcerting.

'Why would they do that?' said Wensley.

'To get them off their hands,' suggested Morgan. 'Sound tactics.'

'There is another possibility. I'm working on the matter now. I don't want to give you theories. Let's stick to facts. And one deplorable fact is that MO5, being new, is laughably short staffed. I'd hardly be exaggerating if I told you that it started with me and an office boy. So I've been poaching. From the Home Office *and* the Foreign Office. And I've picked up some good men. One from the Home Office in particular called Hubert Daines. Now, if either of you happened to have a promising man who could be put in direct touch with Daines, we might be able to organise a useful liaison.'

Morgan looked doubtful. He said, 'I've got a lot of good policemen, but I don't see any of them as Intelligence agents.'

Wensley opened his mouth and shut it again as though to repress something he had been going to say. Kell swivelled round to look at him. 'Come on, Fred,' he said. 'Let's have it.'

'Well, as it happens, there is one youngster in my Force who's got what you might call qualifications. He started life as a game-keeper.'

'Excellent training for all fields of crime.'

'And somehow he's managed to pick up good French and Russian.'

'Couldn't be better. So what's the drawback?'

'The drawback is that he's young and inexperienced. A year and a bit in uniform in a quiet division and less than two years with me. If he tangles with the sort of men you've been talking about, he'll be out of his class and heading for trouble.'

'I appreciate that. But I'm not asking him to tangle with them. Just to observe them and their friends and contacts. There are plenty of Russians who don't carry a bomb in each pocket and a knife up their sleeve. Some of them will surely talk to him. Particularly the girls, if he's young and personable.'

'I don't think he's interested in girls. Though they might be interested in him.'

'Girls are like cats,' said Morgan. 'Shoo them away and they come climbing back on to your lap.'

'Speaking from experience, Dai?' said Wensley.

'Myself, I'm a happily married man. I was just giving you the fruits of my observation.'

'Right,' said Kell. 'That's settled. Send your accomplished young linguist along. And since we don't want to mark him out publicly he'd better come by the back door. He goes in through the India Office and there's a subway under King Charles Street, so he needn't show up in the open at all. I'll give him a pass for both buildings. And impress on him, Fred, that we're looking for observation, not action. He isn't a player. He's a spectator, on the side lines.'

'Always supposing he'll stay there,' said Wensley gloomily.

'When I was told,' said Luke, 'that I had to co-operate with a Foreign Office official, I feared the worst.'

Daines said, 'I know. Morning dress, pompous delivery, developing stomach.'

'Well—'

'And you were correspondingly relieved when you discovered that it was a man you had last seen with his clothes in tatters and his face painted yellow.'

Both men laughed.

Daines said, 'If we're going to work together I shall have to start by giving you my personal interpretation of what happened at Houndsditch and Sidney Street last month. It isn't the popular view. Far from it.'

'I can give you the popular view. In two words – bloody Russians.'

'That's the view of the man in the street. And we mustn't sneer at it. The man in the street is often right when politicians are wrong. The only thing is that politicians not only have to know what people are thinking, sometimes they have to tell them what they ought to think. In this case, it's not difficult. Three policemen dead, three Russians dead. Three all. Not a bad result, for people who think of most things in terms of football.'

'Do you think it's an over-simplification? Or do you think it's wrong?'

Daines said, 'I think it's wrong. And I think it's dangerous.' He paused to gather his thoughts for the benefit of the serious young man sitting opposite. His room looked out over an enclosed courtyard at the back of the building. In the deep silence Luke could hear two pigeons quarrelling over a scrap of food three floors below.

'To understand what happened you have to concentrate on someone who hasn't featured in the published accounts at all. Someone you've never heard of and may never hear of again. One Charles Perelman who came over from Russia six years ago. Nothing against him, except that he seemed to change houses rather often. And whatever house he moved to, soon became a home-from-home for other Russians, many of them criminals. He's a curious character who goes about in a huge cloak and a black sombrero, though it's far from clear whether he really is a terrorist, or is acting the part to keep in with the boys and take their money for rent, for he's usually hard up. And here's the first point to notice. All of the nine men involved in the Houndsditch robbery had lodged with Perelman at one time. Jacob Peters, George Gardstein, Max Smoller, Yourka Dubof, Fritz Svaars, Josef Sokalow, Karl Hoffman, John Rosen and Peter Piatkow.'

Luke, who had been scribbling desperately, looked up to say, 'Is that the one the papers call Peter the Painter?'

'That's the one. For some reason he seems to have appealed to the popular imagination. Right. Consider now what happened to those men. Gardstein was shot, accidentally, in the course of the Houndsditch robbery. Svaars and Sokalow died in the ashes of the Sidney Street house. Peters, Dubof, Rosen and Hoffman are on the run and either have been arrested or will be soon, because the ports are now blocked against them. If you've been keeping the score, what's the answer?'

Luke looked at his scribbles and said, 'Two left. Peter the Painter and Max Smoller.'

'Correct.'

'I suppose they're on the run, too.'

'No amount of running is going to catch that precious pair. They both got across to France, with Perelman's help, on the night those policemen were shot in Houndsditch. Which makes Perelman more than just a casual associate. A close friend of all the men concerned, wouldn't you say?'

'Certainly. A very good friend.'

'Then you could explain why it was it was that Perelman gave away Svaars and Sokalow and led the police to Sidney Street.'

Luke said, 'For God's sake,' and sat with his head in his hands, whilst facts and figures performed a crazy tango in his brain.

Daines watched him sympathetically. 'It's a devil's dance,' he said. 'They never stand still. Forming and re-forming, swapping partners and then linking up again. When you think you understand what they're doing, they're doing something quite different. But one thing's certain. We may have come badly out of this last round of trouble, but it can hardly have pleased the Ochrana.'

'Sorry. The who did you say?'

'The Administration for the Protection of State Institutions and Public Security, the Okhraneniyu ot Delenya, usually shortened to Ochrana. Formed after the assassination of Alexander II in 1881. A very powerful organisation indeed. What *they* were hoping for was that the efforts of this gang would cause such a revulsion of public opinion here that our political masters would be forced to send all or most of the Russian immigrants back to Russia.'

'That's the street cry. "Send the bastards back where they came from."'

'Where the Ochrana would have been waiting for them with open arms. Open arms and a quick death in the Lubianka prison or a slow one in Siberia. But in fact all they achieved by their efforts was a public verdict that substantial justice had been done. Three terrorists for three policemen.'

Luke, who had by this time a fair idea of where Daines was

going said, 'So what you're anticipating is that next time there'll be an outrage, or maybe a series of outrages, that will force the British government to act in the way the Ochrana want.'

'That is, indeed, what we fear.'

'And will that bought-and-sold creature, Perelman, be stage-managing the next production?'

'No. He's exhausted his usefulness. A serious matter like this will be handled seriously. We think that two or three men will be pulling the strings. All I can give you at the moment is their names and a few scraps of information. First, Casimir Treschau, who goes under the name of Otto Trautman—'

'I noticed his name in the papers Silistreau-Morrowitz brought over with him.'

'The more I hear about those papers,' said Daines sadly, 'the more I regret that they went into the drink. They might have painted the whole picture for us. At the moment all we know about Treschau is that he had a big name in Russia as a chemist, that he fell into disfavour and was questioned so roughly by the police that they broke his leg for him. He still limps.'

'Yes. It's an odd dragging limp. I only heard it once, but I think I'd recognise it if I heard it again.'

He told Daines about his night watch over the widow Triboff's house and its unhappy outcome.

'Then you never saw his face.'

'I heard him and felt him, but didn't see him.'

'A pity. Next there's the hard man, the head of their street gang over here, a lout who uses several names, including Zircov and Zmunstrov. His real name's thought to be Molacoff Weil, nick-named in Russian "Three Times".'

Since Daines was waiting for a question, Luke obligingly said, 'What does that mean?'

'You may find the story difficult to credit, but the fact that his compatriots *do* believe it will give you some idea of the man. It seems that one of the procedures of the Ochrana, when looking for information or co-operation, is to strip the prisoner naked and immerse him alternatively in boiling water and cold water. A treatment calculated to unlock the most obstinate tongues.'

'Dear Lord,' said Luke, 'I should be talking before they got me near the boiling water.'

'So would most people. Weil is said to have suffered three immersions before he decided to change sides. Hence the nickname. But the third man is the pick of the bunch. The man whose efforts you encountered in Newcastle – Janis Silistreau, currently going under the name of Ivan Morrowitz. Noted in his own country as a poet and a thinker. All that we have on him at the moment are those excellent photographs that Farnsworth took. We missed him on arrival up here. There was some delay in Farnsworth's message reaching Wensley. But a man of that eminence can't stay hidden for long.'

'Now that you've identified these three men, can't they be arrested and deported?'

'They could only be deported if they were proved to be involved in criminal activities. Not in political activities. A difficult distinction, as you will appreciate. Also, Treschau and Silistreau are public figures. If we laid a finger on them without full justification, our intellectual lefties would be screaming themselves hoarse. Your job will be to keep your eyes open. If you spot any of the three men, let me and Wensley know at once. And,' he added with a smile that softened the words, 'no heroics. If these men catch a spy, their treatment of him is intended as a warning to others.'

5

When Luke reported what Daines had said, Wensley looked up from a photograph he was studying, thought about it briefly and said, 'Report weekly, in writing,' and returned to the photograph. As that seemed to be all he was going to say Luke edged towards the door.

Wensley said, 'Come here a moment.' He pushed the photograph across the desk. 'What do you make of that?'

It was a close-up of a dead man's face. The only remarkable thing about it was a sickle-shaped slash on each cheek.

'I'm afraid it doesn't mean much to me, sir.'

'You wouldn't say it was the sign of a secret society?'

'Difficult to say, sir.'

'Very difficult,' said Wensley.

Luke thought he looked tired and worried and said as much to Joe who had been waiting outside.

'Of course he's tired,' said Joe. 'Poor old sod. Like I told you, he gets landed with any sticky work that's going. A body turns up on Clapham Common, which is miles from his division. But because it's a Russian Jew and because a likely suspect is another Russian it gets shovelled on to Fred's plate. I expect he can live with it. What were his orders for us?'

'To report in writing once a week.'

'What does that mean?'

'That we do what we like and tell him about it once a week.'

'Well,' said Joe, 'I've no complaints about that. Sounds like the recipe for a rest cure. The only thing is, what about Josh? He likes to keep an eye on the Detective Branch.'

What Superintendent Joscelyne thought about it transpired

later that day when he summoned Luke and Joe to his office. His ears were still tingling both from Winston's criticisms and from the indirect but even more hurtful comments of other senior police officers, which had made him truculent in temper and violent in speech.

He said, 'I gather that your job will be to keep an eye on those fornicating Russian bastards. Right? And if keeping an eye on them involves getting a bit rough with them, I'd say get as rough as you like. Don't worry. I'll support you. You understand?'

He glared at each of them in turn. Luke said, 'Yes, sir.'

'No kid gloves. Give them the sort of treatment they gave Tucker and Bentley and Choate. Work together. Watch your step. Keep your eyes open. Don't get caught. Don't get shot. Any questions?'

Since neither of them could think of any questions to ask about these instructions, they were dismissed with an injunction to get on with it and not fuck about.

'Don't get caught,' said Joe. 'I should worry. A champion dodger like me. If a squad of gamekeepers couldn't catch me, what chance have a mob of heavy-footed Ruskies got?'

Luke said, 'Daines isn't stupid. If he thought they were dangerous, I'll go along with it. We keep our heads down.'

'Now you're talking sense,' said Joe. 'Lead me to a comfortable bed and I'll get my head right down on it, no fooling.'

Luke ignored this. He was pursuing his own thoughts. He said, 'You remember what happened, that night I got coshed?'

'I remember what you told me about it.'

'I was following young Tomacoff. He's not important. Just an errand boy. He'd been given a message and told where to go and when. From the way he kept looking at his watch his instructions seem to have been to hang about and not get there before a stated time. Right?'

'Seems logical.'

'But is it? If he'd simply got a message, why couldn't he get there whenever he liked? If the man it was meant for wasn't in, he could always wait. So what was he hanging round for? A dangerous thing for him to do, at that time of night.'

'You tell me.'

'I'll tell you what I think. I think certain precautions had been taken. Routine precautions for men like that. Tomacoff was waiting until his guardian angel was in position. If he was followed, his guardian angel would follow the follower. You follow me?'

'No.'

'But it's obvious. And it's just the sort of drill they would adopt. They're professional terrorists. People who've lived for years in their own country with eyes in the back of their heads. Which is why they've survived.'

'OK,' said Joe patiently. 'You followed Tomacoff. An angel with a sand-bag followed you. So what does it add up to?'

'It adds up to something we should have thought about before. If the man that Tomacoff was going to see was important enough to warrant such elaborate protection he must have been one of their top men. And a man like that wouldn't have been lodged any old where. He'd be in a safe house. Kept by a trusted person.'

'The widow Triboff. That smelly old bag.'

'Old bag she may be. But I've a feeling that if we shook her hard enough something useful might fall out. We'd jumped to the conclusion that her lodger was there by chance. I don't believe it. I think the Triboff house is one of their centres of activity and must be watched.'

'By us?'

'Who else?'

'Starting when?'

'Starting tonight.'

'I thought that was what you meant,' said Joe.

'Most of police work,' Wensley had said, 'is waiting and watching. I once kept it up for thirty-six hours on end. It was a wasted effort. I was watching the wrong house.'

Luke thought about this, as the sky began to pale over the roof and chimney stacks of the widow Triboff's home. This time they had a more comfortable observation post than the doorstep on which he had squatted on the previous occasion. They had broken into an empty house and established themselves at an upstairs window.

Joe was beside him, flat on his back and snoring. It was gone half past seven before he rolled over, grunted, sat up and said, 'How long've I bin asleep?'

'Difficult to say,' said Luke. 'It was two o'clock or thereabouts when you started to snore. You might have been asleep before that.'

'Is that a fact? Well, seeing as how no one turned up, it didn't matter whether I was awake or asleep, did it?'

'What makes you think that no one turned up?'

'If there had been anyone for us to follow, I suppose you'd have woken me up. I mean, we're on the job together, aren't we? Correct me if I'm mistook.' Like most people who feel that they're in the wrong Joe managed to sound aggrieved.

Luke said, 'I never supposed we'd be able to follow anyone. All I wanted to do was to see if someone turned up.'

'And did they?'

'Two people. Neither of them stayed more than a few minutes. The first one –' Luke looked at his scribbled notes – 'dropped in at 3.15 and the second at 4.25. Both were youngsters. One of them could have been Tomacoff. I imagine they were dropping in written messages for collection later. If we'd followed them we might have found out where *they* lived. Hardly worth the trouble, though.'

So what do we do now?'

'We pay a visit – an official visit – to the widow Triboff. Look as fierce and formidable as possible.'

'I can't look formidable when I'm dying of starvation.'

'Work first, breakfast next.'

A double rap on the Triboff door, repeated with increased

emphasis, produced an untidy old lady in a dressing-gown with her hair in rags. Luke showed her his police identity card and pushed past her into the room at the back of the house which seemed to do duty as sitting-room, kitchen and bedroom combined. The old woman followed him, squawking indignantly. Joe followed her to cut off her retreat.

Standing with his back to the window, Luke surveyed the dirty, cluttered room in silence until the old lady's protests had died down to a mumbling and clucking. Then he said, 'Your name is Triboff?' All he got was what might have been a nod. 'I want to know who the two men were who visited you last night. What they came for, and if they brought letters, what you've done with them.'

The widow snapped her toothless jaws shut and said nothing. Luke stepped up to her. When he was so close to her that he could smell her breath and her fear, he repeated the question; with the same result.

He thought, with disgust, she expects me to hit her. Followed by a second thought. However much I hurt her she isn't going to talk. He appeared to change his mind. He said, 'When you've got dressed you'll come along to the police station in Leman Street to answer some questions. If you're not there by nine o'clock you'll be fetched. Which may not be so pleasant. You understand?'

The old woman bobbed her head. Luke could see that she was deeply relieved by this change of plan.

'Then get on with it.' He strode out into the front passage, followed by a mystified Joe. When he reached the front door he snibbed back the catch on the lock and slammed the door behind them. Then they walked away until they were out of sight of the house.

'Give her two minutes,' said Luke.

When they got back they eased the front door open and tiptoed along the passage. The living-room was empty, but someone was moving upstairs and they heard a metallic sound.

'Come on,' said Luke. 'Quickly now.'

The room above the widow's sordid den was, as they saw when they burst into it, an altogether superior apartment. Neat, well warmed and lighted, with a big desk alongside one wall and a bed pushed back against another; it was an office-cum-bedroom, comfortable and ready for use. The heating came from an old-fashioned iron stove into which the widow was trying to push a sheaf of papers. When she saw her visitors she screamed, but did not stop what she was doing.

'Grab her,' said Luke.

Joe sprang into action, twisted the widow's left arm behind her back, frog-marched her across the room and banged her right wrist down on the corner of the desk, loosening her hold on the papers which fell on to the floor. In her anxiety to get rid of them the widow had rolled them into a sheaf which was too large to go between the bars of the stove. All she had succeeded in doing was charring the ends of them.

'Sit her down in that chair,' said Luke.

'Tie her up?'

'No need. She won't run away.'

The events of the last few minutes had knocked most of the fight out of her. She sat in silence as Luke gathered up the papers. He said, 'Now listen to me, Mother Triboff. Do you know a man called Weil? Molacoff Weil?'

The widow started to shake.

'I see that you know the sort of man he is. All right. Unless you answer a few questions I'm going to let him know that you handed over these papers to us, to get yourself out of trouble. *And* that you let us take them away. So what do you think he'll do to you?'

'Feed her into the stove, like as not,' said Joe. But the widow took no notice of him. Her eyes were on Luke and on the papers, which he had unrolled and started to examine. Her lips were working.

Finally she said, 'What do you want?'

'I want to know where the messages are that came last night.

You can't have sent them on yet, because no one has left the house. Also I want to know who's the man who uses this room.'

'And if I tell you, you won't—'

'If you tell us, that's the end of the matter.'

'You've got the messages there.'

Most of the documents were anarchist literature, handbills and circulars, printed by the Anarchist Press in Jubilee Street. From among them Luke extracted two grubby envelopes, neither of them sealed. The notes in them were in Russian, unheaded and unaddressed. The first said, 'The usual place, tomorrow. Bring your two friends with you.' The second said, 'When you go to your workshop watch your back. This is important.'

Luke said, 'What's this "usual place" and this workshop they talk about?'

The old woman shook her head. She knew nothing. All she had to do was pass on messages to people who came to collect them. This seemed reasonable. Luke changed tack. He said, 'Tell me about the man who uses this room. He seems to have made himself pretty comfortable. He must have been here some time.'

'Trout. His name was Trout.'

'Sounds fishy to me,' said Joe, predictably.

'Is that all you can tell us?'

'I know nothing more. He came, he paid his rent, he hobbled away.'

'He had some difficulty in walking?'

'Yes. He was lame.'

Looking through the printed papers whilst he was talking, Luke had spotted one that was handwritten. It seemed to be a receipt of some sort and the important thing was that it had an address on it. Twenty-two Cundy Street. Careful not to seem too interested in it he pushed it into his pocket with the two messages, rolled up the anarchist literature and gave it to Joe. The widow watched him, blinking fearfully.

'If he – if anyone asks,' she said, 'you will tell him that you

took the papers by force. That I tried to burn them, but you pre-
vented me.'

'Very well. That shall be our story. Only changed a little. You
didn't try to burn the papers. You succeeded. That puts you in an
even better light, yes?'

The old lady nodded. Now that Luke had started to speak in
Russian she was following what he said closely, her button eyes
gleaming.

'Second point, if Mr Trout reappears, you get the news to us at
the police station in Leman Street. You know it?'

'The police house, yes.'

'Good. Then, for the moment, goodbye.'

'What next?' said Joe, as they slammed the widow's door
behind them.

'Breakfast,' said Luke. 'Then we might have a look at this
Anarchist Press.'

Later that morning their route to Jubilee Street took them
along Stepney Way and down Sidney Street. Small clumps of
sightseers were still poking around, pocketing slivers of charred
wood as mementoes and staring about them, although there was
nothing to stare at except the forlorn carcass of number 100, half-
burned timbers poking up through the rubble of brickwork and
fallen tiles. A group, halfway down the street, was being
addressed by a small, stout person with an aggressive moustache
and a red nose.

'So what do they come 'ere for?' he was saying. 'And where
do they come from? I can tell you that. I've bin watching 'em.
They come from up there.' He jerked one thumb over his left
shoulder to indicate the upper class end of London. 'They come
to see what poor people like us is forced to live in.'

Luke though that the chain of gold links looped across his
waistcoat was not one of the more obvious signs of poverty.

'Forced, we are, to live among furren muck, men who think as
little of using guns and bombs as we think of blowin' our noses.
So let me ask you a question. 'Oo let 'em in?'

He waited for his audience to oblige with an answer. One of them offered. 'Parliament let 'em in.'

'And oo's responsible to Parliament?'

This defeated his listeners, so he supplied the answer himself.

'It's the bloody 'Ome Seggeratry oo's responsible. Mr Winston bloody Churchill. If I'd my way, 'e'd 'ave bin tossed into the fire along with 'em.'

A policeman on the outskirts of the crowd, who had been listening absentmindedly with his thoughts on his relief and his next meal, now sharpened up. It seemed that the orater was stepping outside permissible limits.

'And what did our blessed 'Ome Seggeratry do? 'E came down 'ere to enjoy the fun. I seen 'im with my own eyes, standing on this very spot, gloatin' over the destruction.'

At this point the policeman drew out his book and made a note and it occurred to Luke that they would be better away. As they moved off down the side street they saw another policeman at the corner of Lindley Street, and a third one at the point where Jubilee Street ran out into the Mile End Road; strategic points where they could keep an eye open for trouble.

Joe said, 'The Anarchist Press is number 37. That'll be right up the far end.' When they reached it and could see round the corner, they were in time to witness a more serious piece of trouble.

A group of four toffs, on a spree, had grabbed a passing youngster. When they found he was Russian they had evidently decided, for no very good reason, that he must be a terrorist and two of them were devoting their attention to teaching him a lesson. They had forced him to his knees and the shorter of his assailants had grabbed his hair and was hitting him in the face. The taller one was kicking him, choosing his targets carefully.

'Bullying,' said Luke. 'And enjoying it. We've got to stop this before they damage him badly.'

'The odds aren't too steep,' said Joe. 'Help is at hand.'

He had noted the policeman at the Lindley Street corner and

before charging in, he blew a blast on his useful whistle. As they arrived the tall attacker aimed a last kick at the boy and transferred his attention to Luke. The taller they come the harder they fall, he thought. Pivoting on one foot he hooked his opponent's ankle from under him and put him on his back with a satisfying thump.

When the policeman cantered up, Joe had the shorter one with his head in chancery under his arm. The other two had bolted, pausing at the corner to look back and signal violently. The message was clear. Luke's opponent scrambled to his feet and ran to join them. Luke watched him go, but made no attempt to follow. Joe loosened his victim, who was purple in the face, grabbed one of his wrists and twisted his arms up behind his back. After which brief flurry of action Luke and Joe introduced themselves.

'Certainly we're charging him,' said Luke. 'Assault and battery. Maybe attempted murder.'

'Not just attempted,' said Joe. In fact the boy on the ground looked unpleasantly corpse-like.

'I don't think he's dead,' said Luke. He bent down to feel his heart and stood up abruptly. 'If you go with the constable – Perry, isn't it? – and see to the formalities, I'll get this one home. Mostly shock and bruises, I think. But the sooner he's in bed the better.'

By this time a small crowd had collected and when Luke asked if anyone knew where the boy lived, several voices volunteered. 'Deickman Street', 'Just round the corner' and 'The shop with the photographs.'

Luke hoisted the boy on to his back. Joe, his prisoner and PC Perry marched off and the crowd started to disperse. Two or three of them followed Luke to point out the shop, easily identifiable from the photographs of marriage groups in the window. One of them ran ahead to knock on the door, which was open by the time Luke arrived.

An elderly couple were standing in the hall. The woman uttered an exclamation of alarm. Luke said, 'Nothing too serious,

Mamma.' He lowered the boy to his feet and he seemed able to stand. The woman put her arms round him and hustled him off.

The man said, 'We must thank you. And introduce ourselves. Jacob and Elzelina Katz. You are – Pagan – yes. Please be seated, Mr Pagan. My wife has medical training. She should shortly be able to reassure you that our son Ivan will be all right. Thanks to your most timely assistance. Whilst we are waiting, might I offer you a glass of schnapps or of brandy?'

Luke voted for brandy. This seemed to him to be exactly the sort of contact he had been told to look for. He said, 'Would you regard it as an impertinence if I asked you to tell me something about yourself?'

'An impertinence, no. I only fear that I might bore you. I have poured out my troubles so often that they come out like water when you turn the tap.'

Luke said, 'Turn it on for me.'

'If you wish me to. It is a sad story, though a common enough one in these parts. Maybe we have been luckier than some. It was – let me see – almost exactly ten years ago that we arrived. Myself, my wife Elzelina and the two children, Dmitry and Ivan. They were six and seven years old. It was only because they were young, you understand, that we were allowed to bring them with us. If they had been a few years older we should have been compelled to leave them behind.'

Outside it had started to rain. A heavy January shower blown in from the east.

'It was raining when we arrived,' said Jacob. He looked back, in silence, to that unforgettable moment: he and his family squatting in the rain on the quay, with their few belongings around them and no idea of what to do next.

'To leave your old life behind,' said Luke, 'and start anew. It must have been a hard decision. What drove you to do it?'

'We came because we had to come. Life for us Jews had been made intolerable. I mean that literally. Impossible to bear. Our language was forbidden. Our books were burnt. Our sons were dragooned into the Army. A Russian recruit faced fifteen years of service. A Jewish boy thirty years. Very few survived it. It was customary to recite the prayers for the dead over our young conscripts. Then, when they were in the Army, they were forced into the Orthodox religion. They underwent a rechristening.'

'Could they have refused?'

'Oh, certainly. What followed such refusal would be a diet of salted food, water being withheld until they agreed to co-operate. Most did. A few resisted until death mercifully carried them away. When our village was uprooted and transferred, with many others, to where they called the Pale of Settlement, conditions became even worse. But I had one advantage over my fellows. My printing and photographic business had prospered. I was even able – you must not laugh – to publish a newspaper. It was a poor little sheet and always cringingly discreet. In the end, even that was frowned on and I was forced to suspend it, but by that time I had money. Not a lot, but enough. I could buy my way out. It would cost me all, or almost all that I had, in payments to the authorities, at all levels, for a permit. Bribes at the frontier would extract what I had left. In fact, I was able to bring out a very small residue of cash. I will not describe to you the method of hiding it, which might shock you. I only know that if it had been discovered, further fees and formalities would have been invented. With that money and the necessary resolution to starve rather than spend all of it on food, I was able to start again. My first work was hand-written. Fortunately I am a good pen-man. Then I was able to buy an old camera. Then a better one. Then set up my printing press again. Now, as you see, we live in a measure of comfort. I can even save money. That enables me to send remittances to my son, Peter. The Ghetto Bank handles such matters.'

'Peter, then, was your elder son?'

'He was fourteen years old, nearly fifteen, when we left. Now he will be twenty-four. He has, mercifully, managed to avoid conscription and tells me that he is doing well as an engineer.'

'That sounds like a happy end to an unhappy story.'

'May it continue happy. I hope it will. But sometimes I fear—'

'Fear what?'

Picking his words with evident care Jacob said, 'Most refugees, ourselves and our friends, view England as a haven. A blessed place, on no account to be disturbed by resort to criminal activities. But, alas, our activists reject such a view.'

When he paused, as though not anxious to proceed, Luke said, 'It seems such a sensible view that one wonders why anyone should reject it.'

'One reason is that they want money. More money than they can possibly get by honest work. But they persuade themselves that there are more lofty reasons. They despise all existing administrations as corrupt capitalistic façades, erected in order to mask the exploitation of the lower orders. Nonsense, of course, but that is the way they have been conditioned to think.'

At this point they were interrupted by the return of Elzelina Katz. She said, 'Ivan is much recovered. It is nothing worse than bruises and scratches, thanks to this kind gentleman. I do not know your name, sir.'

'Luke Pagan. My friend and I have an apartment in Osborne Street. A short way down the High Street. You know it, perhaps?'

'Indeed,' said Jacob. 'I know all the streets round here, having tramped them for custom. I hope you will pardon me for asking what may seem an impertinent question. But are you of the police?'

'Correct. But I wasn't aware that it was so obvious.'

'My unhappy experiences have enabled me to identify a policeman almost at first sight. Ah, here is Ivan. He does indeed appear to have recovered somewhat.'

Luke said, 'Now I, in turn, must ask you an equally impertinent question. What is this child's real name?'

'His real name,' said Jacob. 'I'm not sure I understand.'

'Not Ivan, surely. Would it perhaps be Rebecca? Catherine? Leah?'

In the silence that followed, the members of the Katz family looked at each other. They did not seem greatly alarmed. It was Elzelina who broke the silence. She said, 'Her name is Anna.'

6

Luke was dreaming.

From time to time he grunted, twisting about in bed, unwilling to return to reality. Feeling a hand on his shoulder he opened his eyes.

Joe said, 'You've bin imitating a pig for nigh on half an hour. Must have been a lovely dream. Something happening in a farm yard, was it?'

Luke said, 'If it was, I've forgotten. I never remember dreams for more than five seconds.' This was not true. He could remember it clearly. He had been dreaming about a girl's body in boys' clothes.

Joe, who was already dressed, said, 'Arise and shine and tell me what's on the menu for today.' The rain, which had belted down all night, had stopped and the sun was shining. 'It's a lovely morning. Let's go out and kill someone.'

'We've got a job to do.'

'Don't tell me. I know we're going to watch a house somewhere for someone who isn't there.'

'No. It's what you might call a cleaning job. I told you last night that the boy I picked up turned out to be a girl. I didn't tell you why she was forced to dress like that and how I found out.'

'Let me guess,' said Joe. 'You found out when you laid your hand gently upon his heart to see whether it was beating and felt—'

'Right,' said Luke hastily. 'That's when I found out. Later on I discovered why she was going round dressed as a boy. It seems she and her brother needed jobs and the only ones they could get were at a sweat-shop in a place called Brownsong Court,

85

wherever that may be. It's run by a prime bastard called
Solomon. If a girl entered his employment one of the understood
terms was that she would co-operate with him in every way. In
every way. A session in his private apartment after the day's
work was done, is the usual arrangement.'

'And if they refuse?'

'They lose the job. Which is why Anna went on as a boy. She
reckoned that Solomon would tumble to it sooner or later, but
meanwhile she is pocketing her pay – which, as sweat-shop pay
goes, is fairly generous.'

'And you think we ought to make it clear to Mr Solomon that
we consider his terms of employment irregular.'

'I think it is our duty to do so.'

'How did you propose to set about it?'

'I hadn't worked out all the details.'

'What would be suitable,' said Joe thoughtfully, 'would be a
boot in the crutch. That would keep him quiet for a week or so.
Anyway, more fun than watching an empty house. Lead on.'

Brownsong Court, when they found it, proved to be an
enclosed square in the Spitalfields area, south of the market.
The approach to it was a narrow cobbled lane called
Brownsong Passage. The whole area seemed to have been
taken over by the Jewish fraternity. On the left, as they
approached down Stratford Road, they passed the Jewish
school and a modern synagogue. In Brownsong Passage the
right-hand side was lined with tiny shops that sold old clothes,
sewing-machines and religious medallions. The left-hand side
was occupied by the double frontage of Solomon Enterprises.
Before tackling this, they looked into the square. On the right
and on the far side, it was lined by one-storey houses, each of
which seemed, from the boards at the front doors, to be the
residence of half a dozen different families. To the left, behind
Solomon's spread, stood a branch of that monument to Jewish
industry, the great Ghetto Bank.

'Shonks' corner,' said Joe.

Luke found nothing to disapprove of. Like most Jewish quarters it was neat, functional and, after the recent heavy rain, clean. 'Better than most Gentiles' corners,' he said.

The front door of Solomon's shop was opened by the proprietor himself. Luke, who had expected a Jew in a greasy gaberdine, rubbing his hands together and smiling in a placatory manner, was taken aback to be confronted by a thickset dwarf, wearing a dark, well-cut suit and a scowl. When they had identified themselves as policemen, the scowl disappeared, to be replaced, as he understood the business they had come on, with a smile of seemingly genuine amusement.

'Come in,' he said. 'Come in. Feel free to question all my boys and girls. They make up stories, you understand, to intrigue each other. They will have nothing to tell you that will embarrass me. Of that I am sure. Enlighten me. Who has made this preposterous accusation?'

This was difficult. He could hardly say, 'One of your girls who was dressed as a boy,' so he was forced to fall back on generalities. He said, 'I have heard it from many sources.'

'Indeed,' said the dwarf. 'But you know what girls are. As I said, they like to spread romantic tales. Me, I have no time for such frippery. I work as hard as they do. Or harder.'

By this time they were through the entrance hall and were looking into the two big rooms beyond. In the left-hand room a number of men were working with sewing-machines. In the right-hand one, separated from it by a partition, twenty or more girls were sewing and pressing. When they peered through the door in this partition most of the girls looked up and most of them smiled. None of them looked oppressed.

'My happy family,' said Solomon, beaming at them. 'Though I fear that soon they may have less cause to be happy. Soon I shall be forced to close down part of my business. Maybe I shall retain one of these rooms and work only from the other one. I am being driven out by the large operators. I employ twenty or thirty workers. They use two or three hundred. With mass production they can afford to lower their prices. In the end, maybe, I shall have to close down both rooms.'

Luke decided to terminate what was turning out to be an unproductive visit. In an endeavour to maintain some part of the initiative, he said, 'I may be back with some questions for you later.'

'I shall always be glad to see you,' said Solomon with a warm smile, as he closed the door behind them. When the door was shut the smile was shut off, too.

'Didn't get much change out of him, did we?' said Joe. 'Could be true about those girls. I mean, that they made the running, not him. It's a funny thing about girls. I've noticed. The idea of having it off with a dwarf or a cripple or someone like that seems to titubate them. Do I mean titubate?'

'I think you meant titillate.'

'That's right. Titty-late. Just the word I had in mind. You remember one-legged Jack, back at Bellingham. Girls round him like flies round a jam pot. 'Ullo, who's this?'

They had turned out into the main road and were passing the frontage of the synagogue, when the door swung open and a white-bearded man erupted from the door. He grabbed Luke by the arm, dragged him across the pavement and said, 'You are of the government, yes. Then you will do something quickly. Before worse occurs.'

He pointed to the spot where the forecourt in which they were now standing bordered on the road and Luke saw that water had flowed out of the two storm drains in the gutter and had formed a pool. It was clearly the residue of a much larger pool, almost a lake.

'Come and look,' said the old man. He had such a firm grasp of Luke's arm that Luke could not have thrown him off without hurting him. When they got into the synagogue he could see that the flood, before it receded, had entered the building and covered a section of the floor.

Luke said, 'Must have been the rain last night. Unusually heavy.'

'Never before has such a thing happened. Rain we have had, yes. Storms, yes. But never before a flood. Our building is precious to us, you understand. We cannot stand idly by and see it ruined.'

With the idea of getting away Luke said, 'I'd better report this to the Sanitary Authorities. They'll know what to do.'

This qualified assurance seemed to satisfy the old man, who smiled for the first time, and said, 'That is well. You will make a report. Something will be done. We are proud of our synagogue. It must not be damaged. Noble, is it not?'

Looking about him Luke saw an oblong, uninspiring interior, the only remarkable feature of which was the great window which filled the east wall. 'A masterpiece indeed,' said the old man. 'It is the work of Elias Kazan. You will have heard of him, of course.' Luke felt that it was safe to nod. 'You will observe the motif. In the centre is the Prophet Moses, in his glory. At his feet the spirits of the damned, who are in Purgatory. Along the top, ten great bene-factors and scholars. On the left you can see the blessed Chasdal ibn Shaprut and next to him the learned Johan ibn Janach. I could tell you the story of each one. My name, by the way, is Werfel. Joshua Werfel. I have the charge of this congregation.'

'You are its pastor?'

'I am its rabbi,' said the old man with a smile. 'At your service.'

'I'll keep in touch with you,' said Luke. 'And when we have a moment you shall tell me the story of your window. Meanwhile, I must hurry away. I have much to do.'

One of the things he had to do, he realised, was to deliver his weekly report to Wensley. It was already a day late. He had writ-ten most of it the night before. He decided that he would hand it over as it stood, since their expedition that morning did not seem to have produced anything of importance.

When they reached Leman Street they were told that Wensley was in conference. He would see them as soon as he was free.

Wensley had known and admired Sir Melville Macnaghten since the days when Sir Melville was Chief Constable of the CID and he himself a detective sergeant. The admiration was mutual. Wensley's subsequent promotions had been well earned, but it had done him no harm to have a friend at court. 'A thoughtful man', Wensley had once called Sir Melville and he was demonstrating his thoughtfulness at that moment by coming to Wensley's office to confer rather than getting him up to Scotland Yard. He knew how busy the Clapham Common killing, added to his other preoccupations, had made his subordinate. He had brought Hubert Daines with him.

He said, 'I wanted you to hear, at first hand, what he has been telling me.'

Daines said, 'Our troubles stem, as usual, from the Tsar. A tiresome creature. If only he would stop swinging from left to right and right to left like a demented pendulum, we might know where we stood. One moment his troubles come from the moderates on the right, who want a constitutional government. The next moment from the revolutionaries of the extreme left. The main plank in *their* programme is the assassination of the Tsar, along with most of his ministers, and then, a constant source of irritation to him, there are the *émigrés*, particularly the ones who have reached this country. Protected by our well-known tolerance they sit here like a line of rooks croaking out anti-Tsar propaganda. The Minister of the Interior, Peter Stolypin, is said to be temporarily in favour because he has promised to organise a series of outrages here in London that will force our government to come off the fence.'

'Which they're closer to doing than you might think,' said Sir Melville.

'The Opposition, I'm told, has already prepared a draft bill calling for the return of *émigrés* to their own country. In fact, it doesn't need a bill. It could be effected by an Order in Council under the Aliens Act. The Cabinet is said to be spilt, but it wouldn't take much to move them. If the anarchists' recent plan to bomb the Lord Mayor's show – aborted at the last moment – had come off, that would almost certainly have tipped the balance.'

'So,' said Sir Melville, 'what do you think, Fred?'

Wensley, who had contributed nothing to the discussion so far, pondered for almost a minute. Then he said, 'You ask for my opinion. So be it. What I think is that two very able men have been sent here to organise trouble. Casimir Treschau, or Trautman, and Janis Silistreau, who calls himself Morrowitz. Both well known in Russia. Treschau as a chemist, Silistreau as a poet. And if I had the smallest shred of evidence that they've committed, or were planning to commit, any criminal acts, I'd ask you to send them straight back where they came from.'

'But you haven't?'

'Not yet. So far, they've kept clear of law breaking. It's all secondhand. Organised for them by that bullying lout and gang-boss, Molacoff Weil. Recently, I hear, he's been enlisting a regular private army, mostly young Russians newly arrived, who can't get jobs and would starve without the pittance he doles out.'

'Armed?'

'No. They don't normally carry arms, but I'm certain he's got a cache tucked away somewhere that they can draw on. So, if trouble comes we're going to find ourselves facing guns and bombs with wooden truncheons. There's only one answer. We shall *have* to arm the police.'

'The idea has been put to Winston more than once. He says it's un-English.'

'That's his Liberal principles,' said Daines. 'With a capital "L". They've become very marked since he crossed the floor of the House.'

Wensley said, 'And it isn't just a hard core of young toughs that we're up against. Half the *émigré* population are passively on their side. They act as spies, informers, keepers of safe houses, hiders of arms and ammunition. What they're best at is keeping their eyes open. I can't leave my own office here without the news getting straight back to Weil's crowd. There's a man runs a fish stall at the High Street corner and another one who seems to spend most of his daylight hours sitting outside his shop at the south end of the street. I've no doubt they've got ingenious methods of passing the word to other watchers.'

'But this is intolerable,' said Macnaghten. 'If a police officer can't move about his own manor without spying and harassment—'

'They don't harass me,' said Wensley with a grin. 'They know better than to try anything like that. And I've got a very simple answer. I'm planning to shut my office here for the time being and move down to one of our other stations. Probably the one at Poplar. That area is full of sailors, who don't love the Russians. If trouble's coming, I like to operate from a firm base.'

'And you really think,' said Macnaghten, 'that it will be the sort of trouble which will be difficult to handle.'

'If I could arm my men, I'd handle it easily enough. Once Weil and his gang have been stamped on, the opposition will crumble.'

Macnaghten said, 'I'll put it to Winston, but he's not an easy man to argue with.' As he got up he added, 'There was one other matter, Fred, and I apologise for raising it, knowing how busy you are, but I've had Sir Hector Durrance round my neck lately. It seems that his son, Lance, got involved in a street brawl which ended with his being charged. I'm not clear whether it's breach of the peace or whatever. It could be worked up into something serious and if it ends in a prison sentence it will affect his future career. The witnesses are two of your men.'

'Pagan and Narrabone. I heard about it.'

'And it isn't just Sir Hector. It's his wife. Her father's Viscount Rawley and he's got a lot of pull in political circles. I've got so much on my plate at the moment that I'd like to clear this extra bit off.'

Wensley, who had a good deal on his own plate, said, 'I'll see what I can do.'

When his visitors had gone he sat for a few moments, thinking. He was busier at that moment than he could ever remember being. Two time-consuming matters had come together. The killing of Leon Beron on Clapham Common was exciting increasing interest. It had the dramatic touches calculated to appeal to the press and the public. The apparently motiveless murder. The laceration of the dead man's cheeks. Above all the fact that it had coincided with the Sidney Street seige. Was there any logical connection between them? Had Beron been killed not because he had betrayed his Russian accomplices, but to prevent him from betraying them? And as a warning to anyone who might feel inclined to talk? It was just the sort of pre-emptive strike that would appeal to a trained anarchist.

When Luke and Joe were shown in he pushed the other papers on one side and picked up their report. He said, 'Those two letters you found in the Triboff house. They were in Russian. I see that you've translated them into English in your report. That sentence, "When you go to your workshop", I wonder if you can remember what the word was in Russian.'

'I could look it up. I've got the original at home. But I'm pretty sure it was *"mastyrskaya"*.'

'Could that mean anything else? I take it the letter was meant for Treschau. He's a chemist. Could it mean laboratory?'

'Yes. Addressed to a chemist I suppose it could mean laboratory.'

Wensley resumed his reading. When he had finished he said, 'I take it you investigated 22 Cundy Street.'

'We found that it was a butcher's shop. A kosher butcher.'

'And didn't that strike you as odd?'

Luke and Joe looked at each other. The truth was that as soon as they discovered that it was a butcher's shop, and not a den of anarchists, they had lost interest in it.

'Assume that these messages are meant for Treschau. He's not a Jew. Why should he patronise a kosher butcher?'

'It didn't occur to us,' said Luke. 'Do you think it's important?'

'I haven't any idea whether it's important or not. But when

you're conducting an investigation and you come across something that seems odd, you don't let it go. You follow it up. Would it be possible to watch this shop, discreetly?'

'As it happens,' said Joe, 'it would be dead easy. Coolfin Road runs into Cundy Street and two of the houses at the end of Coolfin Road are a sort of boarding establishment for sailors off the "A" and "B" lines. They run it as a commune.'

'Logical place for it,' agreed Wensley. 'Handy for the Victoria and Albert Docks. What did you mean by a commune?'

'According to Bill Trotter – I told you about him, sir – it's fairly informal. They club together for the rent and use it when their ship's in dock. That means that it's usually half empty.'

'Then there might be a spare room in it? One that both of you could use.'

'Actually, Bill suggested it.'

'What's the arrangement at your place in Osborne Street, if you wanted to get out?'

'The office looks after all that sort of thing. I think it would just be a matter of giving a week's notice.'

Wensley said, 'Then get them to give it. Everything I heard today from Daines and Kell made me certain that we're in for trouble. I'd feel happier about you two if you were tucked away down in the docks among a crowd of friends. One other thing. It seems we may be in for some difficulty over Durrance.'

'You mean that young bully we gave in charge for knocking Anna Katz about? Has there been some trouble there?'

'The trouble with Durrance is that his father's an MP and his mother's the daughter of a viscount. I've got so much to do that I'd like to clear this off. See what you can do.'

'I wonder what he meant by that,' said Joe, when they were by themselves.

'Seemed clear enough to me,' said Luke. 'When we give evidence we're to go easy on young Durrance.'

'If that's what Fred wants, I suppose we've got to do it. Seems a pity. A week or two on the treadmill would have done that blue-blooded nurk a power of good. If I'm to give evidence, you'll have to tell me what to say.'

'Play it by ear,' said Luke.

It turned out to be easy enough.

For a start, the case against Durrance was weakened by the fact that Anna had refused to appear, on the grounds that if she had done so her masquerade as a boy would have come out. Luke, when questioned, agreed that the main assailant, who had been using his boot, had escaped and had not yet been identified. The one they did catch, the prisoner, had been smacking the boy's face.

'You mean,' said the magistrate, 'not punching with his closed fist, but smacking with an open hand.'

Luke agreed that this was what he meant.

The magistrate turned to the prisoner. 'I understand that you have been invited to name the persons who were with you.'

'Yes, sir.'

'And that you refused to do so.'

'Yes, sir.'

'You are aware that if you had been prepared to co-operate it would have had a beneficial effect on your case.'

'Yes, sir.'

'And you still refuse?'

Durrance drew himself up like a soldier on parade and said, 'Yes, sir.'

'Good boy,' said his father, from the back of the court.

The magistrate paused to consider the matter. He said, 'It's our job in these difficult times to discourage irresponsible behaviour of this sort.' He addressed the prisoner. 'In view of the fact that it's a first offence and that your parents have come forward to give you a good character, I shall merely impose a fine. But let me make it clear that should anything of this sort occur again, I shall not hesitate to impose a custodial sentence. You will pay forty shillings and ten shillings towards the costs of the prosecution.'

Durrance, much relieved, left the dock to discharge his debts. His father was smiling happily. Everyone seemed pleased. The only person who was unhappy was Joe. As soon as they were alone together he voiced his displeasure. 'Bloody nurk,' he said, 'standing there like the boy stood on the bloody burning deck. And incidentally, I didn't know you was a capitalist lackey.'

'I'm not,' said Luke, amiably.

'Then why did you come down so heavy on his side?'

'Maybe because I've got better eyesight than you,' said Luke, and would offer no further explanation.

Two days later they were sitting in their Osborne Street quarters, amicably enough, the slight coolness engendered by the Durrance episode having quickly evaporated. They had inspected and approved an attic in the Coolfin Road commune and had arranged to move into it at the end of the following week. They were both reading newspapers. Joe had a copy of *Answers* and was trying to work out one of the ingenious puzzles for which it was famous. Luke was leafing through the badly printed pages of *Rank Pelnis*, the immigrants' newspaper. It was published in Russian and it was his job to extract from it any items of interest, translate them and include them in his weekly report.

'Well, what do you know?' he said. 'Listen to this: "On Wednesday, at 2.30 in the afternoon, there will be held a meeting at the Free Working Men's Club in Jubilee Street. The meeting is sponsored by the SRP and the MSD jointly."'

'And who the hell are they?' said Joe, putting down his paper.

'The SRP are the Socialist Revolutionary Party and the MSD are the Marxist Social Democrats.'

'Add them together and what've you got? A crowd of windbags.'

'I'm not sure,' said Luke. 'The interesting thing is that they should be getting together at all. Normally they don't talk to each other much. The SRP specialise in assassination and bombing. The MSD are more moderate. They believe in expropriation – which is a polite name for robbery – but not in violence. If they're putting together a common programme it should be worth listening to.'

'Might be.'

'But that's not the really interesting thing. It's the last paragraph: "The platform will be graced by the presence of Prince Igor." As we all know, he crossed swords with the Tsar and got turfed out of Russia. "Also by Michael Morrison."'

'The one who calls himself the working man's friend,' said Joe.

'That's the chap. Communist candidate for Deptford at the last election, with as much chance of getting into Parliament as a grasshopper of getting into the Royal Mint. "The third man in this distinguished group on the platform –" wait for it – "will be Julian Spencer-Wells."'

'Well blow me down,' said Joe, 'not our own Julian, who used to bend our ears back in the public bar of the Suffolk Serpent?'

'Must be,' said Luke. He thought of the earnest young man who had sat beside him on the sofa and had wanted to kiss him. He had been much younger then. Infinitely younger. It was a lifetime away.

'Looks like a meeting we ought to get in on,' said Joe. 'Might sneak in at the back somehow. But I've got a feeling it won't be easy.'

'Listen to this: "Entry is by ticket only. Tickets will be allotted, without charge, to paid-up members of the SRP and MSD, who should apply to one of the stewards (names and addresses below) at least one clear day before the date of the meeting."'

'Difficult,' agreed Joe.

'I wondered if maybe Anna's father could help us. He's a printer. If we could get hold of a ticket he could probably copy it for us. With a crowd going in at the door they wouldn't be examined too closely.'

'And how do you suggest we set about getting a ticket for him to copy? You're not hoping I'll put on a false beard and apply to one of the stewards, I hope.'

'You'd lose more than your beard if you tried that. No, I'll have a word with Jacob. He may have some ideas.'

'Anything for an excuse to call on Anna,' said Joe. But this he said to himself.

Next morning, when Luke called at the Katz house, he found Jacob at his desk, examining a page of script with a magnifying glass. He apologised for disturbing him. The old man said he was always welcome and sounded as though he meant it. Whilst they were talking Anna came in from the kitchen. She was wearing a boy's shirt, open at the neck; her sleeves were rolled up and her forearms were speckled with flour.

She said, 'You must excuse my appearance. I have been cooking one of my father's favourite dishes – savoury pancakes. There is plenty for you, if you would condescend to share our midday meal with us.'

'No condescension,' said Luke. 'A pleasure.'

Her father said, 'Of course he must stay. I regard him as a member of the family.'

When Anna had returned to her cooking Luke explained the object of his visit. Jacob listened carefully, them moved across to a cupboard and brought out a cardboard box, full of tickets, neatly packaged,

'Half for the SRP, half for the MSD,' he explained. Noting Luke's look he added, 'You must not suppose that because I work for them that I approve of their objects. I do jobs for anyone who will pay.'

Luke examined the tickets. They were numbered from one to three hundred.

'I doubt whether they will all be used. I have printed a hundred and fifty for each organisation. Nothing easier than to run off two more for you. Only, the numbering would have to be thought of.'

'No problem,' said Luke. 'Pick two numbers at random. Say, eighty-nine and ninety. No one is to know that these particular tickets have been duplicated.'

'Very well,' said Jacob. 'But promise me that when you have used them you will destroy them. I know these people. I would not wish to incur their displeasure.'

Luke said, 'They shall be burned as soon as the meeting's over.'

He thought this development so promising that he would not hold it back for his weekly report. He would let Wensley know about it at once.

When he got to Leman Street he was told that Wensley had moved. 'Gone down to Poplar for a chance of air,' said the desk sergeant. 'Comes back here from time to time.'

'Then I suppose Narrabone and I will be attached to the Poplar Station.'

'If that's what you think, you can think again,' said Superintendent Joscelyne, who had come in and overheard them. 'We can't have you spending all your time chasing anarchists. There's a lot of routine CID work piling up. And we're short-handed in that department.'

This was true, since the CID contingent at Leman Street, apart from Joe and himself, consisted of a junior detective inspector, who was in hospital with stomach trouble, and two over-worked detective sergeants.

'There's no reason you shouldn't tackle both your jobs. You'll report here every evening at five o'clock and I'll give you your instructions for the following day. Understood?'

'It's a swindle,' said Joe when Luke passed this on. 'A bloody swindle. One moment he tells us to spend all our time keeping an eye on the Russians. Next moment it's back to the treadmill.'

'It's a hard life,' said Luke. 'Let's go and look up the old weasel in his new burrow.'

They found Wensley installed in a room which looked south, over the West India Dock and the river. The Poplar Station was under Inspector Paine, who seemed to be proud to be housing the redoubtable DDI. Luke told him about the forthcoming meeting and about his plan for getting into it. As he was speaking he noticed Wensley's face relaxing into a smile and when he had finished and was waiting for some comment, he was awarded a laugh which seemed to start low down in Wensley's stomach and rumbled on for some seconds.

As soon as Wensley could speak he said, 'I could give you a lot of reasons against doing what you propose. I'll let you have the first three that come to my mind. You realise that this meeting will be confined to people who've known each other for years. As soon as you showed your face you'd be spotted as an intruder and would be lucky to get out undamaged. Secondly, we know, or can guess, exactly the sort of nonsense that's going to be spouted. Corrupt capitalistic façades that mask the exploitation of the lower orders by a spurious claim to a democratic electoral system. We've heard all that drip a dozen times. Thirdly, and perhaps even more important, the tickets, you may be certain, will be collected at the door and very carefully checked afterwards. Your duplicates will be spotted and since old Katz is the only person who could have printed them, he'd be for the high jump. Do you want any more reasons?'

Luke, whose face was deep red by this time, muttered, 'No, sir. Three's enough.'

'But I'll tell you what you can do. There's a tobacconist's shop in Jubilee Street almost opposite the working men's club. The owner's a Mr Passmore. He's inclined to be helpful. I've used it myself more than once. You can get a good view of the main entrance to the club from his upstairs windows. I suggest you borrow a pair of binoculars from your Navy friends and make a particular note of anyone who seems to be there in an official capacity – guarding the entrance, vetting people going in, that sort of thing. Hubert Daines has given me a list of men that his outfit have identified so far. Names on this paper, with brief descriptions. If you can fit the names to any of the people you spot, that'll be a lot more useful to you than listening to the hot air they spout in the hall. All the same,' he added, 'interesting about Spencer-Wells. One of the nobs from your village, is he?'

'His father's Lord of the Manor.'

'And would you think his son was a dangerous man?'

'No,' said Luke, who couldn't help smiling at his remembrance of their last encounter. 'I wouldn't call him dangerous.'

7

On the following afternoon Luke and Joe were in Mr Passmore's bedroom, occupying a window seat each. They were equipped with binoculars and had a list of names which they referred to from time to time as they tried to fit them to the members of the little group outside the club door.

Luke read out, 'Indruk Spiridov. Bulky. Bent nose. Ben Levin. Fat, Jewish cast of countenance, sometimes wears earrings. It'd be easier if they'd stand still. Alexei Krustov. Tall and thin, quite young.'

'Yes, I think I've spotted Krustov,' said Joe. 'The one leaning against the door post. Must be all of six foot three. Could judge his height better if he'd stand up straight.'

'Don Katakin. Red hair, worn in ringlets. Red sideburns. Bad teeth. Ivan Luwinski. Tubby and robust. Good pair of shoulders on him – might have been a professional wrestler.

'David Heilmann. Straggling grey beard and moustache. Ears stick out. Prominent nose. It'd be easier to be sure if he'd be kind enough to turn round. Tallish.'

As though to oblige them the man did turn round. Certainly he had a beard and moustache. They were so luxuriant that it was difficult to be certain about the other points.

'Stanislas Grax. Fair haired. Young. There's two or three match that description.'

'Not much doubt about the head boy,' said Joe.

Molacoff Weil had stationed himself in front of the door. No one could get in without coming directly under his scrutiny. 'What a horrible man. Like a rhinoceros on springs.'

Luke noted that Wensley had been right. All tickets were being collected and put on one side. When the last man had gone in the reception committee followed and the doors were shut behind them.

'That's that,' said Joe. 'Time for a cigarette.'

Luke was busy with his weekly report, a serial document to which he added supplements as occasion offered. They had watched the platform trio go in. Julian Spencer-Wells demonstrating his bohemianism by the untidiness of his dress and the length of his hair; Michael Morrison wearing a red tie and a look of importance; and, between them, a tall, dark man who must have been Prince Igor.

'Two characters we didn't see,' said Luke. 'Treschau and Silistreau. Maybe they went in before we got here.'

'Wrong,' said Joe. 'Here they come.'

The two Russians were strolling along the pavement towards the hall and had now reached the foot of the front steps. These ran up to the main entrance to the hall and were flanked by a deepish area on each side, guarded from pedestrians falling into it by an iron-spiked railing. Luke was wondering whether the two Russians were planning to go into the hall, when the front door opened and Molacoff Weil came out and bounced down the steps.

Joe was right, thought Luke. Heavy as a rhinoceros and active as a cat.

The three men stood for a moment at the foot of the steps, laughing at something the donnish-looking Treschau had said. At that moment they were spotted by a reporter. He had been barred from the hall, but saw a chance of an informal interview and came hurrying up. Before he had time to say anything Weil had picked him up and tossed him clear over the iron railing. The Russians then turned about and walked back the way they had come, still laughing.

The reporter had started to scream. Luke wondered if they ought to go to his help, but there were other men already on the spot. They made their way down into the basement by a side gate and reappeared carrying the reporter carefully. One of his legs was dangling and was clearly broken.

'You can put it in your report if you like,' said Joe. 'But the old man won't do anything about it. He don't love the press.'

Wensley had recently been made the subject of a smear attack over his handling of the Clapham Common murder. Objections seemed to centre round the fact that he had taken four other police officers with him to arrest Steinie Morrison.

On the following Monday evening Luke duly reported in at Leman Street. He and Joe had decided to deal with Superintendent Joscelyne's tiresome instructions by putting in an appearance on alternate days. Luckily the Superintendent had not yet got round to organising anything, so Luke escaped. Next day Joe was not so lucky and had to spend Tuesday evening taking statements from a number of women who were possible witnesses in a case of intimidation and extortion.

'They all told different stories,' he said. 'And were all lying their bloody heads off. If the case gets to court, the judge is in for a high old time.'

On the Wednesday, when Luke looked in, the desk sergeant handed him a letter addressed to him at Leman Street. It was postmarked Lavenham. Luke recognised Reverend Millbanke's handwriting. The Rector wrote:

Your father asked me to let you know that Sir George Spencer-Wells died two days ago. He was not a national figure and his death may not have been reported in the London papers. I have been asked to write an obituary notice which will appear in the *Ipswich Herald* next week. The funeral will be at noon on Thursday in Bellingham Parish Church. It will no doubt be largely attended by Sir George's family and friends. When he sees you, your father will explain why he thinks you should be there. I must add that I agree with him. If you show this letter to your superior officer I am sure he will not grudge you a couple of days' leave.

The Superintendent's reaction was predictable. He said, 'You need not report back here until Friday evening. Tell Narrabone that he will have to stand in for you.'

'Do your job *and* mine,' said Joe. '*And* see to moving all our stuff down to Poplar. Roll on retirement.'

'It must have been – let me see –' Hezekiah counted off the days on his gnarled fingers. 'Yes. All of two weeks ago. 'Twas a stroke, so I heard. Seemed he was getting over it. Then, Monday just past, before he could get out of his bed in the morning, his heart gave way.'

Hezekiah said this without any particular feeling. Life and death meant little to the old man.

'Maybe you can guess why I thought you should be here.'

'Yes, I can guess,' said Luke. 'He paid for my Russian lessons, didn't he? The part I couldn't pay myself.'

'He did so. More'n once, after you'd taken yourself off to London, he talked about you. He was sorry you weren't to be a clergyman, but he weren't sorry about you not being a schoolmaster. He thought that was no job for a man. No more did I.'

'I'm glad you think that,' said Luke, and yawned as he spoke. It had been a long day. He had caught the last evening train and his father had picked him up in his trap from Ipswich. It was now close to midnight.

'Tomorrow morning you must have a word with Mrs Parham. Poor old soul. This will have upset her more than most. More than them uncles and aunts and cousins what've come flocking in, never having had a word to say to Sir George while he were alive.'

'Yes. I'd planned to look in and see her,' said Luke, and climbed up to his old bedroom, his mind afloat with memories.

After an early breakfast he made his way across the park to the back door of the hall. He smiled when he remembered that he had once been scared of the ghostly passage inside it. Since that time he had dealt with characters more dangerous than ghosts. Mrs Parham's room was empty, but a maid was sent to fetch her. She came bustling in, kissed Luke warmly and said, 'It *was* good of you to come, but oh dear, oh dear, I hardly know whether I'm standing on my head or my heels. Nine family and five guests, some of them I'd never heard of before. All expecting to be looked after and Parkes in bed with a bad stomach, trying to do too much, silly old man. And everyone coming to me for instructions. But thank the Lord for one thing. When Mr Oliver heard of his father's first attack he didn't waste a minute. Came straight back from Cambridge without finishing his studies and he's been here ever since, working like a Trojan. We couldn't never have got through without him.'

'And Julian?'

Mrs Parham produced a noise which, in a less dignified woman, might have been described as a snort.

'Came down yesterday,' she said. 'Brought a friend with him. Some sort of furriner. As if we hadn't enough people to look after.'

'A foreigner,' said Luke thoughtfully. 'What was his name?'

'I was sure I'd forget his name, so I wrote it down. And now, with all this bustle, I seem to have lost the paper. I was told as he was a poet.'

'A well-known Russian poet,' said Oliver, who had come in without knocking. 'How are you, Luke?'

After a brief pause in which the two young men struggled to accommodate the changes of seven years, Oliver added, 'Wasn't it an extraordinary coincidence – but a very happy one – that when Lance Durrance made a fool of himself in London, the two policemen on hand should both have been from this village.'

As Mrs Parham started to say something, he added, 'Sir Hector and his wife are both here. I'm sure he'd like to meet you and thank you. He's really very grateful. Though I must admit that my first reaction was one of surprise.'

107

Michael Gilbert

'Oh, why?'

'Numerous discourses which I have listened to, from my brother Julian, on the iniquity and unfairness of the possessing classes led me – perhaps wrongly – to think that you would hold similar opinions. Or have your experiences in the last few years changed your views?'

'We don't meet many of the possessing classes in Deptford. And, no. My views haven't really changed.'

'Then, if it's not an impertinent question, why did you do it?'

'The reason's very simple. I've got excellent eyesight.'

'Ah!'

'I spotted you, as you and your friend ran off. Since I'd made up my mind to keep your name out of it, I could hardly see Lance Durrance put down.'

'It crossed my mind that that might be the reason. So, it seems that I'm in your debt, too.'

'Then forget it.'

'No. I really am grateful. I'll tell you why. It's become obvious to me, during the last few days, that Julian is planning to slide out and I'm going to be the one who has to wear Father's shoes. It would hardly have been a good start to my career as Squire of Bellingham if I'd been run in for brawling.'

Mrs Parham again tried to say something, but this time it was Luke who defeated her. He said, 'Tell me, who is this Russian that Julian has brought down with him?'

'He's called Janis Silistreau and I'm told that he's a well-known poet.'

'In London he passes under the name of Ivan Morrowitz. He may have half a dozen other names as well. And he's a very dangerous man.'

'I see,' said Oliver. 'At least, I don't see at all. But I imagine you know what you're talking about. What do you want us to do about him?'

'Nothing. But neither Silistreau nor anyone else must know

that I'm here. I can answer for my father. And I'm sure that you'll be discreet, Mrs P.'

Being introduced into the conversation, Mrs Parham was at last able to insert the question she had been trying to ask. She said, 'You spoke about *two* policemen. Both from hereabouts. Who was the other one?'

'Joe Narrabone.'

'That it can't be,' said Mrs Parham. 'He was a *very* bad boy. Why, if I ever heard of him again, I supposed it would be on a convict ship going to Australia.'

'I think we've stopped sending bad boys to Australia,' said Oliver gravely.

As he walked back to the cottage Luke was thinking how much he preferred the new squire of Bellingham to the peevish boy he had known. He found that his father had already donned his Sunday suit, with a black band round one arm. He had a second band ready for his son.

'I'm sorry,' said Luke. 'But something I've just heard means that I shan't be able to attend the funeral service.'

With a wrinkling of his eyes which indicated that he was intrigued and pleased at the thought of secrecy, his father said, 'What you heard must've bin uncommon serious if it's to keep you out of church, after coming all this way along.'

Luke said, 'Yes. It's serious. Julian has brought down with him a man who mustn't know that I'm here.'

'He'd be a guest, like?'

'Yes. He's a guest.'

'Then he'll sit in the family pew. If you're behind the crusader he'll not see you.'

Luke knew the crusader well. As a boy he had passed the long hours of service speculating about the recumbent Lord Welles lying with his gauntleted hands clasped on his stomach and his ankles crossed. Certainly the monstrous edifice, out of all proportion to the little church, would hide him. It was tempting, but common sense prevailed. He said, 'No. And I must get back to

London before this man does. Could you find out if he's going back today, and if so, what train he's planning to catch?'

'Whatever train it is, Jabez will be driving him. I'll talk to him right away.' The old man's eyes were glinting at the thought of undercover enquiries for hidden ends. When he got back he said, 'The trap's booked for four o'clock, to catch the five o'clock train from Ipswich. If I run you to the station now I'll be back in time for the service and you'll be well ahead of this person. There's a train at half past two. So you've time for a morsel of lunch before you go.'

The morsel proved to be the greater part of a cold pheasant, backed by potatoes baked in their skins and a pint mug of home-brewed ale. Luke fell asleep in the train, came briefly to life at Colchester and slept again until he reached King's Cross. He got through to Wensley from the police call-box at the station, finding him, eventually, at his old office. It seemed that he was fluctuating between Poplar and Leman Street. He said, 'Well done. I'll send some men to cover the five o'clock train. We'd very much like to know where Silistreau's holed up.'

The ground-floor flat in Gooseley Lane, which one of their compatriots had found for Treschau and Silistreau was convenient in a number of ways. It had a back garden which gave directly on to the East Ham recreation ground and this, in turn, on to the East Ham Level which, along with the Ripple Level and the Dagenham Marshes, bordered the north bank of the Thames. The fact of the river being within easy reach was a comfort to both of them. The night was cold and the fire which their new landlord had lit for them flamed cheerfully as Treschau inserted another lump of coal into the heart of the blaze.

'I changed my mind at the last moment,' said Silistreau. 'Instead of taking the train from Ipswich I asked my hosts if they would be good enough to drive me into Stowmarket. From there, with one change at Ely, I was able to catch an express on the Midland Line to St Pancras. I am afraid that the reception committee at King's Cross had a long cold wait. They may be there still.' He warmed his hands at the fire.

'Rather a roundabout route,' said Treschau. 'I take it you had a reason.'

'Of course.'

'Which was?'

'The reason was the presence in the village of a young man called Pagan. Luke Pagan. He is a policeman, stationed in this part of London, but he came originally from Bellingham.'

'Then he had a reason for being there.'

'Certainly. But no reason to take elaborate precautions to conceal his presence. He was lodged with his father, a close-mouthed Kulak, who was in church but said nothing about his son.'

'You found that odd?'

'Very odd. You would have imagined that the proud father would have had his son alongside, and talked about him to everyone who'd listen. But not so. And when I happened to mention the man to Sir George's younger son he, too, affected to know nothing.'

'If you didn't see him and no one would talk about him, how did you know he was there?'

Silistreau smiled. It was a smile with a lot of ice in it. He said, 'The young man made a mistake.'

'Young men are apt to make mistakes,' agreed Treschau. 'What was this one?'

'He spoke to one of the kitchen maids who recognised him and, naturally, mentioned it to everyone in the kitchen. What is news below stairs soon becomes news above stairs.'

'I follow that,' said Treschau. 'What I cannot understand is why this young man should be so interested in you, and you in him.'

'I am interested in him because he was in Newcastle when I arrived. He was hand in glove with the head of Port Security there. It is possible therefore – not certain, but quite possible –

that he may have been shown the papers which were taken from me.'

'Would he have understood them?'

'Yes. He is a competent Russian speaker.'

There was a long pause, broken only when Treschau added a further piece of coal to the fire and the flames leaped up, glinting on his steel spectacles as he leaned forward.

He said, 'Yes. That would be unfortunate.'

Although he had moved his base of operations to Poplar, Wensley had two reasons for maintaining contact with Leman Street. The first was that his laboriously compiled records, the fruit of his years of service in the East End, were filed there in heavy wooden cabinets, which would have been a labour to move and impossible to install in his new quarters at Poplar.

A second reason weighed with him even more heavily.

He had no desire to lose touch with Superintendent Joscelyne, who was his friend though his opposite in almost every respect. Wensley was a detective, who worked partly by instinct and rarely by the book. Joscelyne was a policeman, an excellent example of a regular officer, hidebound if you like, but totally dependable and uninfluenced by fear or favour. Working together they made a formidable pair.

When he arrived at Leman Street on the morning following a long, cold and fruitless wait at King's Cross, Wensley was in no good temper. He found the Superintendent in a state of irritation bordering on outright fury.

'We've got to do something about it,' was his opening salvo. Wensley sat down without speaking and waited for the floodgates to open.

'Last night,' said Joscelyne, 'or rather, in the early hours of this morning, a fire broke out in Osborne Street. You know it?'

'Runs north from Whitechapel Road. Two of my men used to board there.'

'Used to?'

'I understand they were planning to get out some time this week. I advised them to come down to Poplar. I thought they'd be safer among a crowd of friendly sailors.'

'And would the house they were using in Osborne Street have been, by any chance, number 15?'

'I think it was. Yes. Why?'

'Because that house was burned to the ground last night.'

'Not accidentally, I assume.'

'It could hardly have been more open and deliberate.' The outrage in Joscelyne's voice was clear. 'When the brigade got there they found the owners of the house, a German Jew called Reuben and his wife, sitting on the pavement, unable to move, even though they were in some danger. They seemed to be paralysed, from fear or cold or both. In the end, when they had been lifted, almost bodily, and deposited in Whitechapel Hospital, they recovered enough to give some sort of account of what had happened. They occupy the ground floor, which is just a large kitchen, with a bedroom off it. The upper floors are usually let. At that moment, luckily, they were both empty. At about two in the morning they heard sounds of movement in the kitchen and came out to investigate. They found two men busy piling up tables and chairs against the door that led upstairs – which they'd bolted. The men were dressed in black, were masked and were completely terrifying. They gestured to the Reubens who cowered down on to a sofa and sat watching their household furniture being arranged as a bonfire. It seems that one of the most frightening things about the men was the unhurried and deliberate way they set about it all. Finally they soused the pile in some liquid they'd brought with them in a can – petrol, no doubt. When they were quite ready they opened the street door, motioned to the Reubens to step outside, flung a lighted spill into the pile, closed the door and walked off up the street.'

Wensley listened impassively. Then he said, 'So what do you make of it?'

'Clearly they were after your two men. If they'd been upstairs asleep, they'd have been roasted.'

'Yes. It's lucky they'd moved.'

'And I'll tell you another piece of luck we had. Which was that none of our men were in or near Osborne Street at the time. As you know, they patrol in pairs. If they'd looked into the house whilst this was going on the likely result is that we should now have been two good men short.'

'I thought that was what you meant,' said Wensley.

In the silence that followed he and Joscelyne looked at each other. Neither of them seemed inclined to pursue a discussion that had proved sterile. Finally, as though he was answering the first comment that Joscelyne had made, he said, 'There's only one thing we can do. You know it and I know it – we've got to arm our men.'

'And give them full permission to use those arms?'

'Certainly. If they are faced by men who are themselves armed.'

'Or men who they have a reasonable suspicion to think would be armed.'

Wensley thought about this and said, 'It isn't easy. But if I was giving them their instructions I'd keep it simple. I'd say, 'If they shoot at you, you can shoot back.'

'With a bullet already in you.'

'Don't think I don't appreciate the difficulty,' said Wensley. 'In any event we're talking about a situation that won't arise whilst we've got our present Home Secretary.'

'If someone would shoot at *him*, or blow *his* office up, he might be frightened into changing his mind.'

'No,' said Wensley. 'Though he's obstinate as a buffalo.'

'And maddening,' said Joscelyne, 'as my grandmother who could never make her mind up whether she'd dropped a stitch in her knitting or not and used to unravel the whole piece to find out.'

Wensley grinned at this graphic description of the political mind at work. He said, 'All right. Obstinate *and* maddening. I'll grant you both of those. But there's nothing in Winston's early history to suggest he lacks courage. Rather the reverse. He seems to have invited danger, scampering around in the North-west Frontier, and insisting on joining in the fight against the dervishes when no one really wanted him. He seems to enjoy being anywhere where bullets are flying round.'

'Which no doubt accounts,' said Joscelyne gloomily, 'for him turning up to get a front-seat view of the Sidney Street business. It attracted a lot of criticism in Parliament – which he seems to have minded as little as the bullets.'

'Right,' said Wensley. 'That's the Home Secretary we've got. And we can't authorise the use of firearms without his consent. It's a political decision. *But* – that doesn't mean that the politicians have any say in the training of our men. You agree?'

'Certainly not. Training's our job.'

'Very well. Is there any reason we shouldn't pick the men we'd like to arm – say, two squads of twelve or fifteen men under a reliable sergeant – and put them through a course of weapon-training at Woolwich or the Tower?'

'That's certainly an idea,' said Joscelyne.

'The men will have to come from the uniform branch, you understand. We don't want detectives going round with guns in their pockets. You're not over-staffed. Are you going to be able to find that number of men?'

'Not from "H" alone. But I'm sure "J" and "K" will co-operate when it's put to them. And I'll tell you something else. When I'm picking the squads I'll choose as many men as I can get from the ones who were involved in the Sidney Street job.'

'You mean they'd be happy to get their own back?'

'No. For another reason altogether. I think that most of the men who were there would have liked to rush the house, regardless of the risk involved. They weren't allowed to. Result, a lot of people, including those mean-minded characters who write to the papers, have started hinting that they were scared – and they can't answer back. That's not good for morale.'

8

On the days when it was not his turn to report at Leman Street, Joe had taken to sitting, in the late afternoon, in the embrasure of the window of the attic room he shared with Luke and keeping an eye on the kosher butcher's shop which was one along from the corner of Cundy Street. Most of its visitors were Jewish house-wives, who went in, gossiped interminably and came out with bulging shopping baskets. He had given up any real expectation of anything coming out of this surveillance, but Wensley had suggested it and it was an agreeable way of passing the time and fooling himself that he was working.

When he saw Treschau limping along the pavement and turn-ing into the entrance of the shop he was so surprised that, for an appreciable time, he stayed anchored to his seat. However, his plans had been made. He got up, raced down two flights of stairs, out of the front door, across the street and into the porch of the house opposite. From there he could watch the shop, following Treschau if he went forward, getting still further back into the porch if he turned round. After ten minutes he began to wonder if the shop had a back door. No. Here he was, carrying a bulky par-cel, wrapped in brown paper and corded. Which way was he going?

The Russian stood, for almost a minute, outside the shop as though he, himself, was uncertain. Then he turned to the right and went off down the street. Joe was not planning to tread on his heels. In spite of the casual way Treschau was conducting him-self, Joe guessed that he had all his wits about him and eyes in the back of his head. When he had hobbled twenty yards along the pavement, Joe raced across the road junction, turned into

Garvary Road, which ran parallel to Cundy Street and scudded down it, stopping at the corner. Treschau emerged from Cundy Street and moved steadily forward. Soon he was going to reach Prince Regent's Lane and this was where things were going to become tricky.

It was natural to suppose that his man would turn left, since a right turn would simply bring him back to the river. But there were at least six streets crossing Prince Regent's Lane, any one of which he might take before getting back to East Ham, Barking and civilisation. The important thing was to see which turning, if any, he did take. He therefore doubled back to Freemasons Road and went along it, regulating his pace to what he imagined would be that of his quarry and watching each of the side roads in turn. If his man did not appear at any of them, he would have to take the risky course of going down the last of the side roads and prospecting into the main road.

This he was finally forced to do, but without any success. Prince Regent's Lane was as bare as Mother Hubbard's cupboard.

Joe stopped to think. Treschau had not taken any of the left-hand turnings, nor had he gone straight on. There were three streets to the right, but as he suspected, and as he confirmed when he examined them, these were dead ends, leading only to marsh-land. They all ended in a rusty wire fence, easily passable. It was through one of these that Treschau must have gone.

Ahead of him stretched the barren waste of Plaistow Marshes, intersected by dykes and by streams which flowed, sluggishly for the most part, to the River Roding. The embanked edge of that river marked the eastern end of this desolate zone. The only signs of life in it were the brick chimneys of the Gas Light and Coke Company's works away to the south, and to the east, the tiny group of Gallions Cottages. The few and rambling paths which crossed the area had been trampled into slush by the half-wild cattle which grazed in this forgotten corner of east London.

If Treschau had indeed gone that way he could by now be

crouched behind any of the dyke banks, looking back to see if he was being followed. The total disadvantage of his position was clear to Joe. The only tactic was retreat. He retraced his steps to Coolfin Road and found Luke there, who reported all quiet at Leman Street and had brought a veal and ham pie for their supper.

Joe explained what he had been doing and they spread the street map on the table and examined it as they ate.

'Two things I'd like to know,' said Joe. 'Where was he making for and what was he doing with that parcel? He hadn't got nothing with him when he went into the shop. So it must have been something he bought there.'

'Meat, then, of some sort.'

'What for? For a picnic? Or was he going to feed the birds on the marsh?'

'There's only one way of finding out,' said Luke. 'We keep our eyes on him. Next time we see him start out, we get ahead of him. Lie up on the edge of the marsh and see which way he goes.'

Joe said, 'You remember that letter we took off Mother Triboff – "When you go to your workshop, watch your back"?'

'Yes.'

'You told Fred that the word in Russian might be a workshop, or could be a laboratory.'

Luke said, 'Yes, it could be. Though I shouldn't have expected to find a laboratory in the middle of Plaistow Marshes. Next time, we'll find out, perhaps.'

'If there is a next time,' said Joe gloomily. He was aware that he had had a chance and had fluffed it.

On the following Monday evening Jacob Katz was in his work-room, a small apartment leading off the living-room. He was sitting at his desk. This had been positioned, like the easel of an artist, directly under a window which gave him the benefit of the northern light.

A sheet of paper of a curious blue-grey in colour was pinned to a board in front of him. The paper had printed words on it and he was now, very carefully, filling in the spaces between these words in his own handwriting. From time to time he picked up a reading glass to examine the words he had written. These seemed to satisfy him. There was a clean sheet of blotting paper on the desk. He made no attempt to use it, but sat waiting for the words to dry.

He heard the front door open and someone coming in without ringing or knocking. He assumed that it would be Anna or Dmitry. His wife, he knew, was upstairs. He drew the blotting paper over the work he was doing and was half standing up when the door burst open and Molacoff Weil erupted into the room. Jacob sank back into his chair.

'Right,' said Weil. 'That's right. Make yourself quite comfortable. I have things to say to you, old man.'

He extracted a small cigar from his top pocket and had got it well alight before he continued. 'I hope you have no objection to me smoking. Not that it would make the least difference if you did object.'

Jacob said nothing.

'Well, won't you ask what it is I have come to say to you?'

'You are, as I know, a very busy man, so it must be important.'

Jacob managed to speak in a level, conversational voice. But it was clear how much Weil's arrival had upset him.

'You might think so, or you might not think so.' Weil drew on his cigar until the end glowed red. 'What I have to say concerns a young man who has been seen visiting here on more than one occasion lately. You know who I mean. Or do you get so many visitors that you cannot recall this one?'

A belch of cigar smoke.

'I know the man you mean. His name's Pagan and he's a detective constable.'

'Correct. A simple boy, but he works for a man who is not simple. Divisional Detective Inspector Wensley. Known throughout these parts as Venzel, the Weasel. Aah! Dangerous creatures, weasels. Though it is just possible that once in a while it might encounter an animal that was even bigger and more dangerous.' Weil's yellow teeth showed for a moment as he lifted his lip. 'But it is not of the old weasel that I have been sent to talk to you. I have to tell you that the time may be coming when your daughter will be given an important assignment.' Weil had been watching Jacob as he said this and did not fail to notice his reaction. He said, 'She will do what she is told, yes?'

Jacob, again choosing his words very carefully, said, 'She is aware of the position.'

'So. We come to another matter. It concerns another member of your family. Dmitry.'

'My son.'

'Yes. Let us call him that, by all means.'

'What about him?'

'Do I take it that – to use your own words – he is *not* aware of the position?' When Jacob seemed unable to answer, he added, 'I only ask, because I am told he has been opening his mouth rather widely of late. In our country people who open their mouths too widely sometimes end with their lips sewn together.'

During these exchanges Jacob had been aware of something else. Weil, when coming in, had left the front door open. Now someone had followed him in, also without closing the door and was moving softly in the living-room. Very softly, but Jacob's hearing was acute and undimmed by age. He said, 'My son is not aware of the matter you referred to.'

'As well, perhaps, that he should remain in ignorance. The house of ignorance is sometimes more comfortable than the house of knowledge.'

Jacob had nothing to say to this. After depositing a length of cigar ash on the carpet, Weil continued, 'Pagan and an equally young and inexperienced associate of his – I have forgotten his name, if ever I knew it –'

'Narrabone.'

'Is that right?' Weil repeated the name twice. It seemed to cause him some amusement. 'This precious pair recently paid a visit to Solomon's establishment in Brownsong Court. I expect you know it.'

'I know of it.'

'Their excuse for doing so must have been the fact that your son and daughter both work there. Now I am told that Solomon has closed one of his two workshops. He may soon be closing down altogether. This would be a good moment for your children to cease their association with the place. See that they do so.'

As he said this, Weil stood up, moving as though he was on springs, and made his way out of the room, across the room next door and out through the hall, slamming the front door behind him. Jacob judged that whoever it was that had been in the living-room had managed to conceal themselves. He did not resume his work. He knew who the person next door must have been. There was no hurry. He sat down and waited. Sure enough, it was Dmitry. He came in, shutting the door behind him, and said in a voice choked with the fury that was pumping the words up, 'Has that – that person gone?'

'Yes,' said Jacob. 'That person has gone. I am to suppose that you heard what he said.'

'Yes, yes, yes.' Dmitry's face was scarlet. 'I heard him. I heard him bullying you as though you were one of his serfs, cringing before a threat of the knout.'

'Don't talk nonsense,' said Jacob. He was almost as angry now as Dmitry. 'And don't exaggerate.'

'Exaggerating, is it? If I'd looked in, I imagine I'd have seen you crawling on the floor and licking his feet. For God's sake, what's this hold that he's got over you that makes you cringe, instead of sending him about his business.'

Jacob, older and more experienced than the sixteen-year-old boy, regained control of himself first. He said, 'You'd better go to bed. I'll talk to you in the morning.'

Dmitry hesitated. He had been resolving, for some time, to

provoke a showdown and he disliked putting it off. He said, 'Tell me this. From what I heard, Weil clearly knows that I'm not your son.'

'Yes. That's clear.'

'Does he know about Peter?'

'Peter is in Tver, working in the rolling-stock sheds and leading a quiet and useful life. If he knows that, he knows all there is to know about him.'

'Have you heard from him lately?'

'As you well know, I hear from him once a month, thanking me for the money I have managed to send him.'

'Nothing else?'

'He sends news about his family.'

'And he is in no sort of trouble?'

'None,' said Jacob. He said it firmly.

Dmitry looked as though he would have liked to take the matter further, but could think of no way of doing so. As he looked at Jacob's grey face much of the anger drained out of him. He said, 'Whatever the trouble is, you might find it lighter if you were able to share it.'

Jacob sighed and said, 'Go to bed.'

On that same Monday evening Joe had disposed of two irritating jobs that Joscelyne had found for him, was tidying up the dockets of papers on his desk and was preparing to go home when he heard a footstep that he recognised on the stairs outside. It was Wensley, plodding up to his old office.

Joe judged, from the manner of his walk, that his chief had had an exceptionally trying day. He knew, having twice tried to get hold of him, that he had been locked in conference with the lawyers, shifting through the evidence in the Clapham Common murder case. There were more than thirty witnesses for the prosecution and their statements had been checked and rechecked by Richard Muir, the formidable and painstaking Crown Prosecutor. And great care was necessary. The case was not going to be a walkover. The accused was being represented by Edward Abinger, a paladin of the criminal bar, with a junior, Roland Oliver, who was destined to become more famous than his leader. The newspapers of the left had started to describe the accused as a martyr.

Joe hesitated before following his chief upstairs. But he thought that what he had to tell him might at least divert his mind from his immediate worries.

When he went in Wensley pushed aside the heap of depositions on his desk and listened patiently. Then he said, 'Next time, take field glasses with you. Don't try to follow Treschau directly. Circle round, moving only when he does. And keep out of sight. You were a country boy. You understand about field craft.'

Joe agreed that he would find Plaistow Marshes and the East Ham Level a more congenial area for stalking a quarry than the streets of Stepney and Limehouse.

'When Treschau reaches whatever seems to be his destination, pick some spot from which you can watch it. Then you and Pagan can keep it under observation. Continuous observation is the secret of all good police work.'

Joe agreed, but insincerely. In his view the secret of success in police work was energetic action.

Sensing that he was not carrying his audience with him, Wensley said, 'Later, when you're sure you haven't been seen, you can close in. Step at a time. For the moment, what I want to know is what a famous chemist is doing creeping about the marshes with a packet of meat scraps. When we know the answer to that we might be able to take some effective action.'

As he spoke, Wensley had moved across to the window and was staring out over the wharves and buildings to where the Thames ran sparkling under the late February sun. He said, 'Sometimes I find it hard to believe that it was twenty-five years ago that I came up from Somerset. In all that time I haven't seen a meadow with its wildflowers out, and most of the cattle I've seen have been cut up and hanging in butchers' shops. I've sometimes thought I'd like to give it all up and go back. And if I did, very likely I'd be bored silly inside a week. Better to keep it as a lovely dream. Off you go, and remember, keep out of trouble. Because if you get into trouble it will cause me trouble to get you out of it. Understood?'

Joe said that he understood. He didn't take the warning very seriously. He had an infinite belief in his capacity for looking after himself.

That same evening he and Luke had a visitor.

Dmitry had waited until Jacob was busy in his study and Anna had gone up to her own room. He had left the house by the back door, closing it quietly behind him. He was aware of the efficiency of Molacoff Weil's corps of unofficial helpers and he chose a roundabout and zig-zag route, pausing at each corner to look and listen. Helped by the blackness of the night, which had closed down over London like a blanket, he was confident that he could reach his destination unseen and unfollowed.

''Ullo, 'ullo,' said Joe. 'See who's here.' He and Luke were polishing off the remains of the beer that had accompanied their supper. 'If we 'ad a spare glass, we could've given 'im a drop.'

'He certainly looks as if he could do with it,' said Luke. Dmitry's face was white and wet with a mixture of rain and sweat. 'There's a glass in the bathroom.'

'I'll get it,' said Joe. 'And I'll see if I can raise another bottle of beer from Bill. I saw him come in just now and he owes me one.'

When he got back he had something better than beer. It was a bottle of schnapps, part of the fruit of some enterprising smuggling when the *Beatrice* was last at Esbjerg. When Dmitry had downed half a tumbler of this, his face had recovered some of its colour.

He said abruptly, 'I've got something I must tell you. And a favour to ask.'

He said this in English, no doubt out of consideration for Joe.

But Luke had noticed before that his English was, in fact, more fluent than his Russian; not unnaturally when one remembered the age at which he had arrived in London and the life he had lived.

'I have to tell you, first of all, that I am not Jacob's son.'

This did not surprise Luke, who had suspected it when he first saw the family together.

He said, 'But Anna – she's his daughter, is she not?'

'Yes. She is his daughter. I am his nephew. The son of his elder brother, Ivan. My father was shot by the police. Not for any offence. Just because he was rash enough to be out in the street when a pogrom was taking place. After that happened, I was taken care of by Uncle Jacob. When he finally succeeded in leaving Russia I was only six and he declared me as his son. Anna was seven and he was allowed to bring both of us with him. His own son, Peter, was fifteen and was held to be too old to be allowed to leave. Boys of that age, you understand, were wanted as workmen and soldiers. Peter was developing some skill as an engineer and was apprentice to a railway construction company. This was fortunate. It saved him from being called up.'

As Luke listened to Dmitry, a number of things which he had suspected became clear and began to fit together.

He said, 'Let me guess. The Ochrana have arrested Peter, on some trumped-up charge, no doubt, and are holding him as surety for Jacob's help and co-operation.'

'That must be so. He is not a coward. That must be why he crawls to Weil.'

'Does Anna know about it?'

Seeing the look on Dmitry's face, he was sorry he had asked this.

'Yes,' said Dmitry. 'I think she must have been told. I believe that my uncle has already given her messages to deliver and small jobs to do connected with the anarchist ring. He would only do this if he was sure of her.'

'Because of her love for Peter.'

'No,' said Dmitry with a twisted smile. 'She can only have known him as a much older brother and such memories as she has will have faded by now. It is love for her father. She knows that if anything happened to Peter it would be the end of the world for Jacob. Perhaps you will understand if I tell you that when we first came here and had almost no money, a part of what ought to have been spent on food was being sent to his son. Any that was left went, I'm sure, first on food for his wife and us children. For himself, he was prepared to starve if it meant that a few more roubles could go through the Ghetto Bank to Peter.'

The awkward silence which followed was broken by Joe. He said, 'Maybe I'm being dumb. Not an unusual occurrence. But there's two things I can't understand. What's it Jacob can do for them that's so important? He takes lovely wedding photographs and he did print some tickets for one of their meetings, but that was in the line of business. Doesn't seem to me anything to get excited about. And what's even more of a puzzler is why he's so keen on no one going near Ikey Solomon's sweat-shop?'

'Which we hear, anyway, is closing down,' said Luke.

Dmitry said, 'I wonder if the answer to both those questions might not be in the same place.'

They waited for him to explain what he meant. When he seemed reluctant to go on, Joe poured him out another drink and Luke said, 'You can't leave us guessing. Come on. Cough it up.'

'I mean,' said Dmitry, with obvious reluctance, 'that both answers may be in my uncle's desk. Lately he's been so secretive about his work. If anyone comes in – even his wife or daughter – he covers it up. And it's locked away each night.'

'Do you think you might manage to get a quick look at it?'

'I might, perhaps, do that. But it doesn't mean that I should have any idea what it's all about. How am I going to know what's significant? If it concerns Weil and the men who are behind him – I don't even know who they are.'

'Janis Silistreau and Casimir Treschau,' said Luke. 'Or so we think.'

'There it is. You know about them. You'd be able to guess what they're planning. Hints, which would mean nothing to me, might tell you the whole story.'

The forlorn tones in which he said this reminded Luke that they were dealing with a sixteen-year-old boy who needed sympathy more than prodding. Before he could say anything, Joe, smiling in pleasurable anticipation, said, 'Looks like we'll have to do a bit of house-breaking, dunnit?'

'No need for house-breaking.' Dmitry took a purse from his pocket and extracted from it three keys which he laid on the table. 'These are copies. I have been able to take impressions without exciting my uncle's suspicions and one of my friends who works in an ironmonger's shop made these for me. They are not elegant, but they work. This is the key of the desk. That was the most difficult to get. This is the door of my uncle's workroom, which is kept locked at night. This is the back door. The family all sleep upstairs and on the far side of the house.'

'Money for old rope,' said Joe.

'No,' said Luke.

He said it so firmly that the others stared at him. 'Come to your senses, Joe. You and I are members of the police force. Are you seriously suggesting that we commit a burglary?'

Joe, who had been about to suggest just that, opened his mouth and shut it again.

Luke said, 'The most we can ask you to do, Dmitry, is to try to get a look at the papers your uncle's working on. You could make a note of anything that seems significant – names, places, dates, that sort of thing – and pass the information on to us.'

He put the keys back in the purse and handed it to Dmitry. He said, 'There is another way you could help. There's a piece of information that I'd value. If things come to a head it may be of great importance. It's simply this. Just how deeply is Anna committed? You say that she's carried messages and done other small jobs. Would she be prepared to take on something more important?'

'I can tell you one thing about Anna,' said Dmitry. 'And that is that she's a very close-mouthed girl and very unlikely to confide in me.'

'Understood. All we can really ask you for is your opinion.'

'Very well,' said Dmitry slowly. 'I think that if her father put it to her that Peter's safety was at stake, she'd do whatever she was asked to do.'

'However dangerous.'

'In such a case, danger would not be considered.'

'I see,' said Luke. 'Well, thank you. You'd better be getting back before you're missed.'

'I'll see him out,' said Joe, jumping to his feet. 'I can give Bill back what's left of his bottle at the same time.'

He ushered Dmitry to the door and went through, shutting it behind them. Luke heard their footsteps clattering downstairs, after which there was an interval in which he heard their voices but could not pick up any of the words. They seemed to have a lot to say to each other.

Then the front door slammed.

9

Next morning Luke and Joe, having thrown on their clothes, were preparing to go out. Their immediate destination was the Seaman's Café at Tidal Basin. Here they planned to take a leisurely breakfast, after which they would move along, not too fast, to Leman Street to see whether Joscelyne or Wensley had thought up any plans for them.

This programme was destined to be altered.

'Take a look,' said Joe, who was at the window pushing a comb through his unruly hair. 'Isn't that our friend at the end of the street?'

Luke joined him at the window. Even at a distance he had no difficulty in recognising the dragging, limping gait that had once haunted his dreams.

'It's Treschau, all right. Another shopping expedition, do you think? Wait for it. Yes. He's going into the butcher's shop.'

They made for the door, picking up the binoculars which stood ready on the table. Once outside they wasted no time. They slipped across into Garvary Road, scudded down it, crossed Freemasons Road and Prince Regent's Lane and took the centre of the three dead-end streets which led to the marsh.

Joe had already marked down a useful observation post.

The last house in that particular road was empty, and, judging from the state of the garden, had been empty for some time. There was an apology for a summer house at the foot of the garden. Openings in its walls commanded the ends of all three of the approach roads.

'Bound to see him,' said Joe, 'whichever way he comes.'

'Always supposing we've guessed right,' said Luke. 'Did it

never occur to you that he mightn't have come this way at all?'

'If he didn't come this way, which way did he go?'

'He might have been visiting one of the houses in Prince Regent's Lane with a parcel of meat for one of his starving compatriots.'

'No,' said Joe. 'He came this way.'

'How can you be sure?'

'Instinct.'

Luke had nothing to say to this. He had known Joe predict the movements of birds and beasts with unfailing accuracy, so why not human beings, too?

A very slow quarter of an hour crept by. Then they saw Treschau. He was climbing through the fence at the end of the next road along. They focused their glasses on him. He seemed to be following a track which led straight out into the marshes. It ran up to the embanked side of one of the many dykes and they could see that it continued beyond it. No doubt there was some sort of bridge across the dyke, hidden by the bank.

They waited, but Treschau did not reappear.

'Gone to ground,' said Joe. 'Yes. I can see him now. The crafty bastard. He's lying up, under the edge of the bank. You see him? Just to the left of that old willow stump.'

Luke said, 'I'll take your word for it.' Joe, though Luke was loath to admit it, had better eyes than him.

After about five minutes they saw Treschau again. Apparently satisfied that he wasn't being followed he had crossed the dyke and was hobbling forward, clasping his brown paper parcel under one arm. Luke said, 'Off we go. You lead.'

Their plan was to make a circle to the left where the lie of the land would keep them out of sight for most of the way, stopping when they reached a spot from which they could mark their quarry.

Treschau seemed easy and unsuspicious. He went on his way for about half a mile. At this point a rise in the ground took him out of their sight. Fearful of losing him they raced forward across the tussocky ground and climbed the far end of the ridge.

'Heads down now,' said Joe. They went on hands and knees until they reached a clump of bushes on top of the rise. Peering through it they found they were looking both at their quarry and at what was clearly his destination.

They were on the edge of a valley, shut in on two sides, open at both ends. A fair-sized stream ran down the middle of it, widening as it joined the mouth of the River Roding, known in its lower stretches as Barking Creek.

Here a substantial landing-stage had been constructed, large enough to accommodate quite a sizeable boat. There were signs that dredging had taken place to provide the necessary depth of water. At the moment it was occupied only by a two-oared dinghy, attached to a post and bobbing in the current.

But this was not what held their attention.

Above the dock and joined to it by a covered flight of steps, stood a single-storey building, inside a palisade. On each of its two separate wings a chimney was smoking. As they watched they saw the heads of two or three men who were moving about inside the palisade, busy at some job which was hidden from them. Treschau had walked straight in, as though expected.

They settled down to watch.

It was all of two hours before Treschau reappeared. He came out of a gate at the far side of the left-hand building, followed by one of the workmen down the steps to the jetty and climbed into the dinghy. The man loosed the rope, holding it in one hand to steady the boat, then stepped in, unshipped the oars and allowed the current to carry the boat out into the creek. Once there he used the oars only to turn the head of the boat downstream and, with an occasional corrective pull, was soon out on the dimpled grey waters of the Thames. He carried out all these manoeuvres with the unfussed ease of a seaman.

'Tide's starting to make,' said Joe. 'Timed it nicely. A quarter of an hour and he'll be up to Gallions Steps. No sweat.'

'If it's as easy as that, I wonder he didn't come that way.'

'Well, he had to pick up the meat, didn't he? And the tide would have been against him.'

'I suppose that's right,' said Luke. He was trying to make sense out of what he had seen.

The building must be some sort of factory. Tucked away in its little valley it would be hidden from boats passing on the Thames, visible only to one coming down the last stretch of Barking Creek. By approaching it overland, carrying that mysterious parcel, Treschau could keep out of sight pretty well altogether. Once he had disposed of the parcel apparently it mattered less if he was seen and by using the tide he could drift back, comfortably and fairly inconspicuously, to the area of the docks.

This made some sense, but there were still questions to be answered. First, what was the factory making? And if it was a genuine commercial enterprise how could it depend, for any part of its function, on casual parcels of meat scraps?

One thing was clear. They would get no answers unless they succeeded in getting a closer view of what was going on inside that palisade. And they would have to do this without being seen.

Luke put the problem to Joe, who screwed his face up to show that he was working on it. Then he said, 'I might do it. I don't think as you could.'

'All right, Buffalo Bill. Let's have a demonstration. But remember. Everything you see will have to go back to Fred. Every detail. A written report.'

'Fair enough. I'll do the looking. You do the writing.'

This was their normal arrangement. Writing reports was not Joe's strong point.

After a careful survey of the lie of the land he launched himself, flat on his face, down what must have been a tiny tributory, now dry, of the stream in the valley. Its course was marked by clumps of rushes. He moved along it steadily, but very carefully. Twenty yards from the palisade he left the bed of the stream and crawled out into the open.

Luke wondered what he was up to. He had abandoned his

cover and if anyone happened to look out from the palisade he must be spotted. Then he realised that Joe was making for a line of stunted willows, the only sort of trees that grew in that corner of the marshes.

Arrived at the trees he wriggled up the largest of them, steadied himself and parted the thin mask of boughs at the top. The streamlet cannot have been wholly dry, because when Joe turned for a moment to grin at Luke, his teeth showed white in a mask of mud.

Good camouflage, thought Luke. Joe had turned back and resumed observation.

Five minutes. Ten minutes. Then a door in the palisade, which he had not noticed before, opened and a man came out. He was carrying in each hand a heavy bucket made of some dark material and he seemed to be making directly for Joe's tree. He stopped just short of it, emptied the buckets and went back the way he had come.

But Joe had evidently had enough. No sooner had the door shut behind the man than he was down the tree and back into the shelter of the streamlet. When Joe reached him, Luke had his notebook out and pencil poised.

'Let's have it,' he said. 'Whilst it's fresh. We can polish it up later.'

'First thing is, I know what they're up to.'

Luke put down his pencil and stared at Joe. 'How can you possibly know?'

'Simple. It was writ up. On a board over the gate that man came out of. The South London Soap Company.'

'Soap. You're sure it said soap, not soup?'

'I can read, can't I? And what's more I seen them doing it. *If* I might be permitted to tell you about it.'

'Carry on,' said Luke. He saw that Joe was about to develop one of his rare fits of offended dignity. 'All the details, please.'

'Well, like you saw, there's two huts. Log sides, shingle roofs. Both wide open at the end, so you can see right into them. The one on the right's got this very big iron thingummy in it, open at the top and steaming.'

'A cauldron?'

'That sort of thing. I expect that's what they make the soap in. Boiling up the fat what Treschau brought along for them. Isn't that how they make soap?'

'I think they call it a soap kettle. Yes. What else was there?'

'A smaller kettle. Which wasn't steaming. And a row of lockers, but they were shut and I couldn't see inside them; more supplies of fuel, perhaps. Outside the hut there was a tank. V-shaped at the top, flat at the bottom. It was connected with the big boiler inside the hut. There was a pipe running into it at the top, and another one leading into a tank outside the left-hand hut.'

'Same sort of tank?'

'The same size, but the other way round, if you follow me.'

'Flat at the top, and V-shaped at the bottom?'

'Right. Except that in this one the bottom was sloping to the left and it had a pipe which went up the side, and led into the other hut. All clear so far?'

'Clear as a bell. And when we put the report into shape you can draw pictures of those tanks.'

Though no great hand at writing Joe drew admirable sketches. He said, 'One thing I forgot to mention, both those tanks had a second pipe, leading out at the bottom. These went into a cistern full of what looked like ordinary plain cold water. I mean, it wasn't steaming or anything.'

'OK. Now back to the left-hand hut.'

'I couldn't see as well into that one as the right-hand one. But there was a third tank. Not like the others, but round, with an inlet pipe at the top and a forked pipe at the bottom.'

'By the way, that stuff the man was emptying out of the bucket. Could you see what it was?'

'No. Oily stuff of some sort. Now, what else was there?'

He concentrated hard whilst Luke waited with his pencil poised.

'Yes. Two things. Might not be important. I told you the first tank was joined to the second by a pipe. Well this one was much thicker than the outlet pipes which ran down to the water tanks. It seemed to have some sort of cover round it.'

'You mean it was lagged.'

'If that's the word. And one thing more. In the space between the huts I could see two long troughs, one on each side. They were full of earth. I wouldn't have taken much notice of them, except that all the time I was watching, a man was spading the earth out of the right-hand trough and emptying it, through a sieve, into a bucket. When it was full he tipped it into the left-hand trough and started again.'

'What sort of earth?'

'Just earth. I mean, it wasn't sand, or gravel, or clay. Just ordinary earth. The only odd thing I noticed was the colour. It was a sort of pink colour.'

Luke wrote down 'pink earth', but Joe had shot his bolt. He had no more to tell him. He looked at his scribbled notes and hoped that someone would be able to make something out of them. Activity inside the palisade had ceased.

'Maybe it's lunchtime,' said Joe hopefully. 'Nothing much more we can do here, is there?'

'There is one thing I'd like to do. Whilst you were away I've been keeping an eye on those two cottages, back there, alongside the Creek. They're marked on the map as Gallions Cottages. I didn't see anyone going in or out and no smoke from the chimneys. I fancy they must be empty.'

'Like me.'

'We could go back that way and take a look at them.'

The closer they got to the cottages the less habitable did they seem. One of them fronted the creek. A path, just visible in the undergrowth, ran down from it to the water, where there was something which might once upon a time have been a landing stage. This cottage was totally derelict. Most of the slates were gone from the roof and the roof timbers showed, gaunt and blackened, above gaping holes in the walls.

The cottage behind it was in slightly better repair. They walked round it, trying to peer through the windows, but were baffled by the accumulation of filth on the panes. The only inhabitant was a thin black cat which disappeared with a snarl into the wilderness which had once been a garden.

'Poacher,' said Joe. 'If I'd had my gun with me, I'd have shot him.'

This seemed to Luke to be Satan rebuking sin, but he was too busy trying to find a way into the cottage to take up the challenge. The fact that the doors and windows were tightly shut increased his desire to see what was inside.

'Nothing else for it,' said Joe.

He picked up a half-brick, knocked the glass out of one of the windows, wrapped a handkerchief round his hand to protect it and felt round inside for the catch.

'Bound to be rusted solid,' he said. But it opened surprisingly easily. They climbed through into the kitchen.

'Hold it,' said Joe. 'I thought I heard –' He went across to the sink and turned on the tap. The water ran out, rusty at first, but flowing freely. 'Water turned on. That's a bit odd, ennit?'

'Very,' said Luke. Like Joe he was speaking softly.

'You think we might find a couple of dead bodies upstairs? Like it might be the last owners of the cottage, died quietly in their beds a year or two ago and no one bothered to look them up. Wooden' surprise me.'

'Then suppose we go and look for them,' said Luke.

They explored the place cautiously, but found no dead bodies except moths and bluebottles. The two living-rooms downstairs and the two bedrooms upstairs were empty of furniture, fluttering with cobwebs and thick with dust.

'Someone's been here,' said Luke, back downstairs. 'And not long ago.' The prints were clear. Nailed boots or heavy shoes.

'Might be some farm boy,' said Joe. 'Broke in, same as we did, to see what he could nick.'

'Could be,' said Luke.

They followed the footprints which led to the back door, which was bolted top and bottom but not locked. Like the window catches the bolts worked easily. Joe opened them and left the door ajar.

'Keep our line of escape open,' he said. 'I've a bad feeling about this place. When we open a cupboard, a Thing is going to jump out at us. When it does, I can tell you, I shall scarper.'

'Instead of talking nonsense,' said Luke, 'let's follow the prints the other way and see where they lead to.'

'You go first,' said Joe.

The prints took them upstairs, along the passage, passing the two derelict bedrooms, up to a door at the end.

'There it is,' said Joe. 'That's the cupboard I was telling you about.'

'Might be interesting to find out,' said Luke, and opened the door.'

Joe shouted 'Boo' in a loud voice, and then, more soberly, 'Well. Knock me down!'

It was a bathroom. And the surprising thing about it was that it was clean, as was everything in it. There was a basin, with a chair in front of it and one mirror over it and a second one on the wall beside it. When the tap was turned the water ran cold and clear, without any trace of rust.

Luke said, 'Someone must have used this more recently than the tap in the kitchen. And just look at that!'

There was a small fireplace at the end of the room. A fire of dry sticks had been laid in it and a big kettle hung over it.

'Hot and cold water laid on,' said Joe. 'We might be in the Ritz.'

A search of the room produced only a cake of soap, indented with the letters SLSC.

'With the compliments of the South London Soap Company,' said Luke.

Joe said, 'What's it all mean? What's the point of it?' He was staring in disbelief round the room.

'I've no more idea than you have,' said Luke. 'But if we put it in our report maybe someone will tell us.'

'Better take the soap,' said Joe. 'Otherwise they'll think we dreamt the whole thing.'

A difficult point of law having arisen, Mr Justice Darling announced that he would hear arguments from counsel on both sides in private after lunch. He added, with his schoolboy smile, 'I therefore propose to award everyone else a half holiday.'

Accordingly when Luke and Joe arrived at the Poplar Station with their report they found Wensley not only there, but free to listen to them. Hubert Daines was with him and read the report over his shoulder.

Wensley paid them the compliment of reading it right through twice. Then he said, 'First things first. I take it, from the way they accepted Treschau, that the workers in the factory were Russians, or at least were on his side. You agree? Good. In that case there is one simple explanation. The *émigrés* are always on the look-out for cash. The alternative is starvation, so they're prepared to make every effort to get their hands on it. Sometimes by robbery and violence. Might this be, for once, an honest effort to earn it?'

'Except for the curious meat delivery,' said Daines. 'That doesn't seem to me to make any sense at all. And what about that pink earth. Can you fit that in?'

Joe said, 'When I was a kid I remember another boy telling me that he'd been told that soap-makers sometimes put dirt into the soap so that the woman who was doing the washing would see a lot of dirt in the water and think what a good soap it was.'

Daines said, with a smile, 'I was told the same thing at school. And when I was a schoolboy I believed it. Not now. Modern analysts would soon uncover the trick.'

'All right. Forget the earth,' said Wensley. 'Now perhaps you'll explain just exactly what they wanted the meat for. Were the workers threatening to strike if they didn't get a decent mid-day meal?'

'I haven't the remotest idea,' said Daines. 'But that's because I know nothing about soap-making. If I could borrow this report, I could show it to someone who's an expert in the matter and might get you an answer.'

'Hand you anyone in mind?'

'The obvious man would be the chief government analyst. He might be able to solve the problem. The trouble is it normally takes a month to get anything out of him at all.'

'Would it hurry him up if you told him that his report would go to the Home Secretary and that he might have to deliver it in person?'

'I'd almost guarantee it,' said Daines, with a smile.

'Very well. Now I'd like you to tell these young men what you were halfway through telling me when they arrived.'

Daines said, 'Yesterday the Foreign Office got a report from their man in Moscow. The gist of it was that Stolypin, formerly Minister of the Interior, has been promoted. He's now First Minister under the Tsar. A position of great power – and considerable danger. You might say that he's in charge of the execution shed and his own head's on the block. He has expressly undertaken to promote a campaign of terror in London. In fact he stated that the men in charge of the operation were already in position. It would be such an open and provocative campaign that our government would be forced to do what many of its members want to do anyway, and send back to Russia all recently arrived *émigrés*.'

'Regardless of their criminal records?' said Wensley.

'Yes. It would be a matter of sending back all those who had arrived here within – well, whatever was held to be the appropriate number of years. Exceptions might be made in exceptional cases, but apart from that it would be a total clearance.'

'I've no doubt you see what this means,' said Wensley.

Since this was addressed to Luke, he tried to look as though he did.

'What it means is that from now on we've got to keep the

closest watch on the men who we think have been put in charge of this campaign of terror.'

'Treschau and Silistreau.'

'Yes. They're somewhere there.' With a sweep of his arm he indicated the crowded streets and tenements of Stepney and Whitechapel. 'Somewhere there, like scabby rats in their holes, ready to come out and spread the plague. We've seen nothing of Silistreau the poet since we lost him after his return from Norfolk. Treschau the chemist seems to emerge only to undertake his mysterious trip across the marshes. Very well. Don't puzzle your heads about factories and bathrooms. We shall learn the truth about them sooner or later. If Treschau appears again, he *must* be followed back home. I'm not suggesting it will be easy. One of you will have to watch the factory and the other concentrate on the points where, if he comes back by boat, he might disembark. If I had a single detective who was working less than eighteen hours a day I'd lend him to you.'

After this unusually long speech a short silence ensued. It was broken by Luke.

He said, 'I wondered if it might be possible to tackle this from the other end.'

'Explain.'

'Well, sir. You remember Treschau's last hide-out, in the widow Triboff's house. Clearly it wasn't just a place he was lodging at. It looked more like a permanent headquarters. We took away the papers the old woman was trying to burn. But we left a lot behind us. Books and pamphlets and filing cases in the shelves and maybe other papers in the cupboards under the shelves or in the desk. If we made a more methodical search now, might we unearth some indication of where Treschau's bolted to?'

Wensley thought about it. Then he said, 'All right. It might be worth trying. But don't spend too long on it. I want you at your look-out posts.'

'We could do it more quickly if we had some authority for

making the search. The widow's an obstinate old creature and she's likely to obstruct us all she can.'

Daines said, 'I could get you an official certificate of search under the Prevention of Terrorism Act. And if it would help in any way I'd be glad to come with you.'

'I hoped you'd say that,' said Luke. 'Some of those pamphlets looked heavy going.'

It took a little time to get the necessary authority, but by four o'clock on the following afternoon, Luke and Daines were on the Triboff doorstep, armed with an impressive piece of paper, light blue in colour, with the Royal Arms in dark blue at the head of it. Joe had wanted to come with them, but Luke, bearing Wensley's instructions in mind, had vetoed the idea. He said, 'This is a side issue. We're not to take our minds off the real job.' He suggested that Joe should examine the various points at which a dinghy, coming up from Barking Creek, might discharge its passenger. Joe had departed, grumbling.

The Triboff house stood at the end of a row of down-at-heel buildings and a little apart from them. It had a front door opening directly on to the street and a back door leading out to a court-yard and a patch of earth that could hardly be called a garden. Its comparative isolation meant that it could not be directly over-looked by any of its neighbours.

Continued knocking on the front door served only to attract the attention of two or three passers-by. They did not stop, but hurried on, as though to dissociate themselves from the house and its occupant.

'Dozing in front of the kitchen fire,' said Luke. 'Let's try the back.'

The back door was tight shut and hammering on it produced as little result as the assault on the front. Daines consulted the paper he had brought and read out, 'If the occupant will not afford entrance to the searchers they are empowered to enter the house by force, doing as little damage as possible.'

'Right,' said Luke.

There was a spade in the garden shed. He inserted its thin edge into the side of the kitchen window and levered the whole of the decrepit casement out of its frame. 'As little damage as possible,' he said and propped it carefully against the wall. 'After you.'

Daines climbed through the opening and Luke followed him. They stood for a moment, looking round. The ashes in the stove were grey and cold and the clock on the wall had stopped. The silence was absolute.

'There's no one here,' said Luke, voicing the thought that was in both their minds.

They went out into the hall and inspected the two ground-floor rooms. The windows of these, which opened on to the street, were closed, but not shuttered. Upstairs, the front rooms also were empty. They moved along to the big room at the back which occupied the space over the kitchen.

'This was where I found the widow trying to burn the papers,' said Luke.

'Nothing to burn now,' said Daines.

The shelves which had held the books and pamphlets were bare, as was the cupboard under them. The desk was still there, but with nothing on it or in it. Not even a sheet of blotting paper.

'It's a swindle,' said Daines. 'In all the best books the searchers find an odd scrap of blotting paper. Holding it up to a mirror, they read off it the information they're looking for.'

'The Russians must have read the books, too,' said Luke.

'We'll have one more look in the kitchen,' said Daines. 'They might have left something there.'

But the kitchen had been stripped with the same methodical thoroughness as the study. There was food in the larder and plates and cups on the shelves, but no single scrap of paper.

'Too easy,' said Luke. 'Any paper there was would have gone straight into the stove.'

'They certainly cleaned up before they left,' agreed Daines. 'Judging from the state of the food the old lady has been gone for some time. She must have cleared out soon after you visited her.'

'And I know why,' said Luke. 'She was scared stiff of that creature Weil. She's gone into hiding somewhere.'

Outside the dusk was closing in. The house was damp and cold. Luke found himself shivering. A door they had overlooked led to the cellar. It opened on to a flight of worn steps. Luke was glad of his torch and went down carefully.

At the foot of the steps he almost tripped over a bundle of rags on the floor. He turned his torch on it. It was the widow Triboff. Her throat had been cut.

'Found anything?' said Daines, from the kitchen.

'Yes,' said Luke. 'But I don't think you should come down.' He climbed back into the kitchen and said, controlling his voice carefully, 'Like you said, they cleaned up before they left.'

10

Early on the following morning the inhabitants of St Matthew's Row were woken by the sound of an explosion. Peering out nervously they saw that it was the police station in Bethnal Green Road, opposite the end of their street, which had been hit. Smoke was coming from some of its ground-floor windows, but no serious damage seemed to have been done.

PC Miles, who had been on night duty in the charge room and who, though he would have been the last to admit it, had been asleep behind his desk, had been shaken, but not hurt. He had hurried out into the street to reassure and disperse the crowd that was beginning to collect and finding his telephone line unaffected had made a report to Leman Street.

Wensley, looking in on his way to court, had found Miles talking to Joscelyne about it.

''Twasn't nothing really,' he was saying. 'Hardly enough to rattle the tea cups. Damage? Nothing to speak of. We'll need a bit of repainting and a few new tiles.'

'Odd affair altogether,' said Wensley. 'Intended to distract our attention, do you think?'

'What from?' said Joscelyne.

'If I knew that, I'd know what was going to happen next. Meanwhile there's something you could do for me.' He laid on the desk one of the copies he had had made of Luke's report. 'Could you have some enquiries made about this soap company? I'd rather they weren't too official, as I don't want to alert the men behind the company to the fact that we're interested in it.'

'I'll send young Cartwright. He's a champion gossip and he

looks so stupid that people tell him everything and think nothing of it.'

Wensley thanked him, glanced at his watch and hurried off. There was a clear hour before the proceedings at the Old Bailey kicked off, but Muir would be certain to want a post mortem on the previous day's hearing.

It was past five o'clock before he got back to Leman Street, after a day of frustration in which the prosecution witnesses, despite careful coaching, had contradicted each other relentlessly. Abinger had left the court much happier than Muir, who was only comforted by the thought that Wensley's evidence was yet to come and that he, at least, was too crafty and too experienced to be shaken by cross-examination.

'I've got something for you,' said Joscelyne. 'I don't know it'll help. That soap company. It's been in existence for ten years or more and it's entirely run by Russian and Lettish *émigrés*. It's believed to produce a reasonable profit. The raw material for their soap-making is coconut oil, which produces marine soap – that is, soap that can be used in saltwater.'

'Popular on ship-board, I presume.'

'No doubt. And at the wash-houses in the docks. The raw material goes down to Barking Creek once a week, normally on a Tuesday. It goes in a coal-fired scow, which rejoices in the name of the *Red Dragon*, but is known locally as the *Black Stinker* and is reckoned to be the dirtiest boat on the river. On its return trip it brings back the soap, which is dealt with by the SLSC office at the head of the quay.'

'Sounds like a genuine concern,' said Wensley, who had lit his first after-court pipe and was puffing at it. 'Anything else?'

'Not about the factory, but about those cottages. It seems they were occupied about thirty years ago by two brothers, Sam and Ben Gascoyne. They described themselves as fishermen, but had been suspected for a long time of being a link in a very profitable smuggling line. In the end the Revenue caught up with them and there was a fight. Sam was shot dead and Ben and his eldest son were wounded, after which their families abandoned the cottages and came back to Stepney. No one fancied using the cottages and they've stood empty ever since.'

Wensley puffed away and thought about it. It was interesting, but it didn't explain the bathroom. He was about to say so when Joscelyne's telephone rang. He had given orders that he was not to be interrupted and guessed that it must be something important.

Joscelyne listened impassively to the excited voice of his informant and said, 'The DDI's here. When I've had a word with him I'll ring you back.'

Nahum Lockett & Son was the largest and most prestigious jewellery shop in the East End. Its double frontage occupied a commanding position in the Mile End Road. Nahum now played little part in the running of the business, which had been handed over to Abram, the son mentioned in the shop's title. Abram was helped by his wife, Deborah, who presided over the accounts at the cash desk. The shop was large enough to employ three full-time assistants, all of whom had departed promptly when business ceased at six o'clock that Thursday, but Deborah was still at work. A cluster of gaslights above the desk had been left on for her benefit. The rest of the room was in darkness.

Abram, who lived over his shop, as his father and his grandfather had done before him, had moved across to bolt and bar the street door when the two men walked in. As they came through the door they were pulling on masks of knitted fabric, which covered their hair and the top half of their faces, with slits for the eyes, but left the bottom half exposed. As soon as the masks were in place both men pulled guns out from holsters inside their jackets.

Speaking in the rough, largely monosyllabic English which marked him as a recent arrival, the shorter of the two men said, 'Be silent. Both of you. No words.'

Abram was no coward, but he was handicapped by the

presence of his wife. She came out from behind the desk, marched up to the men and said, 'What do you want? The shop's shut. Get out.'

The taller man transferred his gun to his left hand and, with a scything blow of his right arm, knocked the woman to the floor. The other man's gun pointed unwaveringly at Abram.

'One move, one bullet,' he said. 'Through the stomach, perhaps, where you keep all the lovely food you eat every day, yes?'

By this time Deborah was back on her feet, clinging to the cash desk for support, the blood pouring down her face. The short man said, 'You ask what we want. We want many things. First, your daughter.'

'No,' said Deborah. 'No, no and no.'

The Locketts had been married for ten years before Mysie, who was asleep upstairs, had arrived. She was the light of their life and the centre of their existence.

The short man ignored Deborah and addressed himself to Abram. He said, 'You will come with me and we will fetch your daughter. If you do not, my friend will shoot your wife. Not to kill. But in places that will hurt her, badly.'

Abram hesitated. The man said, with a terrible smile which showed a row of jagged teeth, 'You wish to see your wife squirming on the floor? No. Of course not. Come with me. If you do what you are told we shall not hurt the child. Nor you. Come, then. Show me her room. Sooner done, sooner over.'

As he went Deborah made a move, as though to restrain him by force, but Abram shook his head. It was no time for heroics. He led the way, through a door at the back of the shop.

Whilst they were out of the room the tall man, without taking his eyes off Deborah for a moment, proceeded to bolt the front door, top bolt only, and to close the iron shutters which hung behind the door. Then he turned his attention to the shop windows. These were plate glass, guarded by thin steel bars. They had roller blinds, which could be closed, but observation over many nights had told him that it would be a mistake to draw them. The police patrol, which came past every three hours, liked to be able to see into the shop. Meanwhile, if they kept to the back of the dimly lighted shop, he reckoned they had more than two hours in which they could work in safety.

When Abram came back, carrying the child, who was half asleep but not alarmed, he was given his instructions. The presence of the tiny hostage meant that they were obeyed to the letter.

First he had to produce the key to the great safe which was built into the old chimney at the back of the shop. This contained the considerable reserves of the partnership, in the form of bullion, sovereigns and gold. Then he had to open the show cases, where the pick of their jewellery was displayed: necklaces, pendants, rings and bracelets, precious metals and precious stones. These went with the gold into the knapsacks the men had brought with them.

Mysie was beginning to be frightened by the appearance of the strange men with black things on their faces, and by the evident alarm of her father and mother.

She started to cry, a low whimpering.

The tall man said, 'Nearly finished. You have been good. Don't spoil it. We would not wish to wring the neck of such a sweet chicken.'

Deborah, who was holding the child, said, 'Hush, baby. Don't cry. It's all a game.'

Mysie looked doubtful, but stopped crying. The men had packed everything up. They slung the knapsacks over their shoulders and were ready to go. The tall man said, 'One last word. No doubt you will speak to the police. They will ask what we looked like. Be careful that your account is not too exact. You understand me? If any harm comes to us through you, our friends will not be as kind as we have been.'

They unbolted and opened the door and, as they turned away, pulled their masks off and stuffed them into their pockets.

Either their timing was at fault, or the police routine had been altered, because they stepped out into the arms of a two-man police patrol.

For a moment the men stared at each other. Then, as the policemen stepped forward, the robbers raised their guns and fired.

In the excitement of the moment both of them shot at the same man. The two heavy bullets, hitting him in the chest, knocked PC Bellwood backwards on to the ground. Not waiting to mark the effect of their fire the two men doubled away, down one of the alleys that led from the Mile End Road towards the river.

PC Martin hesitated for a moment then, instead of running after them or calling out, knelt down by Bellwood and opened his blood-stained jacket.

It was two passing sailors who took up the chase, running to the mouth of the alley and shouting. A shot which whistled over their heads stopped them for a moment, but they ran valiantly on. The brief pause had given their quarry time to slip into one of the tunnels of darkness at the side of the alley. The two sailors plunged past continuing to shout. When, rounding a turn, they saw that the alley ahead of them was empty, they turned round and came back. Martin was still kneeling beside the body. 'Nothing to be done for him,' he said. 'He's gone.'

Ten minutes later a furious Abram Lockett burst into Joscelyne's office past two protesting policemen. He had brought the sailors with him. He said, 'In case the news hasn't reached you, Superintendent, my shop has been raided, my wife has been assaulted and I have been threatened.'

Joscelyne, who had just put down the telephone, said, 'Yes. We heard.'

His calmness seemed to enrage Abram even further. He said, spluttering so that the words came out in gouts, like water from a partly blocked tap, 'And have you heard? Two of your men were there. One did his duty. The other made no attempt either to stop or chase the murderers. The only people who did anything were these two men. They did start a hue and cry. If more had joined in —'

Wensley raised his hand. It was such a magisterial gesture that Abram cut short what he had been going to say.

Wensley said, 'Superintendent Joscelyne has given orders for the pursuit to be taken up. It may not be immediately effective. If the robbers, as I suspect, were anarchists, they are slippery people, with many holes to hide in. What we have to concentrate on is to see that they don't get out of the country. And you could help us by giving us the most detailed description of the men that you can.'

'I'll do my best,' said Abram. 'The more willingly as they had the impertinence to suggest that it might be bad for me if I gave you too good a description. Very well. But remember that their masks covered their hair and the top part of their faces. First, the shorter man. I'd put his height at five and a half feet. Light build. Light weight. The only bit I could see of his hair was the sideburns. The colour was reddish brown, more red than brown. And he had a filthy row of jagged teeth.'

Joscelyne signalled to the policeman who had been sitting in the corner with a notebook open on his knees. He said, 'You get all that, Miles?'

'Yes, sir.'

'Good. Anything more?'

'Yes. The way he spoke and the sneering reference he made to me having good food to eat , made me think that he was, like you said, one of these Russian anarchists who are swarming into this country.'

Joscelyne said to the policeman, 'Any papers on them will probably be in Russian. That applies to both men.' And to the sailors, 'You saw them without their masks. Can you add anything?'

One of the sailors said, 'It was pretty dark, but when they stopped to shoot at us, they were in front of a lighted window and yes, I did see the smaller one had red hair. It was dressed in tight curls. Almost like a girl.'

'Good. Add that to what you've got, Miles. Now. The other one.'

'He was taller, maybe six foot. Lots of grey hair. It stuck out from under his mask. And a straggly grey beard. Right, Jemmy? You saw more of him than me.'

'I saw his face,' said Jemmy. 'Nor I didn't care for it. With all that grey stuff sprouting round and a great hooked nose sticking out. Like a bird looking out of a bush.'

'Long grey hair and beard. Nose hooked. Got that?'

'Yes, sir.'

'Right. Give it to Inspector Loughton and tell him I want it set up in print. Immediately. We'll need fifty copies. Head it "WANTED" – in big capitals – and under that, "£50 reward for information leading to their apprehension".'

'Please amend that,' said Abram. 'Five hundred pounds reward. I'd give that and more if you get the man who hit my wife.'

The policeman looked at Joscelyne, who nodded. He knew that Abram Lockett's word was as good as his bond.

Wensley said, 'We could probably guess the men's names. The smaller one looks like Don Katakin. The taller one could be David Heilmann. But it might confuse people if we did so. These men change their names as easily as their clothes.'

'And could change their appearance just as easily.'

'No doubt. But if they try to leave they'll have to produce some sort of papers. The ones they brought with them. And if they haven't got their original passports they'll need an identity card issued here. Which will have a photograph on it. If they alter their appearance more than superficially, it won't match the photograph. By tomorrow morning we'll have that leaflet distributed to every point from which ships sail. If they try to get out of the country, I think we shall get them.'

'I'm glad to hear it,' said Abram, obviously impressed by the speed of the police reaction. 'Now could you answer one question?'

'If we can,' said Joscelyne.

'Why don't we arm our own men?'

'We'd like to. But authority has to come from the Home Secretary.'

'Mr Winston Churchill?'

'Yes.'

'Very well. Then I've got a message for Mr Churchill. You might care to pass it on. I happen to be Chairman of the East London Liberal Association. We represent five constituencies which return seven members to Parliament. And I can assure Mr Churchill that unless some definite and positive action – such as arming our own men – is undertaken without delay, then on the next debate on security matters he will find seven of his supporters either abstaining or voting with the Opposition. And since the Liberal majority is so ephemeral that it has to rely on Irish members to make it work, he may not welcome the thought of diminishing it by seven further votes.'

Joscelyne said, 'I shall see – indeed, I shall be delighted to see – that your message reaches him.'

When Abram had departed, mollified by these promises, Joscelyne spread out a street map of the 'H' Division area. He said, 'It will have to be organised as a drive. Taking blocks of houses, sealing them off and going through them from cellar to garret.'

Wensley said, 'I know of a short cut which might get us there more quickly and more easily.'

'Which is –?'

'Mobilise every nark and informer in the area. The thought of £500 will have got their ears pricked up already. Stir that pot and something will come out of it.'

'A joint CID and uniformed operation,' agreed Joscelyne.

It was helpful that the normal hostility between the two branches hardly existed in that division.

'And to be really effective,' said Wensley, 'it's going to need co-ordination – from the top.'

'Any ideas?'

'I'd suggest Chief Superintendent Hawkins is the man to approach. Bert Hawkins is a personal friend of mine. As youngsters we explored the gutters of Bermondsey together. And I happen to know that he's got nothing of particular importance on his plate at the moment. So he should be able to devote his undivided attention to the matter.'

'It'll need all the attention he can spare. You realise it'll be a double job. Rousting these men out of whatever hole they're hiding in, and sealing the ports in case they try to get out of the country. And that will mean co-operation with the London Docks Police and the Customs Authorities.'

'Not only in London. You're assuming that their escape route would be aimed at the Baltic. But remember, it wasn't so with those two men who got away from Sidney Street. In both cases they got across the Channel to France. We'll have to block the south coast ports as well.'

'And there's one other little matter,' said Joscelyne. The enthusiasm that had infected his earlier utterances had disappeared. 'Those sailors saw what happened. Their story will be all over East London. We shall have to put Martin on a charge. Dereliction of duty.'

'I suppose that's right,' said Wensley gloomily.

11

Five days of intense activity ensued, spanning the weekend and continuing into the Tuesday of the following week. Powered by the human dynamo that was Albert Hawkins it covered all five of the East London divisions, turning them upside down and inside out, as a sharp spade driven into the earth beside an ants' nest will lift it up and send its indignant occupants scurrying in all directions.

The main objective was to locate the two men, Katakin and Heilmann, thought to have been involved in the jewel robbery. The fact that they had vanished from their previous lodgings increased the suspicion that they were in fact the wanted men. A second objective, added at Wensley's request, was to find a poet called Janis Silistreau or Ivan Morrowitz and a chemist called Casimir Treschau or Otto Trautman. Both, too, seemed to have vanished.

The search was conducted with method and rigour.

It was entirely unsuccessful. The reason for this was simple.

The blocks of houses in the heart of the search area had often been compared by exasperated policemen to a rabbit warren. The description was apt, since most of the houses were connected at underground level with other houses. Usually the runway was from cellar to cellar, but occasionally it passed under a street to a house opposite. This weighed the odds heavily against the searchers. On one occasion Treschau and Silistreau, observing the approach of the hunters, waited quietly until the search had finished with the house next door and then transferred themselves, unhurriedly, to it. By nightfall they were back in their original house.

Even the thought of the reward had failed to produce the results Wensley had hoped for. One of his most trusted informants had indeed promised to produce the current address of the jewel robbers, but had failed to keep a carefully arranged appointment. Since when it was found that hè, too, had disappeared. One idea was that, warned of impending danger, he had taken himself off to distant parts. Another was that he had been encased in a sack of dry cement and dropped into the Thames.

Whilst all this activity was going forward, Joe – if the expression can conceivably be used about such an open and cheerful person – was sulking.

There were several reasons for this.

Wensley had refused to involve him in the search operations and had kept him chained to observation on the factory and the cottages, reciting, for the ninth or tenth time, his belief in the value of continuous observation. 'It may sound dull,' he had conceded, 'but you'll find it will pay off in the end.'

Then there was the way Luke had been behaving.

First, and worst, he seemed to think that he had some sort of seniority which entitled him to give Joe orders. That they were phrased as advice did not lessen their objectionableness. However – and this produced a grin – he had every intention of disregarding the most earnest of all Luke's prohibitions.

A further black mark against Luke was that he seemed to be associating less and less with Joe and more and more with Hubert Daines. Joe had no objection to Daines as a person – a sound man and a useful friend – but when all was said and done he was a newcomer. Now he seemed to be allocating to himself the position of Luke's oldest friend.

All these uncomfortable thoughts were in Joe's mind as he sat in the hide which he had constructed for himself on the eastern end of the ridge between the factory and the cottages. It was a snug retreat which had taken him several nights to dig, irrigate and furnish with a plank seat and discreet spy-holes, front and rear. The irrigation was necessary since the approach of the vernal equinox had brought a succession of storms with it.

That particular day was better. Banks of cloud promised more rain, but the sky between them was blue. It was after one o'clock and Joe was finishing the lunch he had brought with him, when he spotted the *Red Dragon*, alias the *Black Stinker*, coming down the creek.

Of course, Tuesday. This would be its regular visit to the factory. There was no secrecy about its arrival, which was heralded by a belching cloud of the blackest smoke.

As Joe watched, the boat slackened speed and started to edge in towards the bank. This was unexpected. He had imagined that it would go straight to the factory, a quarter of a mile downstream, round the bend. Nor did it seem to be making for the cottage landing-stage – wisely, Joe considered, since it was derelict and probably so silted up that anything larger than a rowing boat approaching it would be aground before it got there.

So what was it trying to do?

By the time its manoeuvres had brought it to within a few yards from the bank of the river it was practically stationary. Two men now appeared on the forward deck and, as Joe watched with fascinated attention, jumped down into the water, which at that point did not come much above their waists, and started wading ashore. They stirred up a lot of mud as they did so. Meanwhile the boat, with a roaring of its ancient engines and a triumphant puff of smoke, had reversed into midstream and was proceeding on its way.

The two men were now clawing their way up the bank. Joe, who had his binoculars on them, thought he had never seen such a pair of scarecrows. The oily patches on their overalls and the blackness of their faces and hands suggested that they had been working in the stoke-hold. The addition of a coat of river mud and weeds completed their ragamuffin appearance.

Once up the bank they made for the better of the two cottages and were lost to sight behind it. That's the one with the bathroom, thought Joe. And could they just do with it!

This suggested such an intriguing train of thought that he almost missed the arrival of the dinghy. He recognised it as the one they had seen bobbing up and down below the factory. The man in it looked familiar too. He had shipped his oars and was parting the undergrowth carefully with his hands as he forced his way up to the apology for a landing-stage. When he got there he moored the boat, got out his pipe and started to smoke.

The best part of an hour passed.

Then the two men emerged from behind the cottage, each carrying a bulging sack over his shoulder, and picked their way carefully down towards the dinghy. The path ran at an angle to Joe's line of vision and with the sun making one of its fitful appearances he had a very clear view of the men.

Both of them were sprucely dressed.

The shorter one looked like a soldier, on leave perhaps from service in the East. His lightly bronzed face was clean shaven, except for a short military moustache clipped to his upper lip. He was wearing a monocle, attached to the lapel of his coat. Every time it fell out of his eye he paused to replace it.

The taller one might have been a professor. His neat grey hair was slightly curled at the edges and showed the first signs of a bald patch in the centre at the back. The paleness of his clean-shaven face was emphasised by the heavy horn-rimmed spectacles on his prominent nose.

Joe, who had observed them in both their manifestations, knew without any doubt who they were. The taller one was David Heilmann. The two things he could not change were his beak of a nose and his protruding ears. The smaller one, almost as certainly, was Don Katakin. If he had opened his mouth the appearance of his black and broken teeth would have made the identification complete.

One thing was clear. There was not a moment to lose.

His sailor friends had kept him up to date, both with their own sailings and those of the foreign boats which used the Royal Docks. He knew that the SS *Viborg*, a small Danish steamer which carried passengers and goods to Helsingfors and Copenhagen was due out some time that afternoon. The dinghy was already out of sight round the bend. As he extracted himself from his hide Joe realised that if he was going to get back in time to do any good, he would have to move fast.

A minute later he realised something else.

In their usual careful way the opposition had established a screen of watchers to oversee the departure of their two comrades. As he started out he saw three of them and one of them saw him.

Joe swore, loudly and violently. He was not afraid of being caught, confident that he could evade these heavy-footed townsmen and lie up until they got tired of looking for him or if necessary wait until nightfall. But the time element forbade such tactics. He had to get back and get back quick.

As a first step, appearing not to notice the watchers, he set out openly on the way home. After a short distance this brought him below the brow of the intervening slope. As soon as he was out of sight he turned about and crawled, as fast as he could go, towards the river.

Unhappily, like many country boys, he had never learned to swim. His plan was to keep beside the river, under cover of its bank, until he reached the first bridge, which he knew led into a block of buildings south of the recreation ground. Unfortunately it was more than a mile upstream.

Nor was there an easy path beside the river. At some points he had to scramble through rocks and even descend into the river bed itself. Progress was slow. Pausing to listen he could hear the men shouting. There were only two voices and he guessed that they had left one man to block the direct way back and that the other two were closing on the river. One of them was still some distance away, the other was much nearer.

Michael Gilbert

Joe realised that the slowness of his advance was giving them an advantage. If he went on at his present rate both of them would be blocking the bridge before he got there. There was only one thing to do. He had to run for it.

He climbed up from the river bed and took a quick look. Sure enough one of his pursuers was not more than a hundred yards away. He recognised him at once from his height. It was Krustov. Young, tall and thin, the description had said. It had not revealed whether he was a sprinter.

The bridge was in sight, perhaps a hundred yards away. The finish was too close to be comfortable. He had reached and was almost across the plank bridge when Krustov arrived at the far end. Instead of charging across it he steadied himself. Joe went down on hands and knees as the shot came. Then he pulled himself up and doubled down the street ahead.

This was disappointingly empty, with market gardens on one side and shuttered warehouses on the other. Joe had made fifty yards along it before the next shot came. Krustov must have been out of breath, because it went wide. At that moment a greengrocer's cart, drawn by a pony and driven by a boy, came clattering round the corner at the far end of the street.

Joe stopped it by standing in the middle of the road. The driver, who had narrowly avoided running him down, looked upset. Joe said, 'I'm a policeman. I'll have to use your cart.' The boy was clearly in two minds as to whether to allow Joe up, or to whip up his pony and drive away fast. Certainly Joe, after suffering in clothing and general appearance in the river bed, looked more like a tramp than a police officer.

It was Krustov who made up his mind for him. Having got his breath back, he fired again. At fifty yards it was good practice. The bullet hit the railing beside which they were standing and ricocheted off past the boy's head.

This settled all doubts.

'Ruskies eh?' and 'Chasing you, eh?' and 'Hop in quick.'

Joe was already up beside him. With a stamping of hooves the

162

pony turned the cart round and they made for the corner. No more shots came.

'That was good, eh!' said the boy. He had a cheerful freckled face and Joe judged that he was not more than fourteen years old.

'That's just the start,' said Joe. 'Now you drive me to the police station. As quick as you can and devil take anything that gets in our way.'

'Which cop-shop?' said the boy, who clearly regarded the whole matter as an unexpected but welcome break in an otherwise humdrum existence.

Joe had had time to think and had decided that his best course was to make directly for Poplar. It was past four o'clock. Even if Wensley had not yet got out of court, they would at least be close to the Customs House and the departure point of the *Viborg*. The boy needed no encouragement. It was a miracle that the only corpses they left behind them were one cat and one hen.

When they drew up in front of the police station, Joe jumped out and waved his thanks. The boy made no move to drive off. He felt there might be more to come.

Wensley had arrived five minutes before Joe. He listened to what he had to say and started to move before he had finished. As they reached the street he said, 'The Customs Office and the departure pier are up the road. Quickest to run for it.'

'Quicker still to drive,' said Joe and indicated his chariot.

Wensley, who had no false notions of dignity, climbed up on to the driver's bench. There was hardly room for the three of them. Joe, on the outside, clung to Wensley and hoped that providence, which had looked after him so far, would continue to do so.

When they reached the Customs House the policeman on duty recognised Wensley and waved him in. He ran up the stairs, along the corridor and into the room labelled 'Head of Port and Customs'. Mr Warburton, who held this double office, looked up in astonishment. He had never seen Wensley excited before. He tried to say something, but was ruthlessly cut short.

Had the *Viborg* sailed? Yes. Should be heading for Tilbury by now. Could he stop it? Mr Warburton might have said 'How?' but put a question which seemed to him to be even more cogent. He said, 'Why?'

'Because she's got two badly wanted men on board.'

'You can't mean those two men we've been warned about?'

'That's just what I do mean,' said Wensley. 'Can you hold the ship?'

'If I had a very good reason, I might ask the authorities at Tilbury to hold her. They could raise a question about quarantine. Something like that. But it'd have to be a convincing reason.'

He went to the door and shouted, 'Mr Sleight.'

The man who came out of the office next door was immediately classified by Wensley as a red-tape merchant and an obstructionist. This was unfair. Sleight was, in fact, a hard-working subordinate who did his job without fuss.

He answered Wensley's questions calmly.

Certainly the two passengers had been examined. Their tickets had been booked the day before and their luggage was already on board when they arrived only a few minutes before the ship left. It had been held for them. One of them was a Major Eberhardt, of the Royal Danish Army. He was on a six-month attachment to Woolwich to study recent advances in artillery technique. In particular, according to a letter he showed them, the use of shrapnel and the development of the recoil system. The other was Professor Kildebond of Arhus University, on temporary attachment to London University.

Papers? They both held Danish passports, stamped with entry visas six months earlier and temporary residence permits, issued when they entered the country. Yes, one of them was taller than the other, but this had not seemed a valid reason for questioning their credentials.

Wensley abandoned him and transferred his attention to Mr Warburton, who had succeeded by this time in contacting Tilbury on the telephone. It seemed that they were making difficulties about holding the *Viborg*. Particularly as she was a foreign ship.

It would need very high authority before they could interfere with her.

'Only one thing for it,' said Wensley. 'We shall have to go to the top. Save time if I could use your telephone.'

'My office and all that is in it is at your disposal,' said Warburton handsomely.

At his third attempt, Wensley found Sr Melville Macnaghten at his club. When he understood what he was being asked to do, he said, 'Winston's at the Home Office. I've just been talking to his political secretary. He tells me that he's heavily involved in the Ulster business. The only hope of getting him to move in our matter is to go and see him, which I'll do right away. You'd better go back to your own office and stay by your telephone. I'll telephone you as soon as I've got any news for you.'

So, when Wensley reached his office there was nothing for him to do but to wait for the telephone to ring. Joe, who had been hanging round uneasily, was able to fill in some time by organising a letter on Customs House paper for his charioteer, expatiating on the public service he had performed and excusing his abandonment of a vegetable delivery round. He had then visited the Seaman's Café and treated himself to a large meal, after which, finding there was nothing useful he could do, he had taken himself back to his own pad. Luke, he knew, was on duty at Leman Street and unlikely to be back until late. This suited him. He had no intention of going to bed. He had other plans for that night and Luke's absence would be helpful.

As dusk closed down, first softening the outlines of the sheds and derricks, then obscuring them, Wensley sat looking out of the window.

He understood the position that Churchill was in. It was less than a year ago that he had been faced with the riots of Tonypandy and Newport and had dealt with them firmly and successfully – whatever his opponents might say – by refusing to use troops and relying on an unarmed police force. He was unlikely to regard a few Russian scallywags as a more serious threat than a rioting and looting mob of miners and stevedores.

He had reached this point in his thinking when a squeal of brakes in the road outside announced the arrival of the new Daimler motor car which was the pride of Scotland Yard. From the window he saw Macnaghten descend and stop for a word with the police driver. Such a lack of urgency warned him to expect bad news and the look on Macnaghten's face confirmed it.

He settled himself into the chair opposite the desk and said, 'The answer is "no". The Home Secretary will *not* ask his opposite number at the Admiralty to despatch a destroyer to stop and search the *Viborg*. He pointed out that to do so would be an insult to Denmark – could even be construed, if it took place outside her territorial waters, as an act of war. I couldn't argue with that. It was what followed that annoyed me.' He paused and then said, with a smile, 'It annoyed me so much that I nearly threw my own position into the discard, by telling the Home Secretary a few home truths. I'm glad, on the whole, that I didn't. What he said amounted to an accusation that we were panicking. It must be admitted that he had the facts at his fingertips.'

Macnaghten extended his own hand and ticked off the items in the indictment, a finger at a time.

'The widow Triboff. No proof that the Russians were involved. Old women who lived alone often ran into trouble. The fire at the Reubens' house. Was I aware – I wasn't – that the insurance company had rejected their claim on the grounds that no one else had seen the alleged arsonists? Clearly they thought the whole thing was an insurance ramp. The feeble explosion at the Bethnal Green police station demonstrated one thing only. That the *émigrés* were running out of explosives, which might have been expected. They could have smuggled some in when they arrived, but were unlikely to have added to their stock since. After all, dynamite is not something you can buy over the counter. The Lockett robbery. Surely this was a logical development of what he had been saying. The minds of the Russians had turned from terrorism to simple robbery. Something which the police should be able to contain without guns in their pockets. And finally he was not prepared to yield to Abram Lockett's threats. If he thought he could influence the other members of his committee – all of them sound Liberals – let him try. After which devastating speech for the prosecution he added a comment about you.'

'Which was?' said Wensley.

'He said that when you remembered you were a policeman – as in the Clapham Common cases, which he had been following with interest – you did your job excellently. When you plunged into the waters of politics you got out of your depth.'

'Looks as though I shall have to wade ashore, dunnit? Lot of work to do. First thing will be to find out how Heilmann and Katakin got hold of those convincing papers.'

'Agreed. Any ideas?'

'Ideas, plenty. Proof, none. I'll put young Pagan on to that side of it. He's got some useful contacts and it's a help that he speaks Russian. The next thing will be to find out how their new escape route is going to function.'

'Then you think they'll be looking for a new way?'

'Well, they can't hardly use the old one, can they? Not now we know about it.'

'No. I suppose not.'

'Though you have to hand it to them. It was an odds-on winner. All the escaper had to do was sign on as an assistant stoker on the *Dragon* and spread a good layer of soot over his face. He'd be carrying his new outfit in a sack. Wash and brush up at that cottage, put on any bits and pieces of disguise to match his new passport, put his old clothes in the sack for dumping in the river, be rowed to the dock steps and come up a different person.'

'A sort of second birth,' said Macnaghten. 'Do you think Max Smoller and Peter the Painter went out that way?'

'That may have been how they started.'

Macnaghten thought about it. The practical reactions of Wensley seemed to have restored some of his spirits. He said,

'I'll tell you something that may surprise you. I got the impression, a lot of the time, that Winston was arguing with himself. He's got so much on his plate at the moment that he doesn't *want* to think that this new threat is serious. Give him one good reason and he'll change tack fast enough. He's always maintained that consistency is the policy of small minds.'

12

Rabbi Werfel was not feeling easy.

Before coming to England he had suffered, and survived, one of the most savage of the Polish pogroms and he recognised the signs of trouble looming. Walking round into Brownsong Court that morning he had observed that the little shops on the far side of Brownsong Passage had their shutters closed. On the nearside the Solomon sweat-shop had the week before shut down one of its two workrooms and dismissed the male staff. Now he saw that there was a notice on the door advising the girls who worked in the other room that business was suspended. 'For a short time', said the notice. He had a premonition that it would be a very long time. He could see from the faces of the few passers-by that they feared the same.

There was a cold and uncomfortable feeling in the air, a contraction of the scalp, a tingling in the fingers.

He noticed that a number of Russians – mostly young and in his view dangerous – seemed to be the only people still using the Solomon building. They looked confident and aggressive. It was the way the Cossacks had looked before they sealed a Jewish enclave and signalled the start of the massacre; the look of hounds who have been shown the fox.

He was selfish enough to hope that the trouble would be confined to the commercial quarter and that his beloved synagogue would not suffer; and courageous enough to suffer himself provided the synagogue was spared.

He was not the only man who was distressed that morning.

Shortly after breakfast Jacob Katz had received a visit from Luke. He had welcomed him as effusively as ever, but his friendliness had not been returned. That morning Luke was more policeman than friend.

He said, 'Being yourself a printer and photographer I imagine that you will know everyone in this part of London who is in the same line of business.'

Jacob admitted that he knew the names of most of his rivals.

'Let me have a list of them,' said Luke. 'The fullest list possible.'

Jacob promised to do his best. When Luke had gone he sat down at his desk with a local directory and set to work. Wanting something from the desk he took his ring of keys and inserted one of them in the lock. It went in halfway and then stopped. There was something in the lock, jamming it. When he looked closely he could see that it was the broken end of a key. After five minutes of fruitless efforts to fiddle it out he gave up and started to think. And the more he thought about it the less he liked it.

It was clear that someone had been tampering with his desk. It was possible that they had not succeeded in opening it and had broken their key in the attempt. On the other hand, they might have opened the desk, taken what they were looking for and have been unable to extract their key, which must be a roughly made duplicate and a bad fit.

Anna, who came in at this moment, stared at her father in alarm. His face was as white as paper and his hands were shaking. She went up to him, threw her arms round him and hugged him.

After a few moments he disengaged himself gently and said, 'I must have help. The only person I can think of is Molacoff Weil.'

'That animal!'

'Animal he may be. But I am sure he can open that desk. And when we find out what has been taken he will know what to do. Can you get hold of him?'

None of this made much sense to Anna, but she could see that her father was on the verge of collapsing. She said, 'Yes. Yes. I know how to find him. I'll go right away.'

When Weil arrived Jacob was still sitting at his desk. He had made one or two futile attempts to extract the broken key. Weil wasted no time. He selected a heavy poker from the hearth and used it to smash through the lid of the desk. Then he put his hand in and wrenched away the broken pieces.

The desk was empty.

The possibility that Jacob had feared had now become a probability, a hideous probability. He was unable to utter a word.

Weil looked at him curiously. He supposed that Jacob was thinking of himself. If the contents of his desk had got into the wrong hands it could be bad for him. Might even land him in gaol. But what of that? There were worse places than gaol. He had been in one or two himself.

He said, 'You did a lot of work for us, yes?'

Jacob nodded.

'Tickets, programmes, notices. Things like that?'

Another nod.

'And other – more private things.'

Jacob had recovered enough to croak out, 'Yes. Many private things. There were lists I was compiling –'

'Lists of possible supporters.'

'Yes.'

'Unfortunate. But not fatal.' When Jacob said nothing Weil jumped forward. It was a tiger's leap. He picked the old man up by his forearms and shook him. He said, 'So. So there *was* something more. What was it? Speak up.'

He threw Jacob back into his chair. This eruption of violence seemed to have shaken off some of the paralysis which had gripped the old man. He said, 'Those two men who robbed the jeweller's.'

'Katakin and Heilmann. Yes? You did some work for them, so I was told. Photographs and printing. Very private and very satisfactory. What of it?'

Speaking very slowly, almost as though he was forming the words singly, Jacob said, 'I had rough copies. Proofs of the work I was doing.'

'In your desk?'

'I meant to destroy them.'

'Then the man who has them will be able to reconstruct what you were doing.'

'I fear so. Yes.'

It was now clear to Weil that he could not handle the matter alone. But there was one immediate step he could take. He said, 'You know as well as I do who the robber must have been. Dmitry, your so-called son.'

'That seems probable.'

'Probable?' Weil's voice rose. 'Probable? Inevitable. Who else had ready access to this room?'

'Only my wife and my daughter.'

'You suspect them?'

'Certainly not.'

'Speak sense then. It was Dmitry and Dmitry alone who could have got your desk key copied. I know plenty of men who would have done the work. An enquiry among them would no doubt produce the truth. But we have no time for that. We must know *now*. And Dmitry shall tell us. Where is the boy?'

'I'm not sure. He went out early this morning.'

'Where?'

'Around and about. He is looking for a new job. There are a number of people he might be visiting.'

'A new job? Yes, of course. He had been working for Ikey Solomon, had he not?'

'For more than a year.'

'And when Solomon was forced to shut his two rooms, he was told there was no more work for him?'

'For the time being.'

The answer seemed to amuse Weil, who repeated 'for the time being', with curious satisfaction. He said, 'And what about compensation? In Russia, no doubt, the men could have been thrown into the street without ceremony. But not in this country. Where you are so protective of your workmen.'

'Solomon did tell them that when the market revived, he would open up again and they would have their jobs back. Some of the men were not satisfied. They wanted stand-off pay. The difficulty was that none of them had a contract.'

There was a long pause while Weil considered the position carefully. Then he delivered judgment.

'The men must be compensated. Happily, I have some influence with Solomon. I will speak to him at once. I am sure he will co-operate with me.'

Jacob was equally sure. Anyone asked to co-operate with Weil would be likely to do so.

'When the boy comes back tell him that he is to go round, early this evening, to Solomon's workshop. Not a deputation. That would aggravate Solomon. Let him go by himself. He will be paid two weeks' salary, for himself and for the other men in the room. That I promise.'

Jacob hesitated. He placed no reliance on Weil's promises and had a shrewd suspicion of what he was planning to do. He had to think carefully and quickly, weighing advantages and disadvantages. If the papers fell into the hands of the police – and if they understood their significance – the result would be disastrous for him, and through him for his wife and daughter. That was in one scale. In the other scale was the welfare of his adopted son.

A savage glint in Weil's eyes made up his mind for him.

'I'll tell him,' he said.

Dmitry when he understood what was proposed had no hesitation at all. If he had understood that the offer came through Weil he might have jibbed, but Jacob had put it to him as a message received directly from Solomon. The thought of not only getting his money, but of acting as paymaster for the others was a most agreeable one and when he set out at six o'clock that evening he was in high spirits.

It was a clear night with a near full moon. He was too engrossed with his thoughts to take much notice of what was going on around him, but when he turned out of Stratford Road into Brownsong Passage it did seem that the place was unusually quiet. He passed only one man, lounging at the corner, who ignored him.

The front door of Solomon's spread was ajar. He pushed it open and walked through the hallway and into the workroom on the left, in which he had spent so many hours of toil. It was empty and in darkness, but there was a light in the other workshop and he could hear the sounds of movement. Going across, he called out, 'Mr Solomon! Dmitry Katz here. I got your message.'

A voice from the inner room, which he did not recognise, said, 'Splendid. Don't hang about out there, boy. Come along in.'

Dmitry opened the inner door and peered through.

As he stood for a moment, in shocked disbelief of what he saw, he heard the sound of the street door being closed behind him.

Weil's instructions were clear.

He was only to make personal contact with Silistreau in a case of grave emergency. That such a case had now arisen, he had no doubt. The story which Dmitry had sobbed out had made a bad situation worse.

If a visit became imperative, his approach route had been mapped out for him.

It started from a small public house called the Collingwood Arms in East Ham High Street. Here he ordered a glass of beer and settled down to drink it. He disliked beer, but to order anything else in that place might have drawn attention to him.

A careful observer, watching him slouched in his chair, would have recognised his strength. He was a muscular machine, powerfully engined, but not clumsy. The observer might have made the mistake of thinking him stupid. If Weil had been stupid he would not have survived to reach such eminence as he had. He was clear-headed enough to appreciate that Janis Silistreau was his superior as a planner and a tactician. He knew, too, that Silistreau and Treschau were close to the people in Russia who mattered; people who were their paymasters.

He knew all this and resented it.

If, however, as had been promised, the success of the Lockett robbery, combined with their present project, realised enough money to make them independent of Moscow, why then a new regime might be established, a triumvirate in which he, Molacoff Weil, was an equal with Silistreau and Treschau.

Hurry on that day!

Receiving the agreed signal from the landlord, he strolled to the far end of the bar, went out through a side door into the maze of small dark alleys that lay between East Ham High Street and the recreation ground, and set off across the grass to the far corner where, as instructed, he paused for a full minute to look and listen. Then he climbed out into Gooseley Lane and was soon at ease in front of a cheerful fire, with a glass of schnapps in his hand.

'Better than English beer,' suggested Treschau with a smile.

'Much better.'

Silistreau, who was not smiling, said, 'The reason for this visit, please.'

'My reason is that a difficult situation may have arisen. I was informed of it this morning.'

He repeated what Jacob Katz had told him and the steps he had taken.

'Let us deal with this in proper sequence,' said Silistreau. 'The first question is, exactly *what* papers were in that desk?'

'I can only tell you what Katz told me. If he was speaking the truth, much of it was publicity material. There were also some lists.'

'Lists?'

Treschau said, 'I had asked him for the names and addresses and any personal information he could gather about his friends and compatriots who might be inclined to help us.'

'It will not help us that those lists should be in the hands of the police. But it hardly seems a reason to warrant the concern you have shown.'

'If that had been all,' said Weil, 'I would not have troubled you. But the worst came last. It seems he had been stupid enough to retain rough drafts of certain private documents he had been asked to manufacture.'

This produced a long silence. His two listeners looked at each other. Treschau seemed about to say something, but changed his mind at the last moment. Silistreau said, 'Be more precise.'

'I understand – though I had not been consulted in the matter –' Weil tried to keep the pique out of his voice – 'that Katz had been involved in producing Danish passports for our two comrades. Was I right?'

Silistreau nodded.

'I could see that if drafts of these productions came into the hands of the police and if they understood their significance —'

'Which they most certainly would,' said Treschau.

'– this would be unfortunate for Katz. Must, indeed, lead to criminal charges against him. If, to save himself, he involved you, it might be equally unfortunate for you.'

'Certainly,' said Silistreau. He did not appear to be unduly alarmed. Indeed, his chief reaction to this turn in the conversation seemed to be relief.

Weil said, 'It seemed to me that the only people not affected were the holders of those passports, since they have reached sanctuary.'

Silistreau said, 'When you speak like that, I can see that you do not appreciate the position in which this discovery places our two comrades. Previously, the most that the British Government could say was that it *suspected* that their papers might be false. Papers which their own authorities had inspected carefully and passed. A subsequent *suspicion* would not be sufficient to activate another government. Now, however, with the actual drafts in their hands the position is different. They would have clear proof that the papers *are* forgeries.'

'But surely, by now —'

'You knew, I take it, that the *Viborg* was not bound for Esbjerg.'

Weil shook his head. He knew nothing about the *Viborg* and thought this was typical of the way he was treated.

'She is taking the long route, round the northern point of Denmark, then down through the Kattegat to Helsingfors and Copenhagen. You understand what this means?'

'You mean that they will not yet have arrived?'

'Depending on the length of their stay at Helsingfors, the *Viborg* will dock on Saturday or Sunday. Picture to yourself the sort of reception they will receive if a message has already reached the Danish authorities that there is clear proof that their papers are forgeries.'

He looked across at Treschau who said, 'Probably they will not be allowed to land. Possibly they may be returned here. Certainly an application to that effect will be made.'

Silistreau nodded agreement and said, 'Now that you appreciate the position, let us move on to the next question. *Where are those papers now?*'

'I have told you what I did. It was not difficult to make Dmitry speak. It seems there had been a dispute between the two young detectives, Pagan and Narrabone.'

'Pagan?' said Silistreau with a mirthless smile. 'I seem to run across that youth at every turn.'

'On this occasion the attitude he adopted was helpful to us. When it was suggested that they used the keys and ransacked Jacob's desk he said "No". Responsible police officers do not commit burglary.'

'So?'

'Narrabone thought differently. Dmitry also. He handed over the keys, secretly.'

'Then the actual robber was Narrabone.'

'So Dmitry says.'

'Was he telling the truth?'

'By the time we had reached that point in his interrogation he was anxious only to speak the truth.'

Silistreau and Treschau looked at each other, weighing up the situation as it now appeared to them. This repeated interchange of glances was troubling Weil. He was not a clever man, but experience had made him sensitive to atmosphere. It seemed to him that he was being silently accused of having done something wrong.

Silistreau said, 'Narrabone is not a Russian speaker?'

'He may have picked up a few words, nothing more.'

'And in view of the difference between these two young men, we may assume that Narrabone would not have handed the papers over to his colleague.'

Treschau said, 'I agree. He'd have handed them to his superior. To Wensley and to no one else.'

'So. There are really only two places where they may be. If not yet handed on, they will be in the lodging of these two men in Coolfin Road. If handed on, then most probably at Leman Street police station which is, as we know, where Wensley keeps his papers. The next question is, will he have had time to study them?'

Treschau said, 'Very possibly, not yet. The Clapham Common case is close to its end. He will have been in court all day today and will be there tomorrow, when judgment is given.'

'Then there is a chance of undoing –' a sharp look at Weil – 'what has been done. Let us consider the steps to be taken. One of the instructions which we told you to give Katz was that his daughter should cultivate any acquaintance she had with members of the police force. Particularly those stationed at Leman Street and Poplar.'

'Yes. Those instructions were passed on.'

'And she has done what she was told to do?'

'So far as Poplar was concerned no suitable opportunity has presented itself. But there was at Leman Street a Sergeant Gorman. In his case no cultivation was necessary. He was a friend from schooldays and had already indicated a more than general interest in her. She has encouraged him – tactfully.'

'You mean that she has not allowed any intimacy.'

'So her father says. In fact, he disapproves of the whole affair.'

'To the extent of forbidding her to encourage the sergeant any further?'

'No. When he understood the importance we placed on this fortunate chance, he agreed not to oppose the development of the affair.'

'Understanding what would happen if he did so.'

'Understanding it fully,' said Weil with a smile. 'And the matter has turned out even more fortunately than it had seemed originally. On promotion to sergeant, Gorman was placed on night duty. He shares it with another sergeant. They take alternate nights.'

'When is he on next?'

'Tomorrow night. Thursday.'

This answer seemed to please Silistreau. He smiled for the first time that evening and said to Treschau, 'You remember we worked out the way this house could be approached with the minimum of exposure.' Treschau nodded. 'Since the instructions I have to give her are urgent, could I ask you to escort the girl here? I'm sure she'll be happy with you.'

There it was again, thought Weil. Happier with Treschau than with him. Suspicion and distrust everywhere.

'No time to lose,' said Treschau. 'I'll go at once.'

'One thing before I go,' said Weil. 'What am I going to do with Dmitry?'

'Do what you like with him. The time for concealment and knuckling under is past. If the police want a showdown – which I doubt – they shall have it.'

Left to himself Silistreau added another lump of coal to the fire and settled himself back in his chair.

He combined, in unusual fashion, the attributes of a poet and a chess player. As a poet his imagination flowed freely, forwards and backwards, selecting words and notions and arranging them in sequence until they chimed harmoniously. As a chess player he schooled his imagination before it could get out of hand. In any given situation the characters involved could be set out on the board and their moves studied.

The basis of this particular game was secure. He was sure of that. The eldest Katz boy, Peter, was held in reasonable comfort in one of the honeycomb of cells under the Kremlin. He wrote, each week, a carefully considered letter to his father, thanking him for the money he sent and mentioning that, so far, no actual proceedings had been taken against him.

Other pieces had an unfortunate habit of behaving illogically: of flying off at a tangent; of moving when they should be standing still; of standing still when they should be moving. Dmitry had behaved with incredible stupidity. He deserved any punishment he received. There had been moments that evening when he had thought that he might have to upset the board and start again. At one point he had thought that it might be necessary to eliminate Weil, a step which he would have taken without the least hesitation had it been necessary. Fortunately it seemed that Dmitry had either not spoken the whole truth, or had not known it.

Either way, his time scheme was still operative. Just operative.

Thursday evening and Friday morning would be the crucial moments. All of his preliminary moves – the Lockett robbery and its sequel; the operations then taking place at Brownsong Court; the pathetic explosion at Bethnal Green (he smiled when he thought of that); right back to the attack on Carter Farnsworth in Newcastle (he had been lucky there) – all these were moves in the game he had been playing since his arrival in England.

There were risks, certainly, in adhering to his original timetable. He was ready to take steps to minimise those risks. One such step could be taken immediately.

He left the room and climbed the three flights of stairs which led to the room where Olaf lodged. Olaf had been useful to him on a number of occasions. He looked a lot younger than he really was, had curly hair and dressed like a sailor ashore. He was training himself to speak English and already had a good command of the language. Now Silistreau had instructions for him.

'Better, I think,' he concluded, 'that you do it alone.'

'No problem,' said Olaf.

Silistreau could see a great future for Olaf.

He was not to know that he would rise, in the course of time, to a position of such power in Moscow that he was able to dispose of many of Silistreau's closest friends.

13

Mr Justice Darling: Gentlemen, I would now ask you to retire to your room and consider and let me know when you have arrived at a conclusion.

[*Two officers being sworn to take charge of the jury, they retired at 4 p.m. They returned into court at 4.35 p.m.*]

The Deputy Clerk of the Court: Gentlemen, are you agreed upon your verdict?

The Foreman of the Jury: We are.

The Deputy Clerk: Do you find Steinie Morrison guilty or not guilty of the murder of Leon Beron?

The Foreman: We find the prisoner guilty.

The Deputy Clerk: Is that the verdict of you all?

The Foreman: That is the verdict of us all.

Mr Justice Darling: Steinie Morrison, you have been found guilty, after a long, careful and most patient investigation, of the crime of wilful murder. The jury have arrived at the conclusion that you did, either alone or with the help of another, kill that man Leon Beron. My one duty is to pass the judgment which the law awards. It is that you be taken thence to a place of lawful execution; that you be hanged by the neck until your body is dead and may the Lord have mercy on your soul.

The prisoner: I decline such mercy. I do not believe there is a God in heaven either.

Wensley had waited for the verdict of the jury. As soon as the words were spoken he slid out of his seat and was standing by the doorway as the judge finished speaking. This enabled him to get out ahead of the reporters who were rushing for the telephone.

He was making for the conference room at the back, which had been set aside for the use of the prosecution. Muir was a glutton for paper: the more he was offered, the more he devoured. The table was piled with documents, some loose, some strapped into bundles. Less than a quarter of them had been used in the proceedings.

Wensley sat down on one of the hard chairs, cleared room on the table for his elbows and rested his head on his hands.

Reaction was setting in.

It was not what the judge had said. Most of it was routine. It was what he had left out. He had not, as judges often did, expressed his belief in the correctness of the verdict.

His last words to the jury had been, 'Gentlemen, if this case is proved, I know that you have fortitude enough to act upon your conscientious judgment and to say that this man is guilty. But –' and here a pause had seemed to add extra significance to his words – 'if you are not satisfied, you know your duty and I am sure you will do it.'

A plain hint?

Was it possible they had made a mistake?

He was sure, in his own mind, that Morrison and an accomplice had bludgeoned Beron to death. What he was not sure about was whether the Crown had succeeded in proving it conclusively. The marks on the dead man's cheeks had worried him. Were they casual slashes, or were they put there by the terrorists as a warning to anyone who might be tempted to betray them?

He had reached this point when there was a clatter of feet outside, a knock on the door and one of the court attendants put his head in and said, 'There's a gentleman —'

This was as far as he got before Macnaghten, who had followed him down the passage, burst in without ceremony.

Wensley could see that he was angry, but it was not one of those explosions of hot temper that could act as a safety valve. It was a cold fury; a public demonstration of his feelings, which Wensley had witnessed only two or three times before and which always meant trouble.

He said, speaking clearly for all his fury, 'It is a declaration of war. I told you that the Katz boy, Dmitry, had disappeared yesterday.' If he had done so, Wensley had been too wrapped up in the final stages of the trial to attend to him. 'Well, he's turned up. Naked. Hung by his heels from a tree in Victoria Park. With a notice round his neck. In English and in Russian. "Let Authority beware." Also he'd been flogged. With a raw-hide whip, a knout, something of that sort. His back was a mass of blood and bruises.'

'Was that what killed him?'

'No. The doctor said that particular damage was inflicted before death. Some time before.'

'Do we know how he was killed?'

'He'd been strangled. Manually. The marks of two hands round his neck were quite plain. It's a piece of total and open defiance, seen by half a hundred people before the police got the body down. Not only seen, but photographed. It will be in all the papers.'

'They won't like it, sir.'

Wensley could think of no suitable comment. None was needed. Macnaghten was past discussion.

'Do you think I like it? Any confidence people had in the police is being systematically destroyed. They'll be wondering what they're going to find next. Another old man with his head bashed in. Another boy hung up like a joint of meat in a butcher's shop. Soon they'll be scared to go out at night.'

Macnaghten was too angry to sit down. Now he swung on his heel and made for the door, saying, 'Are you coming?'

'Certainly,' said Wensley mildly. 'But I'd like to know exactly where we're going.'

'To the Home Office, of course. So that I can hand in my resignation personally.'

'Right,' said Wensley. 'They might as well have mine at the same time.'

They left the court by the private door at the back, avoiding the crowd that was still milling round the main entrance, and reached Ludgate Hill where they found a cab. As it clattered off, they passed Luke on the pavement, but did not see him.

Luke had spent the day on a self-imposed task which he knew to be pointless. The more he realised this the more obstinately did he pursue it.

There were twelve names of printers and photographers on the list which Jacob had compiled for him and which had reached him just before midday. To these he had added a further six from his own researches. He was determined to visit them all. They had proved unlikely suspects, clearly incapable of carrying out the sort of forgery he had in mind. The suspicion with which he had started had long since hardened into certainty.

The guilty party must be Jacob Katz.

He was an accomplished photographer and an expert printer with up-to-date machinery. He was a binder, too. Some of his best pieces of work, which Anna had shown him with pride, were presentation folders with embossed covers. Lastly and conclusively he was, according to Dmitry, under the thumb of that creature Weil. So why waste a day looking further, when the truth was staring you in the face?

Because, said his inner monitor, you don't want it to be Katz. Because, if Katz was at the heart of the affair, then Anna must be involved. Not as an outsider, not just running messages and doing occasional jobs, but a direct personal involvement. Had not Dmitry admitted that she would do whatever she was ordered to do? As a policeman surely he should welcome the chance of putting such a dangerous person away before she did any further damage.

Terry & Co., newsagents, with a side-line in invitation cards and a printing press which looked as though it had been new at the time of the Battle of Waterloo and had seen hard service since. Cross them off and out into the street again.

From time to time his duty had taken him into prisons. It was the women's prisons that he had found particularly unpleasant. The idea of consigning Anna to the care of those grey-haired, masculine wardresses, who seemed to derive some inner satisfaction from breaking down the girls in their charge, filled him with almost uncontrollable disgust.

A. B. Storrs took photographs, specialising in wedding groups. They had never taken up printing. Too complicated. Cross them off and out into the street once more.

It was darker than it should have been at that time of day in mid-March. The sky overhead was a steely blue, but a thick fringe of cloud had crept up along the eastern edge. The descending sun had spread an unnatural yellow glare across the sky and there was a feeling of undischarged electricity in the air. Storm before long, he thought. A heavy one. Might lift the uncomfortable depression which hung over everything.

The last name on his list was a man who, it turned out, had no shop, only a stall in the precincts of St Paul's Cathedral. He specialised in religious cards which pious ladies would slip into their prayer books. He had no printing press. He drew them by hand. Luke spent no more than two minutes on him before he crossed his name off and, with a feeling of relief at a stupid job done, set off down Ludgate Hill.

When he was halfway down all the clocks in the neighbourhood started to announce the hour of six. A cab clattered past him, but he had no eyes for it.

'I have heard the news,' said Churchill, 'and I surmise from the look of grim determination on your face, Sir Melville, that you may have come to present me with an ultimatum.'

'Not an ultimatum, Minister,' said Macnaghten, 'a decision.'

'Yes?'

'My resignation as Assistant Commissioner.'

'I refuse to accept it,' said Churchill. 'At least until after you have listened to what my visitor has got to tell us. He had only just started on his exposition when you arrived. Allow me – in case you have not met – Sir Vivian Majendie. Sir Melville. I'm sure you know him.'

Macnaghten nodded.

'And you, Inspector.'

'By name, of course,' said Wensley politely.

Sir Vivian Dering Majendie, who had seen service in the Crimea and the Indian Mutiny, preserved, in his mid-seventies, a look of the gunner officer he had once been, but with an academic overlay derived from the countless dissertations which he had been called on to deliver in his office as Government Inspector of Ammunition and Explosives.

He said, 'I shall have to start by dealing with the operation of soap-making – or perhaps you are already familiar with the subject?'

Three heads were shaken.

Winston said, 'We were taught a lot of useless things at Harrow. Nothing about such a practical matter as the making of soap.'

'Nor at Eton,' said Macnaghten, equally regretfully.

'Nor at Monkton Heathfield Village School,' said Wensley with a grin. It pleased him to be able to swap schools with an Etonian and a Harrovian.

'You may therefore proceed, Sir Vivian, on the basis that you have an entirely ignorant audience.'

'Then let us begin at the beginning. Soap can be made from around twenty different raw materials, of which I need only trouble you with two general types. On the one hand there are various vegetable oils, palm oil, olive oil and coconut oil. On the other hand you have animal fats. In both cases the material is boiled or, as the professionals say, saponified. This is carried out in a large soap kettle, such as is clearly shown just inside the right-hand hut. Beside it there is a smaller kettle, which I will come to in a moment. Vigorous boiling and the addition of salt, separates the soap from the spent lyes which are run away through a cock in the base of the kettle and which were, formerly, disposed of as useless.'

'Which would account,' said Churchill, 'for the buckets mentioned in the report.'

'The buckets which were observed in the report – an excellent report by the way – have nothing to do with the disposal of the lyes. They would simply have been run off and dumped. I say, "would have been". Not now. As the result of recent developments, those spent lyes have become potentially more valuable than the soap itself. To understand this you must cast your minds back to what I said about the different raw materials. Different in their treatment and different in their end product. Vegetable oils produce the normal, easily useable and easily saleable soap. Animal fats, used by themselves, produce a soap which is hard, difficult to dissolve and of little sale value.'

He looked at the Home Secretary, as though daring him to interrupt, but Winston, genuinely interested as always in the technique of others, refrained.

'In both cases, when one is proceeding to what I might call part two of the process, the lyes need washing. The lyes of animal fat need less washing than those of vegetable origin. In either case it is a cumbersome process and one can understand why a primitive outfit such as we have here might wish to simplify it. In a modern factory the lyes are made to circulate through labyrinths of lead in such a manner that they pass alternately over and under the partitions. This causes them to deposit any globules of oil which they may hold in suspension. A simpler, though less totally effective, method is to dilute the crude product with water and remove the impurities by distillation. In either case the impurities are collected from time to time and carried away in gutta-percha buckets. Are you with me so far?'

'So far,' said Churchill, apparently unabashed by having had his knuckles rapped, 'I have grasped that normal and saleable soap can be produced from vegetable oil – actually, in this case, coconut oil, I understand.'

Macnaghten nodded.

'The only drawback is that it requires an elaborate washing

process which may perhaps be avoided, or be less elaborate in the case of soap produced from animal fat. The point I find difficult to understand is why, in what you might call the animal fat operation, if the end product is unsaleable, anyone should bother to produce it at all.'

'Precisely,' said Sir Vivian, with the pleasure of a man who has led his audience to a carefully contrived climax. 'In this alternative operation, which would be carried out in the smaller kettle – fed by the animal fat so secretively introduced – the soap itself would indeed be almost useless; but the spent lyes would contain as much as three or four times the amount of the secondary product of such operations.'

'The secondary product?'

'Which is, of course, glycerine.'

The three members of the audience looked at each other, with a perception of what was to come.

'Glycerine,' said Sir Vivian, adding in case his class might be getting out of hand, 'or trihydroxyl propane, has, of course, a wide number of uses in commerce and in medicine. None of these need concern us. Because the presence outside the huts of those two oddly shaped tanks makes the objective in the present case abundantly clear. The one on the right is a separator. The one on the left, connected with it as you will see by a carefully lagged pipe, is a nitrator. Their end product is nitroglycerine.'

This, although it had been expected, produced an effect almost of shock.

Sir Vivian continued, speaking in his level, lecturer's voice, 'The nitroglycerine, a heavy, oily liquid, would first be stored in lead tanks, probably at the back of the left-hand shed. It is exceedingly volatile and astonishingly destructive. Particularly during the process of manufacture. That is why, as you can see from the sketches on the report, both the nitrator and separator have large tanks full of water connected to them below. So that should their contents get out of hand, they can at once be 'drowned'. When I remind you that Alfred Nobel, the first commercial producer of nitroglycerine, not only blew up his own lab-oratory, killing his youngest brother and four other men, but was responsible for the accidental sinking of one steamer at Bremerhaven and another at Panama and, finally, for the total destruction of the Krummel factory at Hamburg, then you may perhaps have some notion of its danger and its power.'

Churchill said, 'One wonders why the production of such lethal stuff was allowed to continue.'

'No one wondered this more anxiously than Alfred Nobel. And that was why he was deeply relieved when by chance it is said he stumbled on a simple but effective answer. This was to impregnate the nitroglycerine into kieselguhr, a pinkish earth which is found, among other places, in Scotland. The earth, when sifted and impregnated with nitroglycerine, produced the final product which made Nobel a millionaire many times over and may be said, without exaggeration, to have changed the shape of the world: dynamite.'

In the silence which followed the word seemed to reverberate. It was an old demon, suddenly reappearing through the trap door. Since the Fenian outrages, nearly thirty years before, the Explosive Substances Act, rigorously enforced, had reduced the threat of the dynamiters to a bad, but distant memory.

Finally Churchill said, 'You are telling us that what was assumed to be a soap factory has become – in part at least – a dynamite factory. It is an alarming idea. How much of this explo-sive might they have in stock?'

'That would depend on how long this new fat-based process has been proceeding alongside the regular work of the factory.'

Wensley, speaking for the first time, said, 'Three months at the outside, I'd guess.'

'Then there are two facts to bear in mind. The advantage of the new process is that it produces glycerine in large quantities. And, once it has been nitrated, the end product is so dangerous that for safety's sake they would treat it with kieselguhr at once. Which means that they could already have a generous supply.'

Churchill, after thinking about this for a moment, turned to Macnaghten and said, 'Then we may take it, Sir Melville, that the ineffective explosion at Bethnal Green was designed by the terrorists to suggest that they were running out of explosives.'

'I think that must be so, Minister.'

'Whereas, in fact, they may have enough for a regular campaign of destruction. Very well. Until you can assure me that this threat has been abated I am prepared to sanction the use of firearms, but only by your specially trained men.'

'Understood.' Macnaghten tried not to make the pleasure in his voice too apparent.

Churchill rose to indicate that the meeting was at an end. His audience waited, anticipating one of the dicta for which he was already becoming famous.

He did not disappoint them.

'As a soldier,' he said, 'my advice is that when your men shoot, they shoot fast and straight. As a politician, my hope is that they will not have to shoot at all.'

Joe's day had been as tiring as Luke's, but a lot more satisfactory.

Although he preferred doing things to thinking about them, given a definite problem he was not incapable of working it through.

'The way I see it,' Wensley had said, 'largely through your efforts – which I'll make it my job to see get reported in the proper quarter – we've succeeded in blocking one of their methods of getting their men inconspicuously to their point of departure in the docks. And a very good method it was.' He passed his hand thoughtfully over his moustache. 'We don't know exactly where that dinghy put them ashore, but whether it was Gallions Steps, Woolwich Pier or Orchard Wharf, they'd have no more than a few hundred yards to go, which was well for them, as that part of London's not friendly to them. Now that this route is barred, how are the next lot going? They're a cautious crowd. They'll have some plan ready. Your job is to find out what it is.'

This might have seemed a task so large and so vague as to be almost impossible, but Joe had certain advantages. In the last few weeks he had examined the landing points mentioned by Wensley and had come to know the area around them. Being a person who made friends wherever he went, he already had a posse of helpers and informants among the sailors, dockers, chandlers, iron-founders, rope-makers, publicans and general hangers-on who lived and worked in Canning Town and East Ham. Moreover, the temperature was rising. Strangers and foreigners, if not actually assaulted, were carefully noted. Joe's plan was to work inwards from the Victoria Docks, asking questions as he went.

He concentrated on the outlying portions, arguing that the Russians would not risk lodging among the maritime population, but would select a departure point in the more neutral commercial fringe to the north and east. It was after eight hours of walking and talking which had left him hoarse and footsore, that he picked up his first promising lead.

He was enjoying a well-earned break in the Collingwood Arms when one of the regulars, a collier and a friend of Joe's, joined him at his table. Joe downed the pint of beer in front of him and gave a repeat order for both of them. When it arrived and had been emptied with equal speed, his friend said, with appreciation, 'Doan 'ang abaht, do yer?' and ordered and brought over two refills. He seemed to be nursing a grievance.

'Not like that bloody furriner we 'ad in 'ere lars night.'

This seemed promising. Joe asked for particulars.

It seemed that a stranger ('a nasty-looking bag of beef') had sat for half an hour looking at his beer and occasionally sipping it ('like a perishing leddy') before making off through the door at the end of the bar and, a crowning insult to the pub and to Great Britain generally, had left half his beer undrunk on the table.

Joe described Weil.

His friend thought it might be, but couldn't be sure. If by any chance Joe wanted to know where the man had gone, he should have a word with old Nancy, who didn't come out much these days – reasonably, since she had lost both her legs in a dockside accident – but sat in her front window in Beckett Avenue watching the world go by.

Five minutes later Joe was talking to old Nancy through her front window. From where she sat she commanded a good view of the recreation ground and she had seen this odd figure ('like a great hape, reely, Mr Narrowbone') climbing in at one end and out at the other into Gooseley Lane. After which, it seemed, he had turned to the left and Nancy had lost sight of him.

Joe thanked her, presented her with a packet of shag tobacco which he kept for such purposes and followed the line she had indicated, across the recreation ground and out into Gooseley Lane.

Here he was at a loss. There were modest two- and three-storey houses on both sides of the lane, with nothing to choose between them. If it was indeed Weil, and Nancy's graphic description of him suggested the possibility, he might have been visiting any of the houses in the lane, or taking one of the turnings off it. The two on the right led out on to the marsh. Could he have been making for Gallions Cottages or the soap factory?

Here Joe's inborn sense of direction came to his aid. If Weil had been making for either of those places he would have gone south when leaving the Collingwood Arms, not east. A sound, if unhelpful, conclusion.

At this point fate dealt him a card off the bottom of the pack.

The lights had been lit in the ground-floor front room of the house immediately on his left and when the owner came across to draw the curtains Joe recognised him. Luke had shown him the excellent photographs, front view and side view, which Carter Farnsworth had taken up in Newcastle months before. Now he was looking at the man himself.

Janis Silistreau, also known as Ivan Morrowitz.

Joe was under no delusions as to the value of his find. He was also sensible enough to realise that there was no step more important than to let Wensley know about it, and that as soon as possible.

He considered telephoning, but decided that a personal report was preferable. It was a choice between Leman Street and Poplar. Wensley had had a camp bed installed in both places and his wife and his two teenaged sons had seen little of him during the fraught and overcrowded month just past. No helpful boy with a cart turning up, he had to rely on public transport. One tram would take him down the Barking Road to Canning Town station, and a second one along the Commercial Road to Leman Street. As he trundled along, at a regulation pace with frequent stops, he thought enviously of his seniors and the motor transport which was becoming increasingly available to them.

Leman Street police station was the second building in that street, separated from its left-hand neighbour by a narrow passage serving the back doors of both buildings. Being dark as well as narrow, the passage was a favourite place in summer for courting couples, and Joe as he went past caught a glimpse of what looked like a closely interlocked pair. Since they broke apart abruptly it seemed that they must have noticed and resented Joe's inspection of them.

Bit cold and damp for back-yard courting, he thought, as he pushed open the door of the police station. This led directly to the charge room.

He was surprised to find it empty.

He had left the street door open and he heard the sound of two pairs of footsteps on the pavement, followed by a pause. Moving across to the door he was in time to identify the couple whose romance his arrival had interrupted.

The man was Sergeant Gorman. The girl was Anna Katz. Stupid little bint. Couldn't think what Luke saw in her. He caught a glimpse of her white and frightened face as she took a last look over her shoulder before disappearing round the corner, into the turmoil of the Whitechapel Road.

By this time Sergeant Gorman was back behind his desk. He looked aggrieved.

'Sorry to interrupt love's young dream,' said Joe, 'but wasn't it a bit rash – just as a suggestion, in times like these – leaving the station empty?'

'What *I* suggest,' said the sergeant heavily, 'is that you members of the soft-shoe brigade mind your own bloody business.'

On the word 'business' the world fell apart in one roaring, blinding, deafening blast, as the heavy charge of dynamite in the next room tore the building apart.

It was echoed by a clap of thunder as the storm which had been rolling up from the North Sea burst over East London and the rain came down in a solid sheet.

14

Luke had supped in one of the many City coffee houses, grateful for a blazing fire and for an opportunity to take the weight off his feet. On his way home he had been deceived, as were many people, by the double explosion.

He had sheltered from the immediate downpour in a doorway. It was only when he noticed that most people were going in the opposite direction to him, all hurrying, some actually running, that he realised something had happened.

He managed to stop one of the hurriers, listened to an incoherent account – explosion – bloody Russians – Leman Street – and turned about and ran, faster than any of them. By the time he got there the rescue team was already at work, the water sluicing off their black rubber coats. One benefit the storm had produced, it had killed any fire which might have followed the explosion.

The blast had brought down the outer wall of the police station and had filled the street with a carpet of brick and broken glass. Luke, picking his way over it, managed to secure the attention of one of the rescue team. When he understood who Luke was, he allowed him through what had once been a door and was now a jagged gap in the wall, into the charge room.

The man indicated an inner wall, which had almost ceased to exist and said, 'We think the stuff was in there.'

'Dynamite?'

'Must have been. Very strong blast. Took out everything above it.' Luke could see clean up to the roof, where the rain was dribbling through a hole. 'It's thrown a heap of stuff into the street. Injured three people who were passing by. One of them badly. The side blast, into this room, picked up the desk sergeant – don't know his name – crushed him against the wall and put his desk on top of him.'

'Sergeant Gorman,' said Luke. 'Did it kill him?'

'He was alive when we picked the bits of the desk off him. Died before we could get him into the ambulance. The other one was luckier – well, a bit luckier.'

'The other one?'

'Young detective. Name of Narrowbone. Something like that. I said he was lucky. The explosion sent the door of that inner room right across this one. Must have come like a shell out of a gun. Knocked the youngster flat, but fell across him. That saved him from the really dangerous stuff – lumps of brick that were coming down all round him.'

'Which hospital?' said Luke urgently.

'Stepney. That's where most of the casualties—'

But Luke had gone.

As the storm passed the rain had eased, but the streets through which Luke ran were empty. He could visualise men and women huddled in their houses, cowed by the double assault from the Almighty and from the enemy. And Joe? The man had said that he had been a bit luckier. What did he mean by that?

At the hospital the grey-haired doctor, who had been talking to the rescuers, was sympathetic. 'Friend of yours, was he? Oh, a colleague. Well, you'll be glad to hear that he's not on the danger list.'

'Then could I possibly have a word with him?'

'Out of the question. He's already been anaesthetised and prepared for the operation.'

'Operation?'

'I'm afraid we had no option. That door that fell on him protected most of his body, but part of his left leg must have been outside it. It was crushed so badly by the stuff that fell on it that it will have to come off.'

Seeing Luke's face he added, 'Only below the knee.'

'Only below the knee,' repeated Luke blankly.

Joe on crutches. Joe, whose pride had been his strength and his ability.

'Might have been worse,' said the doctor. 'A lot worse, when you think that a man a few feet away from him was killed. And I assure you – speaking from cases I've dealt with myself – that the days of sailors stumping round on a peg leg are long past. The artificial limbs they make nowadays are excellent. We'll fit him out with one of the latest types and he'll soon be hopping round like a sparrow.'

But not in the police, thought Luke. There was nothing more to be said and he was about to go when the doctor stopped him.

'You wouldn't be Luke Pagan, by any chance?'

'Yes.'

'Then I've got a message for you. Two messages in fact. I didn't understand them, but I expect you will. He said we were to tell you that Bill Trotter had got the papers. The second was something he said later. He was getting very shaky by then and wasn't easy to hear. It sounded like, "It was Anna who got the sergeant to leave the charge room empty."'

'Yes. I understand that, too,' said Luke. He scribbled his address on a piece of paper. 'Please let me know as soon as I can see him. And when he comes round, tell him I'll deal with the papers – and the other thing.'

The doctor promised to pass those messages as soon as his patient was able to appreciate them. Luke walked home slowly, with his thoughts.

He neither noted nor worried about the fact that he was under observation from the moment he crossed the East India Dock Road. If he had had a thought to spare for it he might have realised that as soon as Wensley shifted his headquarters from Leman Street to Poplar the network of eyes would have moved south.

When he got back he found Bill Trotter waiting for him. He said, 'I'm terribly sorry.' For a moment Luke thought he was talking about Joe, who had been, he knew, a close friend. But apparently it was something else. 'He looked all right. I mean, he could have been off one of the ships. Something like that.'

'*Who* could have been?'

'Why, the man you sent round with a message. At least, that was what he said. He was to wait till you got back. I never thought – well, come up and take a dekko.'

The room looked as though a small typhoon had been through it. Things were scattered everywhere. Bedclothes on the floor; both mattresses ripped up; chairs upended and their cushion seats sliced across. All the cupboard doors were hanging open and where these had contained suits the pockets had been turned inside out and the jackets and trousers added to the pile on the floor.

Luke stared at the chaos. In the light of what had happened to Joe it registered only as a minor irritation. He said, 'We'd better tidy things up a bit.'

'I'm reckoned to be a good hand with a needle,' said Bill. 'I'll soon tack up those mattresses and cushions.'

'That would be kind of you.'

By the time Bill came back a semblance of order had been restored. Bill, seating himself cross-legged like a professional tailor, set about repairing the rents in the mattresses. Whilst he was doing so, Luke told him about Joe.

Bill paused for a moment, said, 'That's bad,' and went on with his work. After a moment he added, 'He once did me a good turn. Did he tell you?'

'Yes, he told me.'

A further interval of silence. Then, 'That man who made all this mess. Was he a Russian?'

'I guess he must have been.'

'Didn't sound like one. More like a squarehead. Do you know what he was looking for?'

'Yes. He was looking for a packet of papers. The ones Joe asked you to look after.'

'I thought it must be that. Get them now if you like.'

'No hurry,' said Luke. 'Please finish what you're doing. You're making an excellent job of it.'

The papers had seemed important once. Now they were nothing more than a routine job. Something to keep his mind off what had happened. Useful because he didn't think he'd sleep much that night.

As midnight was sounding he was sitting on his bed in the restored and tidied room, trying to make out what it was in Jacob Katz's desk that had caused such violent reactions.

First he had had to put the papers into some sort of order. Into one pile went the public notices of Russian and other *émigré* events. Into another the miscellaneous jobs that Jacob had undertaken for other people. Notices of private functions, menus, raffle tickets, fixture lists for local football clubs. When these had been put on one side a more interesting residue remained.

First, there was a list of supposed supporters of the terrorists – some of them surprised Luke considerably. Finally, and he had left them to the last on purpose, there were four double sheets of paper clipped together.

The first two, when spread out, appeared to be a draft of the opening pages of a passport. The main headings – Number of Passport; Name of Bearer; National Status – were in what Luke assumed to be Danish, a language of which he was almost entirely ignorant, but were duplicated, fortunately, in French.

Under *'Nom de Titulaire'* he noted, with growing excitement, *'Harald Knud Eberhardt. Profession: Officier d'Artillerie'*. In the other, *'Hartvig Kildebond. Professeur de l'Université d'Arhus'*. It was clear that these papers had been in front of Jacob Katz whilst he was printing the relevant pages in the forged passports which had allowed Katakin and Heilman to slip out of the country.

Why in the world had he kept them? Stupidity, forgetfulness, or some long-range idea of bargaining with his employers, who would hate to see them coming to light. Whatever the reason, their production would put Jacob behind bars for a long time. He felt no compunction about this. His views on the Katz family had been blown sky-high by the explosion at Leman Street and had come down in twisted and hateful fragments.

The second pair were even more interesting. They followed the same lines as the first pair, but in this case the headings were in Polish, of which Luke had picked up a fair smattering from his Russian tutor, and the duplicate entries were in German.

The holders of these passports, Adam Fredro Krasiki and Juliusz Korgenewski, were both in the Church. Krasiki a priest, *'Geistliche'*, Korgenewski an abbot, *'Abate'*. In both cases the national status was given as Polish. The place of birth in one case was Lodz, in the other, Poznan. From the dates of birth it seemed that both were in their early middle age.

Luke looked at the second pair of documents, while the minutes of the long night ticked away. Clearly the vital question was whether they related to something which had already taken place – Peter the Painter and Max Smoller? – or whether they had been prepared against future contingencies.

Both before and after the Houndsditch and Sidney Street outrages, quite a few wanted Russians, Letts and other Eastern Europeans had vanished from the country. It had been so easy. A mask of soot over the face, a trip down river in the *Black Stinker*, a change of clothing, a new passport, a short paddle in the dinghy, up the dock steps and away.

He could find out from Mr Warburton or the efficient Mr Sleight whether a passport bearing these particulars had been produced to them in the last twelve months. If it had, then too late to shut that stable door. If it had not, it suggested a number of very interesting ideas.

But if they were so interesting, why was he finding it difficult to concentrate on them? There was something at the back of his mind. Something that Bill had said. Something casual and quite unimportant. As he was leaving he had looked out of the window, had noticed that the rain had stopped and had said – yes, that was it – had said how lucky it was, because when the rain was heavy their basement got flooded. Some blockage, no doubt in the storm drain, which they had been pestering the authorities to do something about.

From that point his mind, which was working with the clarity that sometimes comes in the small hours, moved on to the Rabbi Werfel who had had a similar problem. In his case, what could have caused it?

Luke found it easier to think a problem through if he could commit it to paper. He started to sketch the area of Brownsong Court as he remembered it from his visit with Joe.

Stratford Road ran east and west. North of it lay first the Jewish School, with its playground, then the synagogue. A narrow cobbled way ran along the east end of the synagogue, separating it from the back of the Solomon workshop. Next came Brownsong Passage running past the front of Solomon's place and into Brownsong Court. Finally, and more tentatively, he sketched in what he remembered as the only exit from the court, a lane which ran past the south end of the Ghetto Bank, turned right and ran north – to where? He didn't know.

Having blocked in these buildings, roads and passages, he drew a dotted line showing where the storm drain must surely run. Along Stratford Road, certainly. And if it had been blocked, the blockage would be somewhere between the school and the synagogue. If it had been any earlier it would have flooded the school playground. After that the soak-away must turn left, as the land fell away in that direction. But where? The important question was, did it run down the cobbled way between the synagogue and Solomon's place, or down Brownsong Passage?

Luke now found himself assuming that the blockage was not accidental; it was deliberate. Reason forward from this. There were two significant points. First, that Solomon had shut down – had been forced to shut down? – his business. He didn't believe for a moment that it was because of a fall in profits. That was eye-wash. Secondly, that since it had shut down, outsiders had been discouraged. There were reports on the files about this and about young Russians who had been observed going into the presumably empty building.

So what was going on?

Luke thought he could guess. He drew in one further line on his plan. It ran from Solomon's workshop to the synagogue. A tunnel, short and easy to dig. But *if* the storm drain ran in fact down the cobbled way, then it would have to be blocked. If not, every time it rained the tunnel would be flooded.

And the objective was clear. They had been expecting a dramatic demonstration by the Russians. What could be more dramatic than blowing up the main place of Jewish worship in the East End of London? And, looked at from the Ochrana point of view, what more likely to move a hesitating government to take the step they were hoping for? They might be able to laugh off a few Liberal defections. The hostility of the Jewish bloc, so strong in the City and beginning to be felt in government itself – that would be a different matter altogether.

Luke had now so much on his mind that he decided to compose two separate reports. The first would deal with the passports. It would have the four double sheets of paper attached to it. A factual report. No comment needed.

The second was more speculative. He was convinced that he had read the riddle correctly, but there was a lot of guesswork in it.

His conclusion, which he reached after he had finished writing and as four o'clock was striking, was that the first report must go at once. Bill Trotter, or one of the other sailors, would take it for him. As for the other report – he remembered the reproof, all the more stinging for its mildness, which he had earned over his ill-considered scheme to penetrate that meeting – it should go when he had visited the synagogue, spoken to the Rabbi and confirmed one or two of his suppositions.

Having settled all this he lay down to snatch a few minutes' sleep and woke with a start six hours later. He scrambled guiltily into his clothes, sealed up his first report in an envelope addressed to Wensley and took it downstairs. Bill, who was no early riser when not on duty, was still at his breakfast. He agreed, readily enough, to look for Wensley. Since he could hardly be working in the ruins of Leman Street, he would probably be at Poplar, but there were other possibilities. Bill said not to worry, he would contact him. Relieved, Luke started out for the synagogue, where most of the answers he needed could be found.

He was not to know that he was being monitored every yard of the way and would not have turned back if he had known.

He found the Rabbi in his ground-floor study at the back of the tower block which formed the west end of the synagogue, rising above it like the funnel of a steamer. The Rabbi greeted him and offered him coffee. Having had no breakfast, he accepted it gratefully. When it arrived he embarked on explanations. The Rabbi heard him out, nodding his head from time to time. Then he said, 'I can see two objections to your most alarming theory. The first, a minor objection, is that our synagogue is founded upon the rock, both metaphorically and literally. When they were digging out our cellars the builders needed explosives to make the necessary excavation. A tunnel could be dug through it, but it would be a laborious and very noisy job. The second objection is, I think, conclusive. The rainwater soak-away to which you refer runs, in fact, down Brownsong Passage. In front of Solomon's workshop, not behind it. A tunnel starting there and finishing. under our synagogue would *not*, therefore, have to cross it.'

He demonstrated on the plan which Luke had brought with him. Luke said, 'Oh,' and tried to rearrange his ideas. If his theory was nonsensical he was glad that he had taken the trouble to check on it before putting in a report to Wensley.

'However,' said the Rabbi, 'your idea that tunnelling is taking place is not, in itself, farfetched. I have noticed unexplained visitors recently to a place which is now supposedly shut. They might well be digging. Not towards us. But in a different direction.' He picked up a pencil and drew in another line on the plan. 'Not west, but north.'

'North?'

'A short tunnel which, as you can see, *would* cross the soak-away. It would bring them into the vaults of the Ghetto Bank.

Whether their objective would be destruction or plunder I do not know.'

'Both,' said Molacoff Weil.

He had come in quietly and had two other men with him. Before Luke could move they were behind him and had grabbed an arm each. One of them was Ivan Luwinski. Luke had noted him from Mr Passmore's window and had judged him to be a powerful man. He saw no reason to change his opinion as his arms were twisted up so savagely that he fell on to his knees. Weil had brought a rug with him. He covered Luke's head in its stifling folds, pressing it over his nose and mouth.

He heard Weil say, 'Take him the back way. If anyone sees you it is one of your comrades, being taken to the doctor for attention.'

All three men laughed and the laughter was in Luke's ears as his senses slipped away.

15

Luke was lying on the floor of what had been the men's work-room in Solomon's spread. If his legs had not been roped as well as his arms he would have been kicking himself. Had he not done precisely what Joe had been warned against doing? He had got into trouble and had given his senior officers the trouble of getting him out of it.

If they knew about it. And if they could do anything.

In the report which had gone to Wensley there had been no mention of his suspicions or his intentions. Would the Rabbi report what had happened? He had the impression, as he was being carried away like a sack over Luwinski's broad shoulder, that Weil had stayed behind. No doubt he had been warning the Rabbi what would happen to him and his synagogue if he opened his mouth.

Luke had recovered consciousness as soon as the stifling rug had been removed and he had been able to take a few deep breaths. After which he had nothing to do except to keep a count of the passing of time by the chiming of a distant clock and by the regularity with which his guard was changed.

Every half hour a different man would come in. From the state of their elbows and their knees it was clear that they had been working shifts in the tunnel. Neither Weil nor Luwinski had appeared so far. Of the five he had seen he recognised Indruk Spiridov, with his bent nose, and fat Ben Levin from the earrings he wore, two in each ear. There was a fair-haired youngster who might have been Alexei Krustov or Stanislas Grax. The other two were unknown to him.

Levin was the only one who talked much. Some of his remarks were made to Luke, others to the guard who was patrolling

Brownsong Passage. Putting together the bits and pieces of information which they let drop, Luke gathered that the tunnel was
approaching the wall of the bank.

'Any minute now,' said Levin, his earrings clinking together
as he laughed.

Throughout the endless hours one maddening thought had
overridden all others in Luke's mind. He knew that if he were left
alone, for only a few minutes, he could dispose of his bonds.

The men who had tied the knots were not sailors. Also they had
used rope, not cord. Following the hints he had picked up, long
ago, from Houdini, he had already succeeded in getting that first,
vital, stretch in the rope which would allow him to pass his bound
hands down behind his back and over his heels. Once his hands
were in front of him his teeth would soon deal with the clumsy
knots. And he had worked sufficient slack into the rope round his
ankles to ensure that his legs would not be paralysed by cramp.

This was important, because there was a door in the far corner
of the room that looked promising. The bolt was on the inside so
presumably it could be opened. It would lead to a staircase,
which would give him the freedom of the upper storeys.

The spell of duty which started at two thirty had fallen to Ben
Levin. He was the oldest and fattest of his guards and had spent
most of the half hour brushing the earth off his coat and trousers.
After which he had lit a cigarette and sat down to stretch his legs
which seemed to have suffered from cramp.

At a few minutes before three the inner door opened and Weil
came in, followed by the massive Luwinski and a youngster he had
not seen before. When Levin moved towards the door Weil said,
'It's all right, Ben, no more digging. All we have to do now is get the
gas cylinders through. We'll soon have the blow pipes working.'

He pulled a bench up to where Luke was lying and looked
down at the trussed figure with amusement.

'Poor little policeman,' he said. 'No promotion for him now.'

He took a small cigar from the case in his pocket, offered one
to Luwinski, who refused it and lit his own. There was an air of

relaxation about the four men. A job attempted, a job completed. Or nearly so.

'By morning,' said Weil, 'we'll have emptied that strong-room of its Shonks' gold. Tomorrow being their Sabbath they will know nothing of their lost treasure until Sunday morning. By that time it will be safely stowed where no one can find it. Even if they dared to come and look for it. When we add this haul to what our comrades took from the Lockett shop, we shall be plutocrats.' He drew, with pleasure, on his cigar until the tip glowed red.

'What will we do with the money? I'll tell you. We shall expand our forces and pay our men properly; we shall be an army.'

The youngster and Ben Levin smiled broadly at this prospect. Luwinski remained impassive. A masterful character, thought Luke. Second only to Weil.

'But you do not seem to be impressed?' He leant forward and laid the glowing tip of his cigar against Luke's neck.

The casual brutality of the gesture made Luke catch his breath, turning what started as a scream into a grunt.

'Observe,' said Weil, addressing his audience as though he was a surgeon demonstrating in the theatre, 'he did not cry out. That was, would you suppose, because the part of his body where the cigar rested was not among the most sensitive?'

He put the question gravely. The youngster, who had started to dribble, said, 'Suppose we removed his trousers. Might we not find more interesting areas for experiment?'

'We might,' agreed Weil. 'But why should we go to that trouble? Tell me, what is the most sensitive part of the human body?' Answering his own question he said, 'Surely, it is the eye.'

The full horror of this foul suggestion had not had time to register in Luke's mind when they all heard it. A slurring sound, followed by a soft but definite thump. They were still staring when the door flung open and Spiridov came in. 'The tunnel's down,' he said, 'and Alexei's under it.' Without a further thought for their prisoner the four men followed Spiridov out. Luke had supposed that it might take him two minutes to clear his bonds. In less than half that time he was crawling across the floor towards the door he had spotted.

A flight of stairs ran up from behind the door. He climbed them, pausing for a moment at the top to unloose the rope which still hung from one of his ankles. Then he hobbled along the corridor, feeling the strength coming back into his legs.

There were doors on both sides. The rooms they led into would be empty, but would look down on one side on to Brownsong Passage and on the other on to the cobbled way behind the synagogue. There would be guards on both.

At the far end of the corridor a set of steps led up to a trap door. Since the building had only two main storeys this must be some sort of attic. He thought that if he could barricade himself in it, this might win him a breathing space.

He was being driven by horror.

The trap door opened easily enough. The attic was in half darkness. There were no windows, but enough light was filtering through the tiles for him to see that the only contents was a couple of large packing cases.

He moved one of them on to the closed trap door. It was heavy, but even the two together would not hold the bull-like strength of Weil and Luwinski. He sat down on the other case and tried to make himself think.

He knew that it was no good stopping where he was. As soon as his escape was discovered the Russians would come after him. The guards outside would tell them that he had not left the building. As soon as they had searched the bedrooms, the ladder to the loft would beckon them. He must move, but his limbs felt powerless and his mind was confused.

What suggested the next step was a memory. Wensley, cornered on the roof of the brewery during the Sidney Street seige, had escaped by removing tiles and dropping through into the building below. Why should he not do the same, in reverse? Standing on the case, he would be within easy reach of the roof. No sooner thought of than done.

He wrenched at the wooden slats in the ceiling, tearing his fingers in his haste until the blood ran down over his wrists. When he had reached and moved one tile the rest was easy and he soon had a hole big enough to squeeze through. He had come out on the inner slope of the roof that ran down towards the synagogue. He slid forward cautiously and, with his heels in the gutter, peered down into the dimness.

He thought he saw a figure moving at the point where the passageway ran out into Stratford Road. No question, then, of climbing down. But safety was ahead of him. Separated from him only by the width of the passage.

He was level with the top of the parapet which circled the synagogue roof and the gap between the two buildings was not more, he judged, than seven feet. With any sort of running start he could have cleared it easily, but he would have to launch himself from a sitting position with his heels in the gutter. As he looked down, his heart sank. If he failed to reach the parapet and fell, the least he could hope for was two broken legs. The men in the passage would see him fall and would call to the others. And then –

The decision was taken out of his hands. Hearing trampling of feet and a bull-like roar from just below him, he shut his eyes, uttered a prayer and jumped.

He landed against the parapet, with most of the breath driven from his body, and with the cold certainty that, since more of his weight was below the top of the parapet than above it, he would not be able to hoist himself up on to it. It would have been different if the parapet had been sharp edged. Then he might have got a real grip of it and used the strength of his arms to hoist himself up. As it was he faced the bleak realisation that he would have to hang there, his fingers slipping on the rounded surface until they lost the last of their power and he fell.

Like a rock climber whose hand-hold fails him he searched for a toe-hold, the tiniest crack or fissure, to give him if not safety, at least a respite. Careful not to let the movement shake him loose altogether, he explored with his right foot and found the support he was seeking. With a splintering of glass the toe of his shoe went through the blessed Chasdal ibn Shaprut. His left toe felt for and found the learned Johan ibn Janach. With firm supports for both feet he was able to straighten his legs and heave himself over the parapet and on to the lead-lined walk-way which ran round the roof of the synagogue.

At the point where the runway reached the tower block one of the ceiling lights was open and the sound of an organ being played came up to him. The deep notes must have touched a chord in his over-tried mind, for he found himself on his knees, listening with tears running down his face.

'Yes, I see,' said Wensley. 'So, having slipped your bonds, you got up on to the roof and jumped across. Hadn't it occurred to you that you might leave by the rather less dangerous method of getting out of one of the back bedroom windows and down a drain pipe?'

'No good. There was a man – maybe two men – in the alley.'

'Were there indeed?' Wensley looked at his watch and seemed to be working out times.

'I agree it was risky, but I heard them coming up after me. Of course, I wasn't to know that I was going to be helped.'

'Helped?'

'By the blessed Shaprut and the learned Janach.' Luke started to laugh at the thought and having started found it difficult to stop.

Wensley looked at him coldly and then said, 'If you're referring to the stained-glass windows, we've already had one of the Rabbi's young men round to complain about it. He arrived a few minutes before you did. The damage has been put down to the Russians.'

'I'm glad about that,' said Luke. The laughter was draining out of him.

'I think you'd better come along with me. Macnaghten has lent me his machine, so we'll travel in style.'

'Could you tell me where we're going?'

'Back to Brownsong Court, of course.'

'I can't think you'll find anyone there, sir. As soon as

they found I'd gone, surely they'll have scattered.'

'They won't find it easy to scatter,' said Wensley. 'We've had fifty armed men round the place for the last half hour. The first ones to get there may have been the men you saw in the passage.'

'Oh,' said Luke blankly, 'then I needn't have risked that jump.'

'On the contrary. I'm glad you did. If we're going to tackle this crowd I'd much rather do it when they weren't holding you as a hostage. Come along.' He grabbed Luke, not unkindly, by the arm. 'I'll tell you the rest as we go.'

When they were comfortably seated in the car he said, 'This afternoon the Rabbi came round. It had taken him an hour or more to weigh his public duty against his private fears. Came down on the right side in the end. I think that's a good omen. The pendulum's swinging.'

Joscelyne had set up his headquarters in a large draper's shop a few yards east of the entrance to Brownsong Court. The stock in trade had been carefully piled on one side and the superintendent had established himself behind the cashier's desk. Luke, whose mind was turning to fantasy as the day wore on, wondered if he was using the arrangement of overhead wires and little trolleys to send messages to his men, some of whom were sitting behind the counters whilst others were in a room at the back.

'Any trouble?' said Wensley.

'Nothing we couldn't handle,' said Joscelyne. 'Three of their men were patrolling round the building. I sent a section of our chaps to pull them in. When they saw them coming, they shot at them. No. No one was hit. When our men fired back they looked upset. Unfair, they thought. They disappeared into the building and we heard them bolting the door. However, we've got hammers heavy enough to break it down and ladders which'll reach the bedroom windows. All we need is to give the signal.'

He spoke loudly enough for his men to hear. They looked serious, but determined. 'Quite a few of Daddy Tucker and Bob Bentley's friends here,' he added.

Wensley said, 'Fine – I'm sure they'll do a good job. But if you don't mind, I think we ought to try the effect of argument and reason first. Since my grasp of Russian isn't all that hot, I'll take young Pagan along as an interpreter.'

Wensley gave him no time to protest. As Luke followed him, he croaked out, 'Shouldn't we be armed?'

'You could borrow a gun if you felt like it,' said Wensley. 'I've never carried one myself. But I've got a piece of paper which might be equally effective.'

He walked out across Stratford Road and down Brownsong Court and thumped on the door of Solomon's building. After a moment they heard a roar from Weil inside. 'Let 'em in.' The bolts were shot back and they walked through to the back room.

There was a hole in the floor, surrounded by a rampart of earth. Luke counted nine men crowded round Weil, all young except for Spiridov and Levin.

'Say what you've got to say,' said Weil, 'and make it quick. We've got some work to finish.'

'The first thing to tell them,' said Wensley, 'is that we've got thirty-six armed men – trained marksmen – round this building. If you start a gun-fight it will end in a massacre. And a massacre is exactly what your bosses in Russia are playing for. You could say "praying" instead of "playing" if you thought it sounded better.'

Luke wondered whether he had enough control of his own voice to speak at all. He was scared and he was deathly tired. But he realised that this was the moment he had been trained for. Trained by his tutor to turn his thoughts into colloquial Russian; trained by the Rector to think logically; trained by his father to forget fatigue and get on with the job. He found himself able to reproduce what Wensley said – even, in places, to improve on it.

'Right. Now you can read them the first clause in this Order in Council.'

'"All persons coming to this country from abroad during the last three years who have no fixed employment or who have committed or been parties to criminal acts will be returned to the country from which they came."'

'Tell them that if they provoke a battle, this will be laid on the table in the House of Commons on Monday.'

Luke simplified this to 'will become law on Monday'.

'Bluff,' said Weil. 'Pay no heed.'

'You will notice, however, that the two men who were sent here to provoke trouble – Janis Silistreau and Casimir Treschau – have taken steps to look after themselves. They are running away. Their passages were booked on the Polish boat *Gdansk*, leaving this afternoon.'

This indication of the treachery of their leaders had hit them all, thought Luke. Even Weil. The young Russians were beginning to follow every word he said.

'However,' continued Wensley blandly, 'being provided, fortunately, with details of the names under which these two reverend gentlemen planned to travel, we were able to take them into custody, charged with being in possession of false papers. But that was only a holding charge.'

'Don't listen to him,' said Weil. 'When he has finished we will teach him to tell lies. Yes?'

Luke thought that the response of his followers was less enthusiastic than it might have been. Wensley now unmasked his batteries and delivered his next broadside.

'There will be a second charge against them. Because, in belts round their bodies were found all – yes, every piece – of the gold and precious stones stolen from the Lockett shop. They will be charged with organising a robbery which led to the shooting down of PC Bellwood. That charge carries a sentence of death.'

'Nonsense,' said Weil. 'It was not their fault that that stupid policeman got in the way.'

So far Wensley had been addressing his words at large. Now he swung round on Weil and said, 'There will be a more direct charge against you. For the torturing and killing of Dmitry Katz.'

Weil rode this off with a show of indifference, shrugging his shoulders but saying nothing. A fighting animal not to be deflected by words.

'And if you are looking for some reward at the end of your tunnel, I can assure you that there is nothing there. Even if you were allowed to complete your work, you would find an empty strong-room. The contents are being removed, at this moment, to a strong-room on the other side of the building.'

Wensley gathered himself for the final assault. He was ignoring Weil now and addressing himself directly to the younger members of his audience.

'So if you wish to play the game that is being forced on you, where there is no gain at the end – only death, in a gun battle here, or at the hands of the Ochrana who will be waiting for you at the quayside with their tongues hanging out –'

Having no idea of the Russian for this phrase, Luke amended it to 'like slavering wolves'.

'If that is your decision you will follow this besotted man and his ideas to their black and pointless conclusion.'

'They'll follow me all right,' said Weil.

Luke had his eyes on Luwinski, who had been working his way slowly into position behind Weil. He had picked up from somewhere a heavy iron bar. Now he swung it, hitting Weil at the back of his neck.

Weil toppled slowly forward like a felled oak tree.

'That seems to me to be a conclusive answer,' said Wensley with a smile. 'If you will leave all your arms on the table here and go to your homes, I think I can promise you that you will hear no more about your digging. It will be filled in by morning. We'd better go back with you to make sure that no trigger-happy policeman starts the war.'

When they got back to the shop Joscelyne appeared to be more indignant than relieved.

'Do you mean to say,' he said, 'that now that we have got our men keyed up to shoot they'll have to shovel earth instead?'

'A sad anti-climax, I fear,' said Wensley. 'But think how pleased Winston will be.'

Joscelyne said something under his breath about the Home Secretary. It sounded unparliamentary.

16

Luke was sitting in the room which he now occupied alone. He was wondering, as he thought about the year just passed, why he felt so depressed.

Much had happened in that twelve months.

Molacoff Weil, having survived a blow which would have killed nine men out of ten, had been sentenced to death by Mr Justice Avory and had been hanged, impassive to the last. Rumour had it that, coming new to the Bench and beginning to be known as a hanging judge, Avory would have wished to send Treschau and Silistreau to the gallows also, but was too good a lawyer to disregard the contention of the defence that they could not be held liable for the death of PC Bellwood. The best he could do was to award them two sentences of seven years' penal servitude, consecutive not concurrent, one on the charge of travelling on false papers and one on dealing with stolen goods. At the same hearing Jacob Katz received a sentence of seven years for forgery.

It had not been possible to charge Anna since Joe, the only witness of her perfidy, had refused to give evidence. The real offender, as he explained to Luke, was Sergeant Gorman and he was the only one who got actually written off. Anna's wrist had been twisted by her father. She was simply carrying out his instructions. 'And anyway,' said Joe, 'you were soft on her.' Luke had denied this indignantly. Joe knew that he lied. Luke knew it himself, too.

The other results of that wild day's work had been more agreeable. With the departure of the three leaders the threat of organised Russian violence had receded and the *émigré* population had settled down to a comparatively peaceful existence. Wensley had received due credit for this, though it was certainly not the only reason for his promotion to detective chief inspector, which was long overdue and meant that most of his time was now spent at Scotland Yard. It had been repeatedly postponed because his superiors wanted to keep him in the East End, where his knowledge was invaluable.

The South London Soap Company was closed by the authorities. Its proprietors were prosecuted under the Explosives Act and its considerable store of dynamite was removed and destroyed.

Joe, as usual, had fallen on his feet – or the one foot remaining to him. Abram Lockett had been grateful for the return of his property and nursed a hope that the men who had robbed him and assaulted his wife might be brought back and punished. The extradition proceedings were grinding along, the main bone of contention being whether the robbery had been a criminal or a political act. Lockett's gratitude had resulted in the offer to Joe of a well-paid job, with lodging and keep, as security guard on the shop. He had gone straight to it from hospital.

Wensley gone. Joe gone. With the Russians behaving themselves, a lot of routine work with no particular use for his grasp of their language.

And it was raining. When gloom was heavy it always rained.

That was the moment that Hubert Daines arrived. He came with a proposal.

He said, 'I imagine you know nothing about MO5. Same as most people. We were only born four years ago, but we've been a lusty infant, kicking and screaming for our share of the sweets. We've enrolled a lot of people from different fields. The Army, the Law, the Home Office. Even from the War Office, who are notionally our bosses. A lot of our work has been – and still is – office work. But mark my words. If we go to war we will be one of the most important outfits in the country. So, will you consider leaving the police and coming in with us? Your grasp of Russian and French would be a huge asset.'

At almost any other time Luke would probably have said 'No'. What he now said was, 'If you can guarantee a war, yes.'

'I can't absolutely guarantee it, but I'll be extremely surprised if we're not at war with Germany within twelve months.'

Since he said this at the beginning of July 1913 he was wrong. But only by one month.